WENDY PERRIAM has had fourteen novels published to critical acclaim. Expelled from her convent boarding school for heresy, she read history at Oxford and later trod the boards.

After a variety of jobs, ranging from artist's model to carnation debudder, she embarked on a career in advertising, writing in her spare time. In 1980 she became a full-time novelist and is currently working on her fifteenth novel and a second collection of short stories.

Critical acclaim for Wendy Perriam's most recent novel, *Lying*

'Joanna Trollope meets Graham Greene . . . Wendy Perriam is one of our most consistent, and most consistently underrated authors. She rarely fails to deliver the goods; and she does so again here, in a novel of complexity and mounting excitement.' – *Sunday Telegraph*

'An accomplished and intelligent novel by a too-often overlooked novelist who wears her seriousness of purpose lightly.' – *Independent*

'With *Lying* Wendy Perriam returns to brilliant form, with a story that is fast-paced, thought-provoking and original . . . An ordinary love story? Far from it . . . Perriam is a very human writer, for she has both wit and compassion, two qualities that are often mutually exclusive. A pleasure to read from start to finish, *Lying* should be the one novel everyone reads this year.' – *The Tablet*

'In her cleverly plotted fourteenth novel, certainly one of her best, Wendy Perriam explores not just the complicated process of lying in a marriage, but also its ethics . . . She has the knack of being explicit about sex without being crude or embarrassing . . . Perriam teases us to the end with twists and turns in the plot. But just as accomplished is the novel's moral debate.' – *Literary Review*

'It's hard to think of another living author with such searing powers of description and such devastating insight into human behaviour. Her first thirteen novels were outstanding, but so powerful and provocative one felt wrung out after reading them. *Lying* is just as brilliant but with a lighter touch and an engrossing quality that makes it perfect holiday reading.' – *Surrey Comet*

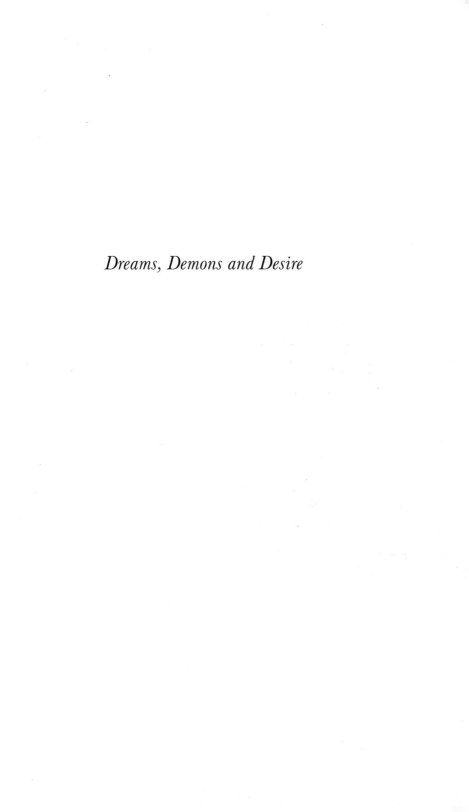

Dreams, Demons and Desire

WENDY PERRIAM

Dreams, Demons and Desire

PETER OWEN
LONDON AND CHESTER SPRINGS

PETER OWEN PUBLISHERS
73 Kenway Road, London SW5 0RE

Peter Owen books are distributed in the USA by
Dufour Editions Inc., Chester Springs, PA 19425-0007

First published in Great Britain 2001
© Wendy Perriam 2001

ISBN 0 7206 1109 1

A catalogue record for this book is available from the British Library

Printed and bound in Great Britain by MPG Books Ltd, Bodmin, Cornwall

Acknowledgments

Some of the stories in this collection have appeared in the
following publications:
The Second Penguin Book of Modern Women's Short Stories
(Michael Joseph), *Best Short Stories 1992* (Heinemann),
Twenty Stories (South East Arts), *Seven Deadly Sins*
(Severn House), *Image, Esquire, The Author.*

For Tara Wynne,
bright star at Curtis Brown,
in appreciation of her rare skills
and unfailing support

Contents

Angelfish

On three nights out of seven Mr Chivers dreamed of purple candlewick. Sometimes they wrapped him in it as his winding sheet; other times it formed the fabric of the universe and everywhere he wandered little purple tufts tripped him up or clung to him like burrs. Occasionally they served it up as bacon with his rubberized fried egg. He often woke screaming. He switched his torch on underneath the blankets and prayed to a purple God that Miss Lineham hadn't woken up as well. Miss Lineham slept with her door open. Maybe she didn't sleep at all, but she retired to her room at ten o'clock sharp, with a purple hairnet and a cup of cocoa, and demanded silence until seven.

Mr Chivers crept out of his tangled bed into the bathroom. There it was: living, breathing candlewick – no dreamstuff this. Purple candlewick bathmat lying exactly parallel to the cold white bath; purple candlewick toilet-seat cover masking the shameful business that went on underneath it. Even the toilet roll was ruched and frilled in purple candlewick.

He stumbled to the basin and inspected his tongue in the mirror. It was shaggy grey, as if a fine mould had settled on it in the night. His bladder was kicking him in the gut, demanding to be emptied. He hitched up his pyjama bottoms and tied the cord more tightly. He dared not risk the jet of urine on white porcelain, not at three a.m. Even in normal daylight hours he preferred to use the public convenience. Miss Lineham's lavatory was a decorative item. He doubted if she even used it herself. She was too refined to pee. He presumed she must evaporate off her waste products in some noiseless, odourless form of osmosis. Even the cistern was shrouded in candlewick. She had turned a cesspool into an ornamental lake. Little matching doilies, hand-crocheted in purple, smirked at him from every surface, standing guard beneath the Harpic, cushioning the Vim. The bathroom boasted little else. Toilet articles were strictly banned. No toothbrush was permitted to flaunt its dripping nakedness in public, no bar of soap to wallow in its own slime. Aftershave was decadent, bath salts an indulgence. Flannels, toothpaste, sponges, razors – all must be locked away in strictest purdah. In the early days, before Mr Chivers realized the perils of exposure, he had rashly left his nail-brush by the basin. Miss Lineham had said nothing. But four mornings running he found the damply accusing object cringing by his breakfast egg. Four mornings running he suffered with indigestion and tension headaches.

Now, he never quitted the bathroom without a thorough scrutiny, going down on his hands and knees in search of slops of water or stray hairs. Still on his knees, he would reposition the bathmat, making sure it was dead centre – not that he ever dared to take a bath. His feet might print obscene naked splodges on the purple candlewick or his city dirt leave a tide-mark impossible to remove. The cleaning rag was folded so squarely on the canister of Vim it would be sedition to disturb it.

He ran just a piddle of water into the basin. If he turned the taps full on, the geyser roared in accusation: Miss Lineham's private spy. He dabbed at his face, then at his private parts, gazing upwards at the prim white ceiling so that he wouldn't get excited. Arousal made the bed creak. He couldn't even eat an apple in bed. The very first bite brought a warning cough from Miss Lineham's open door. There were ways and means, of course, if you were desperate. It was dangerous to chew, but you could graze your teeth very gently, up and down, up and down, against the skin, until the flesh gradually succumbed. Then you held it in your mouth and sucked. The saliva did the rest. It took an hour to dispose of one small Cox's Orange Pippin, and Granny Smiths were more or less impossible.

'I do not consider it hygienic, Mr Chivers, to store perishable foodstuffs among your underclothes. Nor would I have deemed it necessary to supplement the more than adequate diet I supply.'

He couldn't even hide a Cox. Miss Lineham inspected everything in his room, including his underpants. (Cleaning, it was called.) She lined his cufflinks up in twos, sprayed his shoes with foot deodorant.

'Tabloid newspapers, Mr Chivers, are not encouraged in this establishment.'

'I have found it necessary, Mr Chivers, to invest in a new front door mat, and I should like to draw your attention to the fact.'

He never saw her smile. The nearest she got to it was at nine o'clock every evening when she fed her angelfish. The bevelled tank stretched its tropical turquoise luxury along a table in the hall. Jungle plants trailed soft green fingers through the water. Broad-backed leaves and ferny fronds rippled in an effervescent spume of bubbles. And through them glided the fairy fins of three exotic angelfish, one gold, one silver, one marbled black and cream. Their glowing opalescence seemed almost blasphemy in Miss Lineham's fawn and frowning hall. No one else in the house was indulged as were those fish. While the lodgers shivered in their fireless rooms, the angels basked in a constant eighty degrees Fahrenheit. Mr Chivers ate frugally off melamine, but the twelve varieties of super-enriched fishfood lorded it on a silver tray.

Feeding time was a sacred ritual: hall lights turned low, front door locked, parlour blinds firmly closed. Mr Chivers watched through a crack in his bedroom door, peering down through the banisters, awaiting that magic transformation in Miss Lineham's granite face. As the angelfish darted to the surface and nibbled at her dead white fingers, her face turned from stone to petals; the corners of her mouth lifting slightly, so that he could see the tips of plastic teeth.

'My pretty angels,' she whispered, sprinkling Magiflakes like manna. 'My pretty, pretty angels.'

Mr Chivers' pulse raced. There was something about the way her cold eyes sparked and softened, the flirtatious flurry of her hand across the water. He never heard that velvet voice at any other hour; it was sackcloth and hessian when she was snapping at her lodgers.

'Some of us are born to work, Mr Chivers, and some are born to idle.'

'I do not wish Princess Margaret's name to be mentioned in this house again.'

She was even uncharacteristically generous with the fishfood, flinging in fresh pink shrimp and bite-size worm almost with abandon. Everyone else was rationed. Mr Chivers' scant teaspoonful of breakfast marmalade was apportioned out the evening before and sat stiffening in an egg-cup overnight. He never saw the jar. Bacon rashers were cut tastefully in half. And when he had swallowed the last morsel of his one barely buttered piece of toast (thin-sliced from a small loaf), Miss Lineham whisked every comestible swiftly out of sight. Not a crumb nor tealeaf remained to give promise of future sustenance. Even the smell of food crept cravenly away at the touch of Miss Lineham's Airfresh. Five minutes after breakfast the kitchen looked like a morgue or a museum – shining tiles and dead exhibits in sterilized glass jars.

Mr Chivers started eating out. He sprawled in Joe's caff or Dick's diner, elbow-deep in chips, baked beans tumbling down his chin, wallowing in ketchup, gnawing chicken bones. ('*Dogs* eat bones, Mr Chivers, not Civil Service gentlemen.') He ordered both cream and custard on his syrup sponge and slurped it down, savouring every mouthful. Delirious contrast to those tight-lipped breakfasts when Miss Lineham jumped and blinked her eyes every time his teeth made contact with the toast.

He spent more and more time away. He added the public baths to the public convenience, running the bath full to overflowing and shouting above the Niagara of the taps. He set up floods and cataracts, slooshing water over the side of the cracked white tub. He bought a plastic duck and spent reckless hours torpedoing it with the bar of municipal soap. He flung in whole cartonsful of bath salts and turned the water as blue as Miss Lineham's fish-tank. He left hairs in the plug-hole and a rim around the bath. Nobody cared. Nobody pinned crabbed little notes on his door, saying 'Water costs money, Mr Chivers, were you aware?' No one slipped a purple crocheted doiley underneath his soapy bottom.

He discovered a bath with a toilet beside it, for only tenpence extra. Now he ruled the world. He jetted his urine at the stained, un-Harpicked bowl, aiming at the central 'C' in the maker's name, his own initial. Sometimes he took risks or invented games, standing further and further back and still not missing, or stopping and starting the stream, or tracing patterns with it, as if the jet were a golden pencil. That done, he sat on the cracked and germy toilet seat (which had never known the chastening caress of candlewick) and strained and groaned in thunderous ecstasy. He even returned to prunes.

Whatever his excesses in the baths, he was always back in the house by 8.55. Nine p.m. was the angels' feeding time: the high spot of his day. Miss Lineham was often prowling by the door.

'Good evening, Miss Lineham. Lovely weather.'

'Good evening, Mr Chivers. It won't last.'

'Good evening, Miss Lineham. Nice bit of rain for the garden.'

'Good evening, Mr Chivers. They forecast floods.'

Formalities over, he fixed his whole attention on the fish as he walked slowly, slowly past, watching their perfect gills pant in and out, their dramatic ventral fins flowing like fancy ribbons from their underbodies. There were other inhabitants of the tank, inelegant and drably coloured small fry, creeping things that slimed and gobbled on the bottom, the proletariat of snail and loach. He scarcely noticed them; he was too absorbed in the angels: their wide wings and golden eyes, their steady, soothing motion as they meandered in and out of each other's shadows, haloed by their own enchanted fins. He longed to know more about them – what sex they were, what age, their parentage, their origins – but dared not ask; indeed, dared not even loiter by the tank. Only in his fantasy did he lay his cheek against the cold compress of the glass and feel his fingers caressed by foraging mouths, the tickle of peacock tails against his palm.

Cold reality shoved him briskly up the stairs, to cower all evening, a prisoner in his room. He could watch the feeding only in breathless secrecy, craning his neck and peering through the crack, rigid with terror that Miss Lineham's eye might swivel in its socket and meet his own. It never did. She had eyes only for her angelfish; her concrete brow flushing and softening as they flicked their fins and flirted with her hands. Mr Chivers' heartbeat almost cracked the walls. He could feel his supper singing through his veins; jam on the semolina centre of his soul. This was his finale, his golden climax to a sallow day, his after-dinner port, his nuts and wine.

At 9.05 it was over. Gloom descended like a dust-sheet. Miss Lineham disappeared and was stiff and grey again by the time she re-emerged. Mr Chivers drooped in his room, dressing-gown atop his pinstripes. The one-bar fire was removed on March 1 and did not reappear until the last day of October.

'Overheating the system can be dangerous, Mr Chivers.'

'Yes, Miss Lineham.' Three inches of snow outside.

Mr Chivers sat and read. (TV and radio were forbidden in the house.) He bought every aquarist magazine on the market and squandered his Christmas bonus on a *Pictorial Encyclopaedia of Tropical Fish*. Invariably he turned first to the angelfish, studying their breeding habits, learning their Latin names. He traced their showy outlines on sheets of greaseproof paper and coloured them in with a set of Woolworth's crayons. And when at last he fell asleep, marbled bodies and gossamer tails plunged through the spaces in his purple candlewick nightmares and turned them into gleaming silver mesh.

SILVER JUBILEE FESTIVAL OF ANGELFISH
April 15–21

Mr Chivers was reading in bed, his torch concealed beneath the blankets. ('Lights out at eleven, Mr Chivers. Electricity is not a gift from God.') He peered more closely at the print: a full-page advertisement in the glossy new issue of *Fishkeeper's Weekly*. Never before had so much money and attention been lavished on the species. An eccentric Yorkshire millionaire with a passion for *Pterophyllum scalare* was sponsoring a festival in Doncaster, devoted exclusively to angelfish: special breeds, rare specimens, unheard-of colours, generous prizes. All the local pet shops and aquaria had promised back-up displays and exhibitions for the week of the festival. Yorkshire would be awash in angelfish.

Mr Chivers had never been up north. His Easter holiday was due; he was tired of Littlehampton. He placed the magazine underneath his pillow and lay back contentedly. He would book on Inter-City direct to Doncaster and spend an enchanted week among the angels.

April 22. Mr Chivers alighted at King's Cross with an empty wallet and a suitcaseful of dirty shirts. His soul was still in Doncaster. On the tube he plunged through rocky clefts and tangled weed. His suburban train was packed with angelfish. Ghostly albinos plopped between the pages of his newspaper; aggressive all-blacks jostled his elbows and bumped against his knees; foamy lace angels swooped past the windows and swam along the rails. When he got off, water-snails were clinging to his suitcase, bubbles streaming from his nose.

'I took the liberty, Mr Chivers, of moving you to a different room. A new gentleman lodger has arrived who particularly requested a location facing front.'

He jumped. Her voice had startled the rare and fantastic Liu Keung angelfish, which he had just persuaded to nuzzle at his hand. 'Yes, Miss Lineham,' he muttered automatically. He was admiring majestic marbled torsos, the damask splendour of stately tails.

She ushered him into a cold cramped cubicle that looked out across the dustbins. He saw only verdant water-fern reflecting the light from darting silver fins.

'As one of my longest-standing lodgers, Mr Chivers, I knew

I could count on your co-operation. The new gentleman is decidedly artistic and requires a room with good light. I also took the opportunity of replenishing your Airwick and have added the £1.20 to your rent.'

'Thank you, Miss Lineham.' He hardly heard her close the door. He was smiling at two flirtatious silver veil-tails rubbing noses on the ceiling. Their spiky backbones gleamed alluringly through the diaphanous silk of their flesh. He sank smiling on to the bed.

Two hours later Doncaster was fading. Supper had been sausages – the cheaper beef variety with a high percentage of rusk – and mortar-mix potatoes. Mr Chivers discarded a lump in his custard, swilled down the jamless jam tart with tea, then returned upstairs to the beige disapproval of his new back-room. Silver fins and shot-silk tails had vanished, blue water leaked away, leaving only sludge-coloured lino, and purple crocheted water-lily leaves stranded on bare wood. All his possessions had been lined up in rows like orphans awaiting transport to an institution. His chewing-gum was confiscated, his thirteen books (eleven of them on fish) banished to a damp cardboard box marked 'No Deposit, No Return. Lemon Barley Water.'

He changed into his pyjamas and sat staring at his bunions. Miss Lineham would have thrown his feet away if he had been rash enough to leave them in his room. Miss Lineham liked things straight. In his jacket pocket was the crumpled entrance ticket to the festival. He dropped it in the waste-bin.

Nothing left but bed. He slunk into the bathroom to clean his teeth; stopped dead in his tracks. Something was dangerously different – the toilet seat was up! In all his years at Miss Lineham's he had never seen it left up. If some new inmate in his foolishness forgot to replace the cover, Miss Lineham would dart into the bathroom after him and snap it severely shut. Four or five repeats and the tenant was completely cured. Candlewick became part of defecation.

The same with toiletries. An untrained lodger's first few breakfasts were often egg-and-flannel or sausage-and-loofah; the table littered with hang-dog razors and confiscated shaving sticks. Cure was always swift, or had been up till now. Mr New-Boy Gordon had been in residence a week, so what was his orange flannel doing draped across the bath – flagrant, dripping, not even folded? Miss Lineham was at home, so why had she not removed this blushing flag of revolution? Why had no contemptuous note been pushed beneath the offender's door? As far as he could ascertain, she was still in her right mind, watching him at supper with her usual gimlet eye.

'Since you appear to be having so much difficulty, Mr Chivers, in disposing of your second sausage, I shall apportion it to Mr Gordon in future.'

He saw the offending sausage, wreathed in Colman's mustard and Miss Lineham's smiles. She never smiled. Mr Chivers clutched at the basin for support. How could he have been so blind? The new Artistic Gentleman had changed her, found the flinty remnants of her heart and swathed them in his shameless orange flannel. A raw recruit, an upstart, stinking out the house with aftershave, taking artistic licence with the purple candlewick . . .

Mr Chivers strode back to his room and stared in fury at the Stag at Bay. One picture per room. 'Nothing, I repeat nothing, is to be stuck or pinned on to lodgers' bedroom walls.' He hated stags: all that vaunting headgear. It had been a Victorian flower-girl in his previous room – tiro Gordon's room – with nothing on her head but blonde curls and a circlet of roses; a froth of white pantalettes cascading beneath her skirt.

Opening the wardrobe, he surveyed his row of ties, all

limp, all drably coloured. He took out a bar of Cadbury's Wholenut chocolate, hidden in a slipper; put it back again. Wholenut was the riskiest confection on the market. If you bit into a hazelnut, it made a crack to wake the dead. And Miss Lineham was very much alive. He had noticed it at supper. She had hovered over Mr Gordon all through the bread-and-butter pudding, offering him jersey cream from a silver jug. Melamine and custard had always been the rule.

He could hear her now, her brown no-nonsense lace-ups phat-phatting from kitchen to hall. He sprang up from his chair. Feeding time! Every night at Doncaster he had tuned in, in mind and spirit, to that magic ritual, hearing Miss Lineham's fin-enchanted voice winging after him on Inter-City. 'My pretty angels, my pretty pretty angels.'

He crept to his bedroom door and opened it a crack. Useless. His new room was stuck away around a corner, excluding him from the mysteries of the tank. No longer could he peer down through the banisters; he was shut out like a pariah.

He heard the brogues shuffle to a stop and then the sound of voices. Voices? He slunk from his room to the landing, but he could see only squiggled lino and stripy wall. His full-frontal view of the hall had departed with the roses and the pantalettes. He tiptoed along the passage and round the corner to the top of the stairs. Miss Lineham was there in the hall, the radiant feeding-time Miss Lineham, lingering almost coquettishly by the tank. But she was not alone. Standing beside her – unnecessarily close, in fact – was Mr Basil A. F. Gordon; black eyes, white hands, topiary moustache. A spruce white handkerchief burst into late-spring flower from his breast pocket; his trousers were dove-grey (and tight), his jacket softest suede, the colour of muscovado sugar. Mr Chivers clenched his fists. Never before had any mere man, let alone a lodger, been allowed to share in the holy rites. Yet now four hands were trailing in the torrid water, two heads joined as one, two infatuated shadows embracing on the wall behind.

The largest angelfish was nibbling at Mr Gordon's index finger. Mr Chivers could feel the throb and tingle in his own. The new Artistic Gentleman was making stylish patterns with rose-coloured shrimp flakes on turquoise water. All three angels swooped to the surface and kissed his hand. Mr Chivers' palms vibrated with the tiny pressure of their worshipping mouths. Miss Lineham was pointing at a fin. He could hear nothing but a tantalizing murmur, as she confided those intimate details always denied to him – the personal histories of the angelfish, their weaknesses, their gender, their little fads and foibles. He could see her pale mouth opening and shutting almost in time with theirs, the flush on her opalescent skin, the glint in her strange gold eyes.

'My pretty angels,' she was murmuring. 'My pretty pretty angels.' But it was Mr Basil Gordon who had put that extraordinary girlish tremor in her voice.

'May I help you, sir?' enquired the salesman.

'Yes,' said Mr Chivers. 'I want three angelfish. One gold, one silver, one marbled black and cream.'

'Certainly, sir.' The salesman led him over to the corner. The fish were smaller than Miss Lineham's.

'Don't worry, sir; they'll grow to fit the tank.' He made a little flurry with his net. 'You'll be wanting a tank as well, I presume?'

Mr Chivers shook his head.

'You've got a tank? Right, how about a heater? Or a piston pump? Or an under-gravel filter unit?'

'No,' said Mr Chivers. 'Thank you.'

'All right for fishfood, are you?'

'I won't be needing food.'

'Growlux lighting? Stimulates plant life. Choice of blue or green.'

'Just the fish,' Mr Chivers repeated.

He carried them on the bus in a polythene bag fastened with a rubber band, his capacious sponge-bag under the other arm. People stared.

'Not so bright this morning, is it?' remarked the woman at the public baths as she handed him his ticket and his towels.

He didn't answer. He needed all his concentration to conceal the bag of fish beneath his raincoat. His usual cubicle was free. He double-locked the door and slipped the polythene bag into the basin. He didn't release the angels; time enough for that. First, he ran his bath, tipping in almost half a bottle of Blue-Mist Foam, so that azure bubbles frothed above the sides. Next, he unwrapped his plastic duck, followed by his sponges, brushes and flannels, then turned back to the angelfish, wrenching off the rubber band and tossing the bag on to the floor. It landed on its side, jarring the writhing bodies. Slowly, the water leaked away. The fishes flowed out with it, slithering on the shiny tiles. The gold angel twitched and palpitated, leaping six inches in the air, then somersaulting down again with a piteous splat. Mr Chivers paused a moment to admire the markings on the marbled angel, almost identical to Miss Lineham's specimen. Its mouth was opening in a wordless plea, its feeble tail flailing on the tiles.

He climbed into the bath. The water was armpit high; the overflow gurgling down the pipe. He picked up a sponge and slapped his thighs with it. He stuck a crooked foot through a tower of foam. The bubbles were so profuse you could lose whole limbs. Steam was rising from the water, falling again in streams of condensation down the walls. Leaning over the edge of the tub, he saw the silver angelfish plunging and zigzagging in a frenzied attempt to reach the water, its gills pistoning in and out in panic, its eyes almost starting from its head.

Mr Chivers began to sing. The marbled angel had fallen into a drain-hole and was floundering on its back. Mr Chivers loofahed his upper arms. The soap was lost and melting at the bottom of the tub. He stretched and yawned in the benison of steam, watching the fishes all the while. The marbled angel was growing feebler now. Its mouth gaped open, as if it had been unhinged; its eyes were glazing over.

He ran more water, laughing aloud as the hoarse hot tap thundered between his feet. Every time he moved, the bubbles frothed and flurried over the sides. He turned on his belly and lost his chin in foam. The silver angel was only a pale splodge on the tiles, its gills shuttered and inert. The gold angel continued fighting. Its leaps were lower now, but it still did its best to save itself, panting with each agonized contortion. Mr Chivers wallowed in his tub, rocking to and fro, so that the water sloshed and seesawed from one end to the other. A deep pink glow emblazoned him from brow to bunions; bubbles pricked and popped along his limbs. When he sang, the words resounded off the walls, adding a choir and organ to his voice.

The brave gold angel was singing along with him. He could see its mouth gasping open, wheezing out the words, its once-majestic tail trailing like a broken rudder. The other two fish were motionless. Only their eyes stared upwards, as if they were praying for deliverance.

He pulled out the plug, listening to the water chuckle down the waste-pipe. As he stepped out on to the tiles, he was careful to avoid the corpses pathetically marooned there. He dried himself on stiff municipal towels, which he then flung wet and soggy into a corner. Picking up the three small bodies, he placed them in the toilet bowl. They floated on the top, their eyes beseeching, their colours as yet unfaded. There was a flicker of life in the golden angel still. It twitched in shock as it felt itself fall on water. Slowly, it spread its tail and jerked its fins, struggling between triumph and extinction. Mr Chivers stood above it, legs astride. He watched the jet of urine strike and shatter it. Three broken bodies whirled and plummeted in their porcelain goldfish bowl, colliding with each other as the gilded waterfall spewed on.

'My pretty angels,' he murmured, as he traced an L with the last slowing dribble. 'My pretty, pretty angels.'

He pulled the chain and watched them churn and rupture down the bend.

He was humming as he trudged back to his lodgings, his hair slicked down, his shoes high-shined with a wad of toilet paper. The nail-brushes were dried, the flannels folded, the plastic duck caged safely in its sponge-bag. Miss Lineham disapproved of toys.

She met him at the front door. His quiet grey raincoat was neatly belted, his nails were scrubbed with coal tar; his trousers (never tight) were slightly damp around the turn-ups, where they had slipped from their hook on to the bath-house floor.

'Good evening, Miss Lineham. It looks like a storm.'

'Good evening, Mr Chivers. I'm afraid you're wrong. The barometer is rising. Set Fair it says and Set Fair it's going to be. Now, will you kindly go upstairs and wash your hands. I am serving supper early. Mr Gordon has most kindly invited me to see his exhibition and I have no wish to be late.'

Mr Chivers paused by the fish-tank. The golden angel was spiralling lazily towards him, flaunting its outrageous tail, gills throbbing, mouth insolently open. He could see its topaz eyes smiling at him, smiling . . .

He turned away.

'Yes, Miss Lineham,' he whispered. And went upstairs.

Dudley

'You mean Dudley won't be coming with us?'

'I don't see how he can, Joan. The place is terribly small and full of antiques and what-have-you.'

'But he isn't any trouble.' Not for years, anyway. In the early days there had, understandably, been problems.

'It's pushing our luck, though. Suppose something got broken?'

'It won't.'

'Anyway, I've already told her we're leaving him behind.'

Joan snatched up Dudley's rag-doll from the carpet. Disrupting his routine was never wise, as Kevin knew perfectly well. 'I can't think why she's bothered about our bringing him when she's not even going to be there.'

'Perhaps she's worried about muddy footprints. Or hairs on the sofa, or –'

'But Dudley doesn't shed. Couldn't you have told her?'

'Look, just between you and me, I don't think Olwen's all that keen on dogs –'

'Well, in that case, let's not go. You know my opinion of people who don't like dogs.'

'But I *want* to go. It's ages since we've been out of London. I'm looking forward to a breath of country air.'

'Surrey's hardly the country.'

'Of course it is – where Olwen lives, especially. It's right off the beaten track, she says, with lovely woods and a lake. In any case, it would be rude to cry off now.'

'So what happens to poor Duds?'

'I've had a word with Dad, and he says –'

'Oh *no*, not your father.' Joan's voice rose in disapproval. 'He's so peculiar these days.' Dudley wasn't a parcel to be dispatched anywhere, regardless.

'Don't be silly. He's lonely, that's all – he misses Mum. Having Duds will take him out of himself.'

'But can we *trust* him, Kevin?'

'It's only one weekend, for heaven's sake. And he's directly on the route, so it couldn't be more convenient. And if he's the slightest bit worried, all he has to do is phone us at the cottage and we can be with him in under an hour.'

'Aren't you being rather callous?'

'What, consigning Duds to someone who'll spoil him rotten? The way you're going on, Joan, anyone would think I was packing him off to kennels.'

Joan opened the french windows with unnecessary vehemence. It was bad taste to joke about kennels – in her estimation a form of abuse that caused long-term psychological damage, equivalent to prison for dogs, and in fact no better than the shelter. 'Shelter' was a misnomer, suggesting a place of love and safety, admirable in theory – it was the reality that fell short.

'Dudley!' she called, stepping out into the small square of garden. 'Come to Mumma.' Obedient as always, he raced towards her and jumped straight into her arms, a boisterous bundle of golden fur. Cradling him against her chest, she gazed into his dark, soulful eyes. Kevin's weak, short-sighted blue eyes could never communicate such depths of trust. 'Precious,' she whispered, caressing the soft curls on his tummy, 'you know I wouldn't leave you for the world. It's Dadda – he doesn't want to upset Auntie Olwen. She's his new boss, you see, so I suppose he has to show willing.' Although to some extent it was selfishness on Kevin's part. There was no disputing that he needed a break from work, but he might at least have considered other possibilities: a hotel that welcomed dogs, for instance. 'Anyway, we won't be far away, my sweet, and we can talk on the phone if you need to.'

Dudley's 'talking' was a marvel. He could bark on command, sing along to the radio and, even more ingenious, contribute to a conversation with knowing little whines and yelps – just as he was doing now. He understood practically every word you said to him: he would prick up his ears, cock his head to one side and concentrate on the nuances of your voice. In fact his way of communicating was more honest and direct than human speech with its evasions and hypocrisies.

She carried him inside, bestowing a kiss on the velvety skin above his nose. Kevin was sitting on the edge of the sofa, shoulders hunched, staring into space. Perhaps she had judged him too harshly. After all, it was only his long hours that allowed *her* to stay at home with Dudley. But the job was increasingly stressful, and two years running he'd been passed over for promotion and hadn't even received a pay rise. No, on second thoughts, they couldn't afford hotels.

She went to sit beside him, placing Dudley gently in his lap. 'It's all right,' she murmured, giving each of them an affectionate pat. 'He understands.'

With a savage kick Joan sent the duvet flying off the end of the bed. Stupid bloody thing! She was used to a living breathing body on her stomach, not an insensate sack of feathers. She hadn't slept alone for years. She and Kevin had separate rooms, of course – he'd long since given up all that tedious nonsense of sniffing about and mounting her. Dudley was more subtle. Nothing crude, just sensuous strokings, joyous little cuddles. The bed was cold without him; she sleepless, desolate. And he would be missing *her* – howling, for all she knew. Maurice might not even realize, being deaf in his left ear. And that appalling basket he'd produced, centuries old and smelly. Baskets were fine for less sensitive dogs, but Dudley would feel insulted and unloved. She sat up in bed, tempted to ring Maurice there and then. Except that would mean disturbing Kevin, who was sleeping downstairs on the sofa.

Or maybe not sleeping. Like her, he had grown more and more anxious last night as they sat thinking of things they had forgotten to include on the long typed list of Do's and Don't's – not to give Duds chicken bones or let him near the dustbin; that he preferred bacon chews to beef ones, and he must never, ever, be deprived of his squeaky mouse. Oblivious to the attractions of Olwen's landscaped garden and the majestic views and country air, they had spent their time phoning Maurice with a succession of new instructions. Finally, at one a.m., they had crawled into their respective beds, feeling remorseful, guilty and thoroughly out of sorts.

'More tea?'

'No thanks.'

'Toast?'

'I haven't eaten this piece yet.'

Joan spread her own slice of toast with 'I Can't Believe It's Not Butter'. She could believe it, only too well. Olwen had left provisions – low-cholesterol, low-fat, low-taste. But what made breakfast truly low was Dudley's continued absence. There was no point cooking porridge when he wasn't there to enjoy his little bowlful, topped with cream, or trekking to the village butcher for home-made prime pork sausages if he couldn't have his share. And the place seemed oppressively quiet without his pattering feet and spirited bark, the frantic flurries he'd make in pursuit of a fly or daddy-long-legs.

'It's a nice day,' she remarked, without conviction.

Kevin didn't even bother to look up. Their conversations usually hinged on Dudley – his exploits, his achievements, his appetite, his mood.

She daubed a spoonful of marmalade (low-calorie, low-sugar) on her cold and flabby toast. 'I suppose now we're here we ought to see the sights.'

'What sights?'

'I thought you said there were lovely woods.'

They caught each other's eye, both knowing that a wood without a dog was like a bat without a ball.

'And a lake . . .'

The same applied.

'OK.' Kevin pushed his chair back. 'Finish your toast and we'll make a move.'

In silence again they drove to Cransham Woods – no lively quivering presence in the back, no impassioned yelps at the sight of a squirrel or another dog.

'Pretty church,' Joan said, at length.

A grunt in response.

She tried again. 'At least the roads are quiet.' Kevin was regretting the weekend, she knew. Women had greater insight than men – she could have told him how bereft he'd feel, but, no, he wouldn't listen. And now he was suffering more than she was, blaming himself, on top of everything else.

She opened her window a few inches. The car tended to get stuffy in warm weather. 'They said it'll be getting hotter this afternoon – right up into the seventies. I just hope your father keeps Duds' water bowl topped up.'

'It's on the list.'

'Yes, but will he read the list?'

Kevin took his foot off the accelerator. 'D'you think we ought to phone?'

'Yes, definitely. Let's stop in the next village.' Joan opened her purse and shook out a handful of coins. 'And I'll speak to him, if you don't mind. He takes more notice of me.'

'Maurice? It's Joan again. We just wanted to be sure . . . Oh, I see. Good. Well, better safe than sorry. Look, could I have a word with him? . . . All right, all right, keep your hair on. No, I don't think we're fussing unduly . . .'

She returned to Kevin, visibly shaken. 'He *swore* at me, would you believe. He said Duds had got three bloody bowls of water, and he'd had dogs before I was born or thought of, and did we take him for a halfwit.'

'Oh, you know Dad. It's just his blood pressure.'

'God! I hadn't thought of that. Suppose something awful happens and he has to be carted away in an ambulance. Duds would be left on his own.'

'Joan, it's only *mild* blood pressure. He's had it for years.'

'All the same . . .'

'Look, we'll ring again at lunchtime, OK?'

She nodded, staring out of the window at the fields of ripening barley and, beyond, the green-hazed hills. Yet what she saw was Dudley, superimposed in the foreground: tail drooping, eyes haunted, as he sat trembling in a deserted house after the ambulancemen had left.

They parked next to a Range Rover just disgorging a trio of border collies in a flurry of black and white.

Joan felt a pang of envy – no, worse than envy, murderous hate, directed at Olwen. The odd pawmark on the carpet was nothing compared with a dog alone and traumatized.

She watched the collies frolic around their owners as the

happy party set off along the winding path. Cransham Woods was a canine paradise, full of tantalizing smells, sticks asking to be fetched, muddy puddles to explore, drifts of leaves to roll in. But, deprived of Dudley, they had no recourse to such vicarious delights. Just as they, the dogless, were debarred from all communication: the mutual sniffings and greetings, the exchange of names and ages, the easy camaraderie. They walked on in resentful silence, aware that it was Dudley who alerted them to the sights and sounds that made a place alive: rabbits lolloping for cover, birds squawking in a tree, thrilling little rustles in the undergrowth. Today the woods were a cardboard cut-out, sapless, meaningless.

'Tired?' Kevin asked, after hours, it seemed, of aimless trudging.

'No,' she snapped. He was beginning to annoy her – the tuneless way he whistled through his teeth and that dreadful old anorak he should have thrown out years ago.

'What do you want to do for lunch?'

'Don't mind. You choose.'

'Well, how about a pub lunch, and then something more substantial tonight?'

'OK. Let's turn back. I noticed a pub just before we stopped – the Hare and Hounds.'

The Hare and Hounds was quaint – ivy-covered, thatched and hung inside with prints of bewhiskered Victorian grandees, although the shaven-headed barman, with his silver eyebrow-stud, seemed aggressively at odds with his surroundings.

Kevin approached the bar with some apprehension. 'What do you fancy, Joan?'

'Oh, orange juice'll do.'

She chose a seat in the corner, grimacing as Kevin returned with the drinks. Did he always have to spill them? Mopping the puddle from the table, she studied the menu chalked up on the blackboard. Dudley was particularly partial to steak and kidney pie – not just the meat, the pastry, too. And he loved sausages, of course. He also had a sweet tooth, his favourite being treacle tart and custard. She was so used to choosing what he liked that she scanned the board in a haze of indecision.

'I . . . I think I'll have a ploughman's.'

'Cheese gives you indigestion, Joan.'

'Yes, so it does. Well . . . steak and kidney pie then.'

'And sausages for me. Followed by treacle tart.'

There was a long wait before the food came. Kevin embarked on a second pint of beer, wiping a fleck of foam from his moustache. 'It's not bad, as pubs go. None of that ghastly Muzak.'

She jiggled the ice cubes in the bottom of her glass. Listening to Muzak would at least have helped to pass the time.

After another fifteen minutes a girl clumped over with two loaded plates. She was wearing absurdly high platform shoes and a skirt barely longer than a pie-frill. Joan noticed Kevin's gaze travel up the expanse of black-stockinged leg. Was he still capable, she wondered? – not that she cared much either way. Her main concern was getting through the dome of greasy pastry the girl had put in front of her. Eating seemed hardly worth the effort without Dudley's dark beseeching eyes observing her every mouthful, his eager tongue lolling at the ready. Dogs were so appreciative of their food. They didn't push it listlessly around the plate or complain that it was wrongly cooked or discard bits of gristle. Every scrap was relished, the plate itself licked clean. And their enjoyment was infectious, of course.

She tried a mouthful of pie. It might as well have been Polyfilla for all the pleasure it afforded, and Kevin was clearly faring little better. The whole point of a sausage was that you saved a knob for Dudley. Indeed, other people often did the same. Many a friendship had resulted from Dudley's habit of fixing anyone engaged in eating with his not-to-be-resisted gaze. True, she had to take care that he wasn't offered chips, or fish with fiddly bones, but the odd piece of pasty here, or half a sandwich there, gave him such sheer happiness it would be churlish to refuse. He was a trifle overweight, admittedly, but, when she thought of the bag of skin and bone rescued by the shelter, resurrection seemed not too strong a word. It had been touch and go at first, and even after several months they hadn't dared relax their vigilance. The vitamins, the Complan, the home-cooked chicken breast and herring roe – all had been worth the trouble and expense. There was no doubt in her mind that people who turfed a starving animal out into the street should be whipped to within an inch of their lives.

She pushed her plate away.

Kevin looked up. 'Not hungry?'

'No. And I don't think I could cope with dinner out tonight. Let's buy a bit of ham or something and eat it at the cottage.' Then we could go to bed much earlier, she didn't add. And Sunday would come sooner: Dudley day, reprieve day.

'Just as you like. Funnily enough, I'm not hungry either.'

'What about your treacle tart?'

He shook his head. 'Couldn't face it.'

Sunday. Church bells. Although what they had to be so flaming cheerful about Joan couldn't understand. She consulted her watch for the tenth time since getting up. They *could* set off straight away, but they'd told Maurice afternoon and she didn't like to phone again after that ridiculous row last night. Maurice had overreacted, as usual. Any normal person would understand that she wasn't casting aspersions on his physical and mental faculties – she was simply ringing to remind him that Dudley's cod-liver oil should be mixed with moist food, not dry.

'Well, what's it to be today, Joan? The lake or . . . ?' Kevin was washing up the breakfast things, armoured in Olwen's yellow rubber gloves.

'Those damn bells are getting on my nerves! No wonder church attendance is falling if people have to listen to that racket.'

'Campanology,' Kevin said, pausing with a plate in his hand and his head cocked to one side like Dudley.

'What?'

'That's what it's called.'

'What what's called?'

'Bell-ringing.'

'I don't care what it's called. I prefer to hear myself speak, thank you very much.'

'Well, let's go out then. We really ought to see the lake. Olwen's bound to ask me about it. We could take a picnic, if you like – the stuff we didn't eat last night.'

'How far is it?'

'Oh, only a few minutes in the car.'

'All right,' she said grudgingly. They had got through the nights, at least. Last night had been horrendous. She dreamed she was in a shelter, banished to an outside kennel with neither food nor water, her coat disgustingly matted and tangled, and the bleeding stump of her tail throbbing with pain. She looked at her watch yet again, willing the hands to move faster: still six hours to go.

The lake was less secluded than they'd thought – in fact quite a popular tourist spot: children paddling, people feeding ducks, and dogs, naturally, of every shape and size.

Joan stood at the water's edge, idly surveying a spaniel's silken ears and the feather-duster tail of a Pomeranian. Other breeds were attractive enough in their way, but she had never seen a dog with such a magnificent coat as Dudley: a rich golden brown, like sherry, and extravagantly long. On his chest the hair shaded into cream, and there was another adorable little patch of cream outlining his nose. He was the ideal size for a dog: small enough to be cuddled yet big enough to walk for miles without flagging. In fact this was just the time for his Sunday morning outing. When *The Archers* had finished (Kevin, like his father, was an inveterate fan) they'd have their usual quick coffee and fig roll, then drive to the park on the dot of 11.30. No chance of being late with Dudley barking a reminder – he was more reliable than an alarm clock. All the way there, he'd peer out of the car window, keen to be racing around after a frisbee or a ball.

'Fetch!' she shouted suddenly, hurling a stick into the lake. 'Go on, Dudley, *fetch!*'

Kevin lost no time in joining in the game. 'Good boy!' he crowed as Dudley came hurtling back and laid the stick at their feet. Drops of water spattered their legs as he shook his dripping coat. '*Again,*' his brown eyes pleaded.

Kevin flung the stick as far as he could. Dudley was a powerful swimmer and soon outstripped the other dogs floundering in the shallows. Joan watched proudly as he paddled back to the shore, the stick held firmly in his mouth. Some dogs simply dropped their sticks or gave up halfway through. Others had never learned the art of retrieving and just looked blankly at their owners. But, despite his tragic start in life, Dudley was now patently more intelligent than the general run of dogs. Of course it had taken time and patience on her part. He had needed stimulation and well-regulated playtime. She had encouraged games like hide-and-seek and hunt-the-slipper and helped him overcome his fears. Fortunately water wasn't one of them.

And yes, here he was, back in record time, prancing round with a volley of effusive barks, urging them to throw the stick again. A little girl came running over to stroke him. 'Isn't he *gorgeous*!' she exclaimed.

'Gorgeously muddy!' they laughed.

All at once, he dashed back into the water, in pursuit not of a stick this time but a frantic and indignant coot. They couldn't help but smile, especially when the coot spoiled the sport by flying off, much to Dudley's perplexity. But he took it in good part. His sulks and temper tantrums were now a thing of the past.

'He needs a good long run,' said Kevin, 'after being cooped up yesterday. Let's walk all round the lake and tire him out.'

'Good idea. Then he'll sleep well. He hardly got a wink last night, whatever Maurice said.'

They struck out along the path, Dudley darting ahead but constantly gambolling back again, as if he couldn't bear to let them out of his sight.

'I'm sure he feels sorry for us, having just two legs.'

'So he should!' Kevin unconsciously quickened his pace. 'And we'd certainly be better off with tails.'

True, thought Joan, glancing at Dudley's long curly one. If Kevin had a tail he would be easier to live with. He baffled her at times, sitting in blank silence behind the newspaper or putting on his don't-ask-me-how-I-am face, whereas a tail would signal instantly whether he was happy or morose.

At present he was euphoric – practically wagging his tail off. And she felt just the same, now that Dudley was restored to them. She gave Kevin's arm a squeeze. Even the shabby anorak didn't annoy her any more. On the contrary. With money so tight, it was decent of him not to buy new clothes.

'All right, dear?' he asked fondly, linking his arm through hers.

She nodded. 'I'm glad we came. Aren't you?'

'*Very* glad. Dudley's in his element. He needed a change from the park. It's too confining for an adventurous dog like him, although I hadn't actually realized till today.'

'The air's cleaner here, as well. Willesden's so polluted. It can't be good for his lungs. If only you could get another job, dear, we could move out of London altogether.'

'Yes, but who'd take me on at my age?'

'Don't put yourself down. You've still got a lot to . . . All right, Dudley, we're coming! Yes, I know we're slow compared with you, but . . .'

'Oh, Lord!' said Kevin. 'What's that he's found? The remains of a rabbit, by the looks of it. Leave it, Duds. *Leave*, I said.'

'Oh, isn't he an angel? To drop something quite so tempting.'

'All credit to your training, Joan.'

She felt the blood rush to her cheeks. Compliments were rare. 'You helped, dear,' she murmured, recalling their joint sessions at weekends; she teaching 'sit and stay' while Kevin proffered the food rewards and reinforced her praises.

They continued arm in arm along the lakeside path, which was bordered by a thicket of rhododendron bushes, resplendent in full purple bloom. Cupping one of the flowers in her hand, she looked at it more closely, struck by the contrast between the mauve silk of the petals and the dark green leathery leaves. There weren't any flowers in their garden at home – they had made it into a play area, with a miniature obstacle course and a sand-pit, to stimulate Dudley's creative self-expression. 'What are these things?' she asked, poking her finger into the frilly purple bell. 'Stamens, isn't it?'

'Mm. Or pistils, maybe.'

'*Pistols?*'

'No, dear, with an i. It's the female part – the stamens are male.'

'Male?' she repeated, brushing pollen from her finger. 'They're like tiny bunches of bulrushes, with those powdery brown tips.'

'The trouble is,' Kevin mused, 'we don't get *time* to look. Not normally. Life's such a dreadful rush.'

'We must go away more often, then. D'you think Olwen might lend us the cottage again?'

'Yes, probably. But what about Duds?'

'Kevin . . .' Joan gripped his arm to emphasize her point, 'what we need to do is *introduce* him to Olwen, and I bet you anything you like she'll be completely captivated. It happens every time. That friend of yours, for instance, who said dogs were dirty and dangerous – within half an hour of meeting Duds he was holding his paw and telling him what a beautiful boy he was.'

'Of course! Why didn't we think of it before? We'll invite her for Sunday tea and she and Dudley can get to know each other.'

'And I'll lay on a nice spread. D'you think she'd like my date and walnut . . . ? No, Duds, you're far too big to get down that rabbit-hole.'

'He's really into rabbits today – dead or alive!'

'Do you remember that time he actually caught a rabbit? He was so surprised he didn't know what to do with it.'

Kevin laughed. 'Oh, yes. The expression on his face!'

The three of them walked on, Kevin whistling again, melodiously this time. She recognized the tune: 'Spread a Little Happiness'. It was good to see him so content, his tight-set jaw relaxed.

He broke off in mid-phrase. 'Oh, look, a perfect picnic place! And not a soul around.'

The path had widened out to a grassy clearing, with half a dozen rustic wooden picnic tables dotted here and there, and a handsome weeping willow admiring its reflection in the lake.

'Let's stop and have a bite to eat. I'm getting jolly peckish!' With some difficulty Kevin shrugged the rucksack off his shoulders. (He was more used to carrying an umbrella and a briefcase.) He handed it to Joan, who put it on the table and started unpacking the provisions.

'Dudley, what *are* you thinking of?' Kevin held up a reproving finger – their naughty boy was standing on his hind legs, sniffing at the food.

'Sit!' Joan ordered sharply. Even now, Dudley could revert to his bad habits if they didn't maintain strict but loving discipline. You owed that to a dog.

Dudley sat, his eyes fixed on the sandwich box, his moist black nose twitching in anticipation.

'Thank goodness I brought sausages.' Joan unwrapped a greaseproof-paper package – again much to Dudley's interest.

'He'll like the pâté, too.'

'You don't think it's too rich for him?'

'Well, a bit, maybe. But it is his special day.'

'*Down*, Duds! Sit means sit, you know that. If you want a sausage, what do you say?'

Dudley barked his usual 'please'.

'That's better! We don't forget our manners, do we, just because we're on holiday.' She offered him the sausage, which he devoured in a single gulp. 'I'll make a pâté sandwich for him. It'll be more digestible like that.'

'Yes, and if you let me have that cake tin I'll put him some water in it.'

At the mention of cake, festoons of saliva began to drool

from Dudley's mouth, soon developing into quivering liquid stalactites. And as Joan removed the chocolate sponge from the tin he made an unexpected leap at it.

'Manners!' scolded Joan, although secretly she found his passion exciting. A bone, a walk, a sausage, even a staling, shop-bought cake – all sent him into transports of delight. And that in turn awakened some strange urge in her: one she hardly dared admit. 'Not yet, Dudsy, darling. We save choccy things for dessert. And we clean our teethies afterwards with our new doggy toothbrush, don't we?'

Kevin filled the tin from the bottle of Highland Spring. Luckily it was the still sort, not the sparkling (thanks to Joan's indigestion; fizzy drinks played havoc with her stomach). As he bent to put the tin down Dudley all but knocked him over in his eagerness to get to it.

Joan watched anxiously as he lapped in feverish haste. Had Maurice skimped on water? Three bowlsful, he'd said, which had struck her as weird at the time. (Providing three of something would surely only confuse a dog.) It could be that his mind was failing. At his age, brain cells shrivelled at a frightening rate – she'd heard it on the radio last week. Never, under any circumstances, would she leave Dudley there again. In the space of less than forty-eight hours her poor bewildered darling had begun to show signs of disturbance – alarming in a dog who'd already suffered abuse.

Eyeing him with concern, she made his little sandwich – well, not so little, actually. He deserved a treat after what he'd been through, and this time she didn't mean his early life.

She fed it to him in bite-sized pieces, in order to spin out his enjoyment, then gave him the end of her sausage. She was glad now she'd bought the sausages, although cooking them last night had seemed a thankless chore, simply a way of keeping busy, keeping grief at bay. Things were returning to normal, thank God. They were a family once more, reunited, going through the comforting routines: Dudley gazing enraptured at his Dadda, big brown eyes following every movement of his hand from plate to mouth and back again, until finally he was rewarded with a titbit. A few days of careful retraining, a little extra love, and their poppet would be his usual dependable self. In fact life was looking up – regular breaks in the country, Kevin less at risk of a coronary, and Duds idolized by his devoted Auntie Olwen.

She took a sip of water: it tasted like champagne. The weather, too, was flawless; the sky a well-mannered blue and the clouds so white and fluffy they looked as if they'd been washed and groomed for the cloud equivalent of a dog show. A gentle breeze was ruffling the weeping willow, although, far from weeping, its long silvery-green tresses sparkled beneath the steady smile of the sun.

'More water, dear?' she asked, first refilling Dudley's bowl.

Kevin held out his perspex beaker, marbled blue and white, to match the sandwich box. Like everything of Olwen's, the picnic set was stylish – nothing but the best. They must put it back exactly as they'd found it and be sure to leave the cottage spotless. In fact they ought to make a move soon if they were going to be at Maurice's by four. Yet she felt mesmerized by the rippling lake, the tranquillity, the warmth . . . In any case, they all needed to relax after the traumas of the weekend, and it would certainly do Dudley good to stay longer in this idyllic spot.

'I think I'll have a little shut-eye,' she said, getting up from the bench.

'I wouldn't advise lying on the grass, dear. We should have brought a picnic rug.'

'There didn't seem much point.'

'Lie down here.' Kevin spread his anorak on the grass, then

folded the empty rucksack to make her a pillow. She was touched by his thoughtfulness – how lucky she was to have two devoted males.

She settled Dudley beside her, pressing her face against his tawny fur. He, too, snuggled close, as if they had been parted for years instead of just two nights. Whispering endearments, she ran her hands from the top of his head to the very tip of his tail. They had learned falteringly over the years how to please each other.

Kevin's breathing had deepened. He was already asleep, she saw: arms folded on the picnic table, head resting on the wood. He must have been dead tired to nod off in such an uncomfortable position.

She, too, closed her eyes, and let the sun beam down on her as she caressed Dudley's chest and tummy. He responded instantly, stretching out his paws in an ecstasy of pleasure and making tiny contented grunts. 'My precious lamb,' she murmured, enlacing her fingers through his fur. 'We'll never be parted again – I swear.'

It was getting on for seven when they drove into Clifton Close.

'We're terribly late,' Kevin fretted, as he parked outside The Hollies. 'I hope Dad isn't worried.'

'I doubt it. He's never had much sense of time. No, Duds, you can't get out. We'll only be a second. Here's your squeaky mouse. Stay! *Sit!* Good boy.'

Joan gave him a reassuring wave as she and Kevin hurried up the crazy-paving path. The ding-dong chime had scarcely died away when the door was flung open by an unrecognizable Maurice: ashen-faced, wild-eyed.

'*There* you are!' he burst out, clutching Kevin by the shoulder. 'I've been half dead with worry.'

'Oh, come on, Dad. I know we're late, but –'

'God, I don't know how to tell you! Forgive me, please forgive me. I never thought . . .' He broke off, close to tears, blinked several times, then continued in a sobbing spate of words. 'He's . . . gone. He's disappeared. Yes, just like that. One minute he was there and the next . . . I've tried everything, been everywhere – searched the streets, knocked on every door . . . I phoned the cottage, but you'd left. I even phoned the police. Fat lot of use *they* were. Said dogs went missing all the time. But I don't see how he could have gone – I watched him like a hawk, never let him out of my sight. No, I lie – I did have a quick dekko at the golf. But Duds was there beside me, safe and sound. I've been at my wits' end. I know you'll say –'

'Maurice, will you *please* be quiet!' Joan steered him and Kevin inside the door and shut it with a decisive click. 'Right, let's get things straight. First of all, I assume it's Dudley you're talking about?'

'Of course it's Dudley! What the hell do you think I –'

'There's no need to be rude, Dad.'

'It's all right, Kevin. Leave this to me. Now, Maurice, would you kindly make an effort and try to remember what time it was when you first noticed Dudley had gone?'

'I'm not a total cretin, Joan. I remember perfectly well. It was eleven thirty, bang on. I know because *The Archers* had finished and I'd just turned on the . . .'

Joan caught Kevin's eye. They smiled at one another.

Eleven thirty.

Of course.

Scar

The wind slapped her face as she walked down to the beach, buffeted her body, snatched at her scarf. Irritable, like Josh of late. And dominant, like him again, trying to mould and sculpt her to its will. She should never have come. The best of the day was over, the morning sunshine gone, leaving a concrete-coloured sky and a sense of mournful heaviness on everything. The season was over, too; the beach deserted, more or less. Over. A word she would have to get used to.

She stood looking at the sea. Unlike the wind it seemed tired, heaving itself laboriously back and forth and dribbling out a froth of slobber, the drool of an old man. Perhaps it was exhausted by the effort of pandering to the hordes of summer visitors and now wanted to be left in peace. Yet if Josh were here it would have rallied soon enough, laid on a decent show: crashing waves, clouds of spray, dramatic sound-effects. Things gave of their best for Josh. As *she* had. Before the operation.

Instinctively her hand groped down, as if she could feel the scar through her coat. 'A beautiful scar,' the surgeon had pronounced. Beautiful?

Pulling the coat around her, she kept a protective hand

across her stomach. It would be worse in the summer, in more revealing clothes.

She glanced up at the familiar shape of the headland, which Josh had once described as a recumbent lion. Today even the lion seemed dejected, its head slumped on its paws, its whole posture suggesting defeat. Sometimes she thought of Josh as a lion: powerful, unpredictable.

It was too cold to stand around, so she set off across the beach, struck by the absence of smells. No salt tang, no whiff of dead fish or seaweed. Had she lost her sense of smell along with so much else? There was space at least in abundance: the horizon stretching to infinity beneath a vast grey sky. And time. Enough to walk to infinity and back.

She could make out a couple of figures in the distance. As she drew nearer they took on shape and colour: a woman in a turquoise floral swimsuit and a boy of about nine or ten. The woman had evidently been swimming. Her hair hung wet and straggly, and she was shaking out a towel from the pile of belongings on the sand. A masochist, no doubt, to brave the sea in November. Clutching the towel around her, she began struggling out of her costume. Joanne glimpsed udder-like breasts, mottled lumpy thighs, and averted her eyes in distaste. Although who was *she* to feel superior? Her own breasts might be firm, her thighs slim and tanned, but she was damaged goods since the op.

The child had built a sandcastle, an ambitious structure with turrets and a moat. As she moved closer to examine it, he suddenly seized his spade and flailed viciously at his handi-work, jabbing and poking at the battlements and towers. Wet gobbets of sand spattered on to her legs as he demolished the last rampart, then ground it underfoot.

'Don't!' she implored him silently. 'Don't destroy things. Good things.'

But there was no point getting upset. That's how it had all started to go wrong. Josh hated tears, and she had been weepy after coming out of hospital.

The boy flung down his spade with a scowl. Neither he nor the woman had spoken, to each other or to her. Odd, she thought. Unnatural. Were they mother and son, or just two loners on the same stretch of beach? Did your husband leave? she wanted to ask. Your father disappear?

She and Josh had never married. 'It's commitment that counts,' he often said, 'not some fatuous ceremony.'

She turned away, her feet dragging in the sand. Stupid to be self-pitying. Thousands of people were on their own. Single. Widowed. Divorced. Once she had been to a singles bar – years ago, with a girlfriend. The females there seemed predatory: lynx-eyed, ready to pounce. She never went again.

At the waterline was a scum of detritus where the sea had disgorged its lunch: plastic bottles, dented cans, bits of ragged fishing net, a length of hairy rope. She, too, had little appetite. Since Josh had left she'd barely eaten anything. Her mouth felt dry and furred, as if she'd been contaminated somehow. She thought longingly of tea. Tea for shock. And loss. Kindly people offered it after a bereavement or an operation; made sure that it was sweet and strong. Men were rarely both. You had to choose. With Josh, she'd chosen strong. Yet one small scar had unnerved him.

Perhaps it wasn't so small, though. It seemed to be getting bigger every day and assumed grotesque proportions in her mind: a livid purple weal branding her whole body.

Clutching her stomach, she trudged towards the promenade. The café might be open, the one Josh liked, with its silver jugs and old-fashioned sugar-lumps. If she sat at their usual table she might pick up a faint trace of him: his smell, his aura, an echo of his voice.

'Closed' said the sign. Well, what did she expect? Losing a partner meant losing their favourite haunts, losing their friends and relatives. She no longer had claim on this lonely sweep of coast. It was Josh's place. He had grown up here; his sister still lived locally. On previous visits they'd stayed in her cottage, but the door would now be barred. In any case, the seaside was for pleasure, not for grief.

And what madness to have driven so far, when she had to return to London the same day. No, she wouldn't return. Without Josh, the flat wasn't home. Just four confining walls. It seemed smaller, paradoxically, with only one person there.

She tramped on, past the café. The promenade was deserted, like the beach, apart from an elderly woman, another piece of jetsam, washed up on a battered wooden bench. Had life spat her out, discarded her as old and ineffectual? She, too, might have a scar. Perhaps she had lived alone for decades, rejected by a husband who couldn't cope with disfigurement.

A scar was always with you. A puckered ridge, unpleasant to the touch, with eighteen stitchmarks either side: a loathsome extra tattoo. Before the op Josh loved to kiss her stomach, would let his mouth steal slowly further down. Mere memories now . . .

She approached the woman, not wanting to intrude yet desperate for the sound of a human voice. Silence could be frightening. Josh's conversation had kept her magnificently alive. Without it she was foundering.

She sat down on the edge of the bench, murmuring a tentative hello.

The woman didn't respond. Deaf, perhaps. Or foreign. She looked the epitome of Englishness, with her watery blue eyes, big white plastic handbag, sparse head of thistledown. The wind was puffing at the thistledown like a dandelion clock – one o'clock, two o'clock . . . Joanne half expected wispy little clumps of white to float off with every puff. Three o'clock, four o'clock . . . It was only half past three, in fact, but the light was dull and grudging, as if the sun had lost heart and abandoned all pretence of doing its job. Like her. It felt strange having time on her hands, especially at the weekend. Weekends with Josh were a whirl – eating, drinking, partying, lightning trips to Paris or down here to the sea. And making love, of course, often twice a night. Until the operation. No sex for eight weeks, the surgeon ordered. Even after that it hurt. And she'd begun turning off the lights before they undressed. They had never made love in the dark before. Josh liked to see her body.

Had done. Once.

Did the old woman still think about sex? Being kissed, straddled, tongued, touched. Made to feel precious and important. At what age did you lose the urge? Fifty? Sixty? Seventy? Soon she would be an old crone herself. She had already aged two decades in two weeks.

'The wind's nasty, isn't it?' she said. People talked about the weather when nothing else was left. Only rain and wind and mist.

No reply. Had she become invisible? There had been a programme on the radio last week: a physicist and a biologist discussing whether anything existed outside oneself. Perhaps the old lady was no more than a mirage. She, too. Josh had been her identity.

She stood up. Why torture herself. 'It's over,' she said out loud.

The woman jumped. For a moment they stared at each other. The weak blue eyes were watering in the wind; the wrinkled mouth forming wordless words. Then the woman shambled to her feet and hobbled off along the promenade.

Joanne watched her go. The last remaining human in a

depopulated world. A world crumbling, like the cliff-face. She had seen a notice further back: 'Danger. Falling rocks.' In the past, whole tracts of land had toppled into the sea. Species become extinct. Rivers silted up. So why should a trifling scar matter quite so much?

Because it mattered to Josh, that's why. Besides, it wasn't just the scar. She had also lost her confidence. 'You're different,' he kept saying. 'You're so tense, you can't let go.'

That was the surgeon's fault. She detested him, the surgeon: his butcher's hands, his empty eyes, his life's work of creating scars.

The sky was the colour of ashes. There hadn't been a sunset. No point. Why should Nature put on a grand display of gold and scarlet if Josh wasn't here to admire it? She suddenly realized that, back in London, he would be ten minutes further into darkness than she was on the coast. Maybe already in bed with some other woman, one with a perfect unscarred body. Blonde, as he liked. Whorls of golden pubic hair. Huge violet eyes. Voluptuous breasts. And of course utterly at ease in her body; never tensing with pain or trying to hide her stomach with her hands. She and Josh would laugh together, not cry. He'd push grapes into her cunt and suck them out one by one by one. Or hang cherries over her nipples and bite playfully at the stalks. They'd eat ice cream in bed, like the lovers in the ads, or pass softened squares of chocolate from her open mouth to his. He'd lick the chocolate spittle from her breasts; flick his probing tongue-tip into the secret cavern of her navel.

Morning now. They were showering together. Entwined, again, while the jet of water pounded down, colluding and applauding. His slithery, soap-slicked hands a contrast to the barb of his chin. Drying each other. The velvet graze of the towel as he thrust it between her legs. The sense of ecstatic closeness that lasted all day. All night.

'You're so beautiful,' he whispered, kissing her stomach; letting his mouth steal slowly, slowly down. 'I love you, Joanne.'

No, not Joanne. Joanne had changed. Joanne was too tense to let go.

Impetuously, she turned on her heel. The glare of the streetlamps was harsh; any light unkind. The beach would be more merciful. No moon. No stars. Dark enough to hide.

With every step she seemed to dissolve into the night, becoming part of the vast, shadowy blur where sky merged into earth. Dense, swollen-bellied clouds crouched above the headland, as if they, too, sought protection.

The sea was waiting for her. No longer tired, it reached out eagerly as her feet slid over the sand, its soft swishing voice wooing and cajoling. She could hear her lover's name in the soft hiss of the waves breaking on the rocks. 'Josh-sshhh,' they insisted, 'Josh-sshhhhh . . .'

She unbuttoned her coat, let it fall; kicked off her shoes, wrenched her sweater over her head. The wind pestered jealously, tousling her hair, groping her chest, trying to drag her away from the water. Could she really be so damaged if wind and sea were fighting to possess her?

Contemptuous of its rival, the sea crept up and up, moving inexorably towards her, sighing with impatience.

Naked, she ran to meet it across the clammy, clinging sand, gooseflesh pimpling her arms, her whole body taut with cold. Flirtatious wavelets frilled across her feet, cupped her ankles, caressed her skin. She shivered in anticipation as the water rippled upwards, inch by sensuous inch, past her calves, her knees and slowly up her thighs; the tantalizing flurries advancing and retreating; up and back, up and back. She closed her eyes as an icy jolt tingled round her groin, sending exquisite shudders through her limbs.

The sea was spinning out its pleasure, lapping against her

stomach, probing the secret cavern of her navel. Untroubled by the scar, it gently fingered the ridge, explored the tiny stitch-marks, cherishing the puckered skin as a special, precious part of her.

And now its voracious mouth was sucking at her breasts; tempestuous water swirling back and forth. Her nipples stiffened in response. She was breathing fast, crying out, a fierce eddy of excitement surging up between her legs. Nothing had changed. Of course she could let go. She was alive again. Ecstatic. The sea, too, churned and threshed, unable to hold back, suddenly exploding in a squall of spume and spray.

Gasping, she plunged below the surface, exulting in the ferocious shock of cold.

'Come to me,' the sea crooned as it enveloped her triumphantly. 'You're so beautiful, Joanne. Come back.'

Petits Pois

Dot peered at the label on the bag of *petits pois*: 'Specially selected small, sweet, tender peas . . .' She slammed the bag into her trolley. She had been small and sweet once. She grabbed another packet – a different brand this time. 'The youngest, freshest, most succulent peas – only the smallest and sweetest are selected . . .' Cruel, she thought, throwing half a dozen packets in the trolley.

The cold breath of the freezer was welcome on her face. She wiped her damp forehead with her sleeve. It was the weight that made her sweat. But these days everything was bigger, not just her: newspapers, planes, children, buildings, shops. This supermarket had practically grown into a village: delicatessen, florist, café, pharmacy . . . Although without the friendliness of a real village. Most of the shoppers were on their own, independent tug-boats chugging along picking up cargo but avoiding contact with all other craft. She wished she could board someone else's boat, or had a friend with her – better still a son or daughter and a little flock of grandchildren.

Round the corner, in baby foods, a woman with an already groaningly full trolley was amassing quantities of jars: strained turkey dinner, bone broth, creamed apricot dessert. She seemed impervious to the wrangling of her children, two small boys spoiling for a fight. Dot watched in disapproval as several tins of powdered baby milk were added to the hoard. (*She* had planned to breast-feed. If Nature gave you milk, you should use it.) She glanced enviously at the piles of stuff she would have no cause to buy: Cheerios, fish-fingers, Monster Munch, Jelly-Pots. And everything in multi-packs: six of this, ten of that, a dozen cans of ginger beer, two dozen packets of crisps. The woman was a nurturer, feeding up the future generation; an overflowing store cupboard, an inexhaustible drinking fountain. As *she* had planned to be.

Wandering on, past household goods and washing powders, she found herself at men's toiletries. She ought to buy something for Dennis for their wedding anniversary. Except he was bound to have forgotten and would be embarrassed if she gave him a present. Only Dennis could forget a ruby wedding. Forty years – a lifetime. Her children would have remembered, trooping over with their families, filling the house with noise and laughter, bringing expensive gifts. Although, to be fair to Dennis, he did bring her gifts every day – produce from the allotment: armfuls of gangling runner beans, reptilian-skinned marrows, potatoes with strange blemishes, beetroots that bloodied her hands. Such abundance meant hard work – hours of peeling, chopping, boiling, blanching, freezing – and amounted to far more, of course, than just two of them could eat. But you only clocked up forty years of marriage by indulging a husband's hobbies. Over time, you learned to praise his courgettes, admire his first tiny knobbly cucumbers, commiserate over bifurcated carrots, ignore mud on the kitchen floor.

She turned her attention to the shelf of body-sprays, picking up a black aerosol called Impulse. She removed the cap and sniffed it: sandalwood and musk. Dennis smelled of bonfire smoke and compost. And he rarely did things on impulse. The other names were equally exotic: Cossack, Gypsy, Cavalier. She had never met such men. The one boyfriend she'd had before Dennis was sandy-haired and freckled and a civil engineer.

Perhaps she'd buy herself a spray. Allure sounded nice, or Pleasure Zone. But cellulite didn't constitute a pleasure zone, and varicose veins were hardly alluring. She wheeled her trolley briskly past the display – no point wasting time on what might have been.

She joined the queue at the checkout, seizing the bags of *petits pois* and clumping them down on the counter. Why in God's name had she bought them? For the adjectives, of course. 'Young, sweet, special, tender, fresh . . .' Adjectives that made her weep.

When she got home she hid the peas in the freezer, although it was a struggle fitting them in between the scores of tightly packed cartons. They could do with a second freezer. Except it would only encourage Dennis to take a second allotment and then she'd never see him at all. Already he worked there every day – longer hours than he used to at the office. Not that she was idle either. Right now there was a batch of raspberries waiting to be made into jam and several pounds of loganberries to bottle. But first she'd sit down with a cup of tea and a piece of Tartan shortbread. One biscuit couldn't hurt. It was the pregnancies that had done the damage. She had lost the babies but not the weight. Four miscarriages, two stillbirths. After the sixth they'd given up.

She bit into the shortbread, scattering crumbs and sugar on her skirt. The skirt was a dreary colour, like mushroom soup. You didn't wear bright colours when you were size 18 or above. Miserable, mouldy shades were recommended, so as not to draw attention to yourself. Nice to be thin. And have a different name. Dot was absurd for someone pushing thirteen stone, suggesting as it did an infinitesimal speck, not a monster-sized blot on the landscape. It was also perilously close to dotty. And Dot and Den was worse, inviting jokes about the Flowerpot Men. She preferred to call him Dennis, but he'd been Den before they married. Before the pregnancies. A full-time job, the pregnancies – swelling and contracting, swelling and contracting. Losing babies. Gaining weight. Eating for two. Ending up as one again.

Dr Menkes had told her she had got it out of proportion. It was high time she put all that behind her, he said, and started enjoying her retirement, rather than dwelling on the past. What he really meant was that now she had her pension book she should be thinking about death, not birth. She thought about both. Constantly. In any case, the two were linked: embryos flushed down the sluice, new-born babies measured for their coffins. And it wasn't in the past. She still dreamed about confinements every night: lungless, limbless babies strangled by the umbilical cord or thrown out with the waste. Nor had she retired, except from failing to have children. And, as for getting things out of proportion, that was, frankly, an insult. What could be more terrible than six uprooted babies?

She helped herself to another piece of shortbread. A hundred and sixty calories. A shame food couldn't talk. Shortbread she imagined as comfortable and kindly, telling her (in a soft Scots burr) not to worry about calories or heartless, childless doctors. And they could discuss her plans for livening up the kitchen. 'New blinds, do you think?' she asked the empty biscuit packet. 'Sunshine yellow? Cheerful.'

No answer. As usual. Well, time to wash the fruit. The water ran ruby-red. Rubies seemed to be everywhere. In the Bible, even – something about a virtuous woman being valued far above rubies. *She* was a virtuous woman, but only through lack of opportunity. Men weren't exactly queuing up.

While the fruit was draining, she got out the preserving pan and opened the bags of sugar. She should have bought a card for Dennis – a big showy one, with '40' on. Better to remind him than let the date pass unremarked. He'd be out all day at the County Show with his onions and his prize-size marrow, but they would have the evening to celebrate.

There wasn't room on the kitchen table for the jam jars. It was covered with the newspapers Dennis had left in a jumbled heap before rushing off to sow more winter spinach. As she gathered them up, a headline caught her eye: 'Miracle Baby for Granny, 62.'

Sixty-two. Her age. She read on avidly, amazed to think that a woman long past the menopause could actually give birth. It hadn't come cheap, of course. The drugs, the scans, the egg donation, the team of high-powered obstetricians, had cost almost as much as this house. Yet wouldn't any childless woman give up house and home and all she possessed for a miracle like that?

She shut her eyes and pictured the donor egg: a small, sweet, tender, specially selected egg. Which would hatch into a perfect baby. Yes, she could feel it in her arms, a living breathing baby at last, not a corpse in a shawl.

'Don't be daft, Dot. When the poor kid's twenty I'll be eighty-odd. Or pushing up the daisies, more like.'

'No, listen, Den, age needn't be a barrier. There are other modern miracles – people living to a hundred and ten with all their faculties intact. Incredible new transplants. You name it, they can replace it: brains, spleens, bladders, wombs.'

It was useless – she'd never persuade him. He didn't even want a child any more. He already had a nurseryful of babies: Little Gem, dwarf beans, baby beets, seedlings in profusion. She alone was barren.

Miserably she started weighing out the sugar. Seven

pounds, the *Mail* had said – a bouncing, healthy boy. She could see him on the scales, a perfectly formed infant, with her eyes and Den's lean build. If you had a child, you couldn't die. Your genes lived on, your memory lived on.

If only . . . But she'd need Den's consent, his sperm. She assumed there was still sperm. He'd lost interest long ago, but he could do it at the hospital with a nice young nurse on hand . . .

No – that would be all wrong. Too casual for such an extraordinary conception. Couldn't she tie it in with tomorrow's anniversary? Cook a special dinner, with candles and champagne. Then, when he was nicely relaxed, produce a little jar.

She must make him see how important it was, how all she'd ever wanted was a family. And if he was worried about the money side, they could take out a loan, remortgage the house, even raid his pension fund. They would probably argue the whole evening, but she'd win him round in the end. She had to. This was her last hope.

No time for jam – there was the menu to work out. The raspberries could go into a soufflé, for dessert. And something meaty for the main course, with masses of fresh vegetables. The starter was more of a problem. Dennis hadn't the patience to fiddle about with artichokes or harpoon prawns from a glutinous mess of lettuce. Soup would be the best. Yes, of course – pea soup. (No more guilt then about buying the *petits pois*. Buying any vegetables was a crime in Dennis's book.) She would pour her devotion into the most perfect soup imaginable: young, sweet, tender, fresh and succulent . . .

She unzipped her ruby-red dress and sprayed eau de cologne on her breasts. She felt as hot and frazzled as the overcooked meat, and her hair-do had collapsed like the soufflé. The dress was a mistake. It looked garish now and cheap. And the new dangly earrings hurt.

Tugging them off, she limped downstairs to the kitchen. It would be a relief to get back into comfortable shoes and out of these ridiculous high heels. She turned the gas to low. The *potage de petits pois* had been simmering so long there wouldn't be a shred of goodness left in it. Dennis might at least have rung. True he didn't know about the dinner – she had decided to surprise him – but he'd promised to be back by seven, and it was now twenty-five to nine. It was obvious that he'd forgotten the date; he hadn't bought her so much as a card. Her card to him was waiting on the table, propped against the vase of roses – red, naturally.

She had a good mind to chuck the dinner in the bin, change into her dressing-gown and bloody well go to bed on her . . .

'Dot?'

She tensed. She hadn't heard his key in the lock, but heavy footsteps were crossing the hall.

'Sorry I'm late, love. I had a hell of a time getting home. Terrible tailback on the A23. Jammed solid for miles, it was.'

He appeared at the kitchen door, rubbing his eyes wearily. But then he blinked at her in surprise. 'Whatever's that you're wearing? Bit bright for you, isn't it?'

'Your dinner's ruined, Den.'

'Don't worry, love. I'm not hungry anyway. I had a bite to eat at the show. Well, more than a bite. I met old Arthur Cosgrove and we –'

'I've spent all day cooking, I'll have you know.'

'Never mind, dear. It'll keep.'

'Keep? Soufflé won't keep. And I've made a special soup –'

'What sort of soup?'

'Er . . . cauliflower and leek. And it'll boil dry if we don't eat it soon.'

'I'm not sure I could face it, Dot. I've got a filthy headache. Traffic fumes, most probably. Look, I'll take a couple of aspirins and see how I feel then, OK?'

She slammed out of the back door and stood trembling on the patio. He'd had the nerve to criticize her dress. When she'd spent the whole of Friday traipsing from shop to shop. Thin, disdainful salesgirls questioning her taste, steering her away from resplendent red creations towards rails of dull brown sacks. And now Dennis, too, wilfully failed to understand. Red for rubies, red for love. She had to look her brightest best, not just for him, for the baby. No child would want a fat, frumpy mother encased in compost-brown.

Dennis didn't want her anyway. Or the special dinner. He hadn't even glanced at the table in the dining-room: the lace cloth and best bone china, the napkins twisted into damask swans, the perfumed candle and cut-glass vase of roses. She'd had to buy the roses. There was no room in the garden for flowers. Like the allotment, it was full of his children: strawberries coddled in straw cots, melons in glass incubators, tomatoes tucked up tenderly in Gro-bags. Proud father that he was, he'd carefully chosen his tomatoes' names: Tiny Tim, Isabelle, Golden Boy, Ailsa Craig. Her babies, too, had names: Futility, Frustration, Disappointment, Might-Have-Been.

She stumbled along the path between the beds, almost losing her footing in the gloom. Yes, here were all his progeny: fresh sprigs reaching out to her with tiny curling tendrils, every bed crammed with healthy offspring, fed, watered, mulched and cosseted. There wasn't room for another child – their child.

She stopped by the parsley patch. Earlier, she had picked parsley for the soup. Added dill and basil, a subtle blend of seasonings to enhance the home-made stock. Her loving preparations were so much wasted effort – like her loving preparations for the babies: knitted matinée jackets, hand-embroidered layettes, antenatal classes, extra vitamins. All had proved a mockery. And this time it was worse. The child wasn't even conceived. She had no foetus to mourn, no full-term corpse to embrace. Her womb was uninhabited.

Veering off the path, she groped her way towards the waste patch at the bottom of the garden. It was choked with weeds: groundsel, thistles, docks. And a deadly nightshade plant she had noticed a few days ago. Deadly was how she felt. Towards other men, as well as Dennis. Those callous gynaecologists who'd told her to forget about babies and take up a hobby instead; Dr Menkes, who'd said she must lose three stone – no excuses; her brother, who called her Fatso; her father, who'd wanted a boy; Mr Ward at primary school, who wrote 'Doesn't try' on her report. She had spent her whole life trying.

It was hard to see in the darkness, but eventually she managed to locate the spindly plant. 'You're gorgeous, aren't you?' she whispered, stroking a finger along its downy stem. 'With your black berries and green leaves. Belladonna – beautiful woman.'

She plucked two of the berries and two of the leaves and bore them triumphantly back to the house. The air was cool and refreshing; the sky jewelled with little diamanté chips. The garden smells of bonfire smoke and mist gave way in the kitchen to the reek of charring meat. No matter. It was the soup she was concerned with, and Den, fortunately, was still upstairs.

Putting an apron over her dress, she squashed the berries with the back of a spoon. Inside were tiny seeds, suspended in a viscous ruby-red pulp. Incredible – the colour was exactly right. She placed the pulp in a saucer, then shredded the leaves finely with a knife. Giving the soup a final stir, she ladled it into two thick china bowls and divided pulp and seeds between them. She smiled to see the reddish tinge swirled amidst the green. How pretty it looked, how unusual. And the freshly shredded leaves would make a perfect garnish.

'Den!' she called. 'Soup's on the table.' The kitchen table. Why bother using the dining-room? He wouldn't want red roses, Royal Doulton, damask swans.

She called again from the bottom of the stairs. 'If you're not hungry, Den, we'll just have the soup, OK?'

She heard him coming downstairs, the little click as the door opened. 'Feeling better?' she asked.

'Yes, thanks. Sorry I was ratty, love.'

'That's all right.'

'I don't know what got into me. I feel awful now, snapping at you like –'

'I said, it doesn't matter. Now hurry up, the soup's getting cold.' Although hot or cold made little difference – either would be effective. It was time they made an end of it; Dennis with his headaches, she with her empty womb. If you couldn't reproduce, Nature had no use for you. You were expendable, superfluous, ready for the scrap heap.

Dennis sat down at the table. There wasn't a cloth. Just stained Formica, everyday china and a strange unsettling odour from the deadly nightshade leaves.

She picked up her spoon and held it poised above the bowl, imagining the seizures as the poison took effect. Like the pain of her two labours. She would scream and writhe for hours. Then nothing at the end of it. Silence. Void. Stillbirth. Stilldeath.

'Dot, just a minute. Before we start, there's, er, something I . . .' Gently prising the spoon from her fingers, he placed a little package in her hand. 'Happy anniversary,' he said, giving her an awkward kiss on the cheek.

She stared at him in shock. The package felt hard and

dangerous in her palm. A miniature bomb, about to explode. He had planned to murder her.

'Well, aren't you going to open it?'

Slowly she peeled off the gift-wrap. He had used gift-wrap only to deceive her, just as she had disguised the poison in the soup. Her fingers were clumsy with fear, and she was sweating so much her dress seemed glued to her back. The kitchen clock was ticking in a loud, aggressive fashion – ticking like a time-bomb.

She glanced at Den. He smiled. As *she* had smiled to see the reddish stippling in the soup.

'Come on, love. It won't bite!'

She drew out a little blue box. A padded box. A ring box. She lifted the lid. There, enthroned on blue plush, was a ruby ring.

She sat, drinking in the colour: loganberries, raspberries, deadly nightshade pulp. Then tentatively she touched the shining stone. Was it a real ruby? You couldn't always tell. Had the pregnancies been real? Milk in her breasts, stretch-marks on her stomach – could she have imagined them? Imagined panting through the contractions, bearing down in the last, most painful stage?

'What's wrong, Dot? Don't you like it? I went everywhere to find a really nice one. And look . . .' Leaning over, he extracted a tiny piece of paper from the lid. 'This came with it – stuff about rubies. It's fascinating.' He unfolded the leaflet and read aloud: ' "The ruby symbolizes longevity and love . . ." '

Longevity. She gazed at her bowl of soup. The red tinge had disappeared, lost in the green of the soup, hidden by the garnish. Belladonna – beautiful woman. She would be beautiful in death.

'Dot, what's the matter? You haven't said a word. Aren't you going to try it on?'

She picked up not the ring but the leaflet. The tiny print seemed to dance before her eyes. 'The ancients believed the ruby could banish grief . . .'

Grief. Forty years of grief. Banished at a stroke by one small stone.

'They even used the ruby as an antidote to poison.'

She looked at Den in wonderment. An antidote to poison. He had not only remembered, he was offering her the most powerful stone in the world. 'Thank you,' she whispered, as he slid the ring on her finger, above her wedding band. Then she took a first spoonful of soup, rolling it around her tongue to revel in the unfamiliar flavours, before letting it slip slowly, sweetly down. 'Let's eat, Den. Celebrate.'

Obediently he dipped his spoon in his bowl, swirled some soup around his mouth and swallowed with a slight grimace. 'Mm,' he said. 'Unusual.'

The ruby sparkled on her wedding finger as their spoons rose and fell, rose and fell, together and in harmony.

She scraped the last green debris from her bowl, aware of the ruby's brilliant winking eye, watching them, protecting them. Then, putting down her spoon, she reached across the table. It was a long time since she had held his hand, but she gripped it now, in love. 'Happy anniversary, Den. And many more to come.'

Annunciation

'Look, it just isn't possible. I *can't* be. I haven't . . . you know . . .'

The doctor gave a chilly smile that combined disbelief with pity. 'I'm sorry, Miss Brett, there isn't the slightest shadow of doubt. The test is positive. And now I've examined you, I'd say you're about eleven weeks.'

'Eleven weeks? You're joking!'

'Far from it. This is hardly a laughing matter. Now think back to late March. Did anything . . . happen between you and your boyfriend?'

'I haven't got a boyfriend.'

'Well, this male friend you mentioned?'

'Oh, Joe, you mean.' Mary hooked her feet round the rungs of the chair, to connect with something solid. This couldn't be happening. It was unreal. Grotesque. Joe would never forgive her. Except there was nothing to forgive. 'It's not like that, Doctor. Joe and I don't . . . He's a lot older than I am, to start with, and –'

'Age has nothing to do with it. Even men in their eighties have been known to father children. Anyway, I thought you said you lived together?'

'Not in the sense of sleep with. We have a sort of . . . arrangement.'

'Arrangement? I'm afraid I don't understand.'

She stared hopelessly at the doctor's gleaming brogues. Brogues, for Christ's sake! No wonder he didn't understand. He probably wore a thermal vest as well. There were little rows of holes in the toes of his shoes, like tiny open mouths, black o's of accusation. 'Joe's – well – *there* for me. He cares. And I . . . I . . .' How could she explain? The relationship was unique.

The doctor was kneading his hands together, as if rubbing in invisible balm. 'Perhaps you don't realize that pregnancy can occur without actual penetrative sex. For example, if this, er, Joe ejaculated outside your body but –'

'Look, I've *told* you – I've never even seen him naked, let alone . . .'

'Perhaps some other man, then.'

'There isn't any other man.'

The doctor's sigh succeeded in conveying both contempt and incredulity. 'Well, I suppose it might have been a stranger. It is just possible that someone could have spiked your drink.'

'I don't drink.'

'Oh, it needn't be alcohol. They could put it in a soft drink. There are drugs around these days with very powerful sedative effects. If a man slipped you something like that and then had sex with you, the chances are you *wouldn't* remember afterwards.'

'Surely I'd remember having the drink, though? And I haven't been in a pub for months.'

'So you're expecting me to believe –'

'I don't care what you believe. The important thing is what I'm going to *do*. I can't have the baby. It's out of the question.' Mary scrabbled in her bag for a tissue but found only a lipsticked one imprinted with a mocking cupid's bow. She pressed it hard against her eyes. She mustn't cry. She wouldn't.

'Am I to understand that you want an abortion, Miss Brett?'

'Of course I don't want one. The very thought makes me sick. But there's no alternative.'

'There's always an alternative. I can put you in touch with –'

'No!'

'What about your parents? Would they be prepared to help?'

'Don't be stupid! They'd die of shock. Or shame.' She did a quick mental calculation: eleven weeks – nearly three months. Another six months would bring it to late December. Christmas with the family. Fraught enough at the best of times, without her going into labour just as her father was carving the turkey.

'Well, as you seem to have so little support I suggest you see a counsellor. Then you can discuss the matter in detail before making any decision.'

'No – I've made up my mind. How soon can you get me in?'

'I'm not sure I *can* get you in, if you're talking about the NHS. The cut-off period at Kingston Hospital is twelve weeks.'

'Well, that's OK, if you say I'm only eleven.'

'I'm afraid things don't work as quickly as that. By the time I get you an appointment you'll be thirteen or fourteen weeks.'

'Surely you can speed it up?'

'I'm sorry, no. I can't.'

'You *won't*, you mean. I suppose you're one of these pro-lifers. Well, I'm pro-life myself. But this particular life is one I just can't cope with. So' – she stood up abruptly and grabbed her bag and jacket – 'if you won't help me, I'll have to go elsewhere. Goodbye. And thanks for nothing.'

Exactly a week later she was standing at the gates of Durston Lodge. With its mullioned windows and porticoed front door it looked more like a smart hotel than a nursing home. Perhaps there'd be colour telly in the rooms and a hospitality tray with those tiny milks that wouldn't open and mini-packets of biscuits. Her stomach rumbled at the thought. But the instructions said no food or drink after midnight.

The gravelled drive was lined with azalea bushes, their bright orange-red too jaunty for a slaughterhouse. She broke off a flower and sniffed it. The cloying scent reminded her of funerals: lilies clamped to a coffin, carnation cushions smothering a corpse.

'PLEASE RING AND ENTER' said a discreet notice on the door. She read it over and over, doing neither. All week she'd been psyching herself up, but now she was actually here her courage was draining away like water through a sieve. She was an hour early, in any case, and they wouldn't want her hanging around cluttering the place up. Better to walk into town and kill time. A hideous word, kill. Although it didn't always mean death. You could kill two birds with one stone. Or your shoes could be killing you. Or you could be dressed to kill. As *she* was – in black from head to toe: black jeans, black shirt, black jacket. She had put on black mascara, too, strictly against the rules. No make-up, they'd said, or jewellery. But she felt naked with pale lashes. Felt naked anyway.

The stately grey-stone mansion seemed to glower at her in disapproval. Strange it was so deserted; no faces at the windows, no other patients arriving. Perhaps the death business was slack just now.

Turning away, she walked slowly down the drive again, then trudged towards the town. It was cold for June, with swollen grey clouds that looked twenty weeks gone at least. Her shoulder-bag weighed heavy, as if the taint of her deceit had turned each £10 note to lead. She had never lied to Joe before, but no way could she tell him why she needed so much money and needed it so fast. He was a simple man – in the best sense: he believed what he was told.

Bring cash, they'd said, not a cheque. The largest amount of cash she had ever seen all at once. You had to hand it over before the operation. Afterwards, presumably, you'd be too knackered to count notes. Or perhaps they were afraid you'd do a runner.

She squeezed her way through the crowds of dawdling shoppers. How odd that they could laugh and joke, poke around the bargain rails, riffle through racks of CDs. Why should anyone want anything except not to have to return to Durston Lodge? And how did they eat without throwing up? A couple in motorbike leathers were sharing a burger oozing ketchup-blood and cheese-pus. And across the road a family of four were guzzling ice-cream cornets topped with choco-late flake. Murderers weren't allowed to eat. They were con-demned to fast; to feel ravenous and sick at once. And lonely. She watched the happy family stroll off down the street; the couple in leathers feed each other chips. A foetus was no com-pany – a pathetic little creature crouched inside her body, snivelling at its fate. But she couldn't change her mind. Not now.

The shops gradually petered out and she found herself in a dismal road lined with pollarded trees. Their new growth had been hacked off, and the stunted limbs reminded her of thalidomide babies: hands sprouting direct from the trunk, with no arms in between. It was nearly time for her own hack-ing and lopping. She would just walk to the church on the cor-ner before going back to the clinic.

It was a Catholic church, she discovered: Our Lady Immaculate. On impulse she went in and was instantly assailed by the familiar smells of piety and candle-wax and by a sudden desperate longing for her faith. Once, she had believed it all:

Resurrection, miracles, water into wine, wine into God's blood. Her parents were still mega-devout; not just Sunday Mass but rosaries, novenas, pilgrimage to Lourdes. Praying for *her*, no doubt – the sinner, the black sheep.

She sat in the back pew and gazed at the stained-glass window to her left: the Virgin, kneeling, flaxen-haired, a lily clasped in her small white hands, and facing her a magnificent angel with shining golden wings, surrounded by an aureole of light. As a child, she had loved the Annunciation story – an angel swooping into Mary's life and changing it at a stroke. Making a chit of a girl the most important person in the world. Yet Mary was so laid back (or naïve), accepting such amazing stuff without the smallest doubt, just murmuring submissively, 'Be it done unto me according to Thy word.' *She* would have told the angel to fuck off. Or at least wanted to know the ins and outs before agreeing to anything. But then she wasn't a saint like Mary. The nuns were forever saying how privileged she was to have the Blessed Virgin's name. 'The pity is, you don't live up to it.'

They were always plain, nuns. In real life, anyway. In films they were young and pretty (or sweetly old and wise) and doted on the children in their care. But, outside Hollywood, a nun was likely to have bad breath and a moustache, killer instincts towards God's little ones and the explosive temperament of a belching rusty boiler.

She glanced from the stained-glass Virgin to the spiteful hands on her watch. Twenty minutes to go. No point being late.

She genuflected, for old times' sake, crossed herself with holy water and emerged into the street. Trudging back past the aborted trees, she tried to keep her mind on simple things: cracks in the pavement, numbers on front gates, an inquisitive pink lupin poking above the fence.

Soon she reached the shops again and the hordes of munch-ing, jabbering zombies buying things they didn't want. But who was she to criticize? *She* was buying death.

All at once she stumbled to a halt, blinded by a dazzling shaft of light. Rubbing her eyes in confusion, she squinted through the glare and saw a radiant figure rearing up in front of her. He – and he did look male, with brawny arms and a muscular build – seemed to be wearing a long white dress. His bleached-blond hair stood up in punkish spikes, and attached to his shoulders was a pair of shining golden wings.

'Hi, Mary,' he said – his voice was undoubtedly male – 'I have a message for you. A bit late in the day, I'm afraid. I was supposed to give it to you three months ago, but what with one thing and another . . . Still, better late than never, and . . .'

'Hang on. What the hell are you talking about? Who are you?'

'The name's Gabriel. Or Gay if you prefer. Between you and me,' he leaned down confidingly, 'most angels *are* gay – we just don't broadcast the fact.'

She peered incredulously at his nose-ring and the small gold eyebrow-stud. 'If you're trying to tell me you're an angel . . .'

'I could hardly be anything else with these sodding great things, now, could I?' The wings on his back opened and closed, displaying their impressive span. 'They're an encum-brance, I can tell you, especially in towns. I'm afraid the Old Man's a bit of a reactionary. But not to worry – *you*'re in His good books. In fact you've been chosen for a very important job. You're going to have a child, and –'

'That's just where you're wrong. I'm *not*. I've arranged to get rid of it. In' – she consulted her watch – 'exactly twelve minutes' time.'

'Look, for God's sake – and I mean God's – you can't abort

this kid. He's special. He's going to be a King, the Son of the Most High.'

'Cut the crap, OK?'

'You're a bit thrown. Understandably. But everything's under control, Mary.'

'It won't be if I don't get to Durston Lodge. Piss off and annoy somebody else! I haven't time for practical jokes.'

'This isn't a joke. Far from it. Besides, my job's on the line. If you turn the assignment down you'll change the entire course of history and I'll have to carry the can.'

'Not my problem – sorry. Now kindly get out of my way. And if you harass me again I'll ask Joe to –'

'Oh, shit!' The angel gave a dramatic groan. 'I was supposed to tell Joe, too. Raphael was going to do it, but he's on sabbatical. And it went clean out of my head. Still, if I buzz off round there straight away, it shouldn't be too –'

'Stop! Wait! Don't you dare go near Joe . . .'

'Cool it, Mary! You are in a state. Mind you, I can sympathize. This must have been one hell of a shock.'

'It was. It is.' She bit her lip, clenched her firsts, struggling to hold back the tears. 'I . . . still can't take it in.'

'I've really fucked up, haven't I? You see, I was meant to explain, before it actually happened, how you'd come to be pregnant.'

'No one can explain. They . . . they all assume I'm lying.'

'I can't say I'm surprised. It is rather a difficult concept, even for us archangels. But look, think of it as a sort of celestial AID, without the hassle of test-tubes – the donor being the Holy Ghost. Actually, you should be over the moon. The Holy Ghost is pretty damn choosy, I can tell you! He doesn't go putting it about. This is strictly a one-off. And remember, Mary, He picked you out of all the women in the world. Fame at a stroke! Just think what it means – your picture everywhere, people on their knees to you, churches built in your honour, statues put up, litanies composed, an entry in the Guinness Book of Records. I could go on – there's yards of it – but I really must be getting off to Joe's now. He'll do his nut if he finds you're up the spout and I haven't warned him in advance. And I'll get the blame, of course. Goodbye. God bless! Keep your pecker up.'

With a rush of wings and a last flare of light, Gabriel vanished as mysteriously as he had come. The day turned dull and grey again, and she was left staring at '50p off Persil Automatic' blazoned across Sainsbury's window.

She leaned shakily against the glass, the angel's words resounding in her head: people on their knees to you, churches built in your honour, statues put up, litanies composed . . .

She must be dreaming, surely – a girl with two GCSEs and a dead-end job in Boots, chosen by the Holy Ghost over every other woman in the world. She linked her hands across her stomach: not a snivelling foetus, not an alien growth, but God within her, the Son of the Most High.

'Spare some change, love?'

Only now did she notice the scruff of an old man sprawled in a disused doorway, an empty bottle protruding from his pocket.

'I don't know about change, but if this is any help . . .' She pulled the bulky envelope out of her bag and thrust the wad of £10 notes – £300 in total – into his grimy hand.

Joe would understand. Well, Joseph, it should be now, she supposed, if he was to be God's foster-father.

'Joseph,' she murmured, practising, 'we're both in this together.' At this very moment he would be listening to Gabriel's message with his usual unwavering trust. She crumpled up the clinic leaflet and chucked it in a litter bin. Time to go home. Joseph would make her a nice cheese and mushroom omelette, then set to work on the cot. How lucky he was such a brilliant carpenter.

Just one more thing – the most important thing of all. Without embarrassment, she fell to her knees on the hard, cold, dirty pavement vacated by the tramp. She bowed her head, closed her eyes and murmured in thrilling submission:

'Be it done unto me according to Thy word.'

Gambledown

'And where do you live?' Claire asked. Boring question. But so was the party.

'Norton Ashberry.'

Claire bit sharply into a lemon-slice. 'Norton *Ashberry*?'

'It's a tiny village in Suffolk. Well, hardly a village – no pub or shop or . . .'

Beyond the heads of the voluble Hampstead guests Claire watched the horizon unfurl, rolling back and back until there was nothing but an infinite sky brooding over Suffolk fields. Bare black soil rippled into wind-stroked wheat and, in the distance, a self-important church-tower pointed up to God, declaring its unshakeable faith.

'And where do *you* live?'

Claire dragged herself back to London. 'Kensington – the unfashionable part. But this is quite extraordinary. I used to spend practically all my school holidays in Norton Ashberry.'

'Good gracious, what a coincidence! Most people have never even heard of it.'

'My best friend lived there. On a farm called Gambledown.'

'Oh, yes, along that lane by the river. It changed hands fairly recently, and a couple called Westcott bought it. I don't know when your friend left, but . . .'

'Years ago.' Decades. She hadn't seen Bridget since 1969. They had gone their separate ways, only meeting again at the funeral, when their friendship seemed to have died along with Bridget's mother. The day had been overcast, the naked trees shivery and gaunt – all wrong for a plump, sunny-natured farmer's wife. And then the shock of a prosaic crematorium instead of the old stone church, and afterwards fiddly little cocktail snacks that dissolved to grease and nothing in your mouth. Mrs Carter believed in solid meals (sides of home-cured ham, huge slabs of ginger cake) and must have shuddered in her grave-clothes to see her friends so ill-served.

The lemon was making her eyes smart. It would be unthinkable to cry in the middle of this formal gathering. Bridget hadn't cried, not even when the hideous pink velvet curtains slithered round the coffin. *She* had sobbed throughout.

'Have you lived there long?' she asked, the bitter taste of the lemon lingering in her mouth. 'I mean, do you know if the farm has changed much?' She recoiled at a fleeting image of cool grey flagstone floors submerged under carpet tiles, or a barren modern kitchen supplanting the scrubbed-raw wooden table and belching black range.

'Oh, I shouldn't think so. Nothing in Norton Ashberry ever seems to change. Well, the post office closed down last year, but apart from that . . .'

'I'd love to see it again. It's so much a part of my childhood – my real home, in a way. You see, my parents lived in India, and . . .' Embarrassed, she broke off. Why should this unknown woman want to hear the saga? It wasn't even original. Hundreds of children with parents abroad were packed off to boarding school and farmed out in the holidays – in her case, farmed out literally: the best thing ever to happen in her life. She might have been unlucky and landed up in an airless

London flat or been parked with virtual strangers. Stout, dependable Mrs Carter seemed inordinately safer than her own beautiful, brittle mother. 'Just hearing the name brings back such vivid memories.' How could any child fail to be happy at a farm called Gambledown – even the nervous, sickly child she had been?

'Well, look, perhaps I could arrange something. I know we've only just met, but why don't you come up one weekend and I'll give Mrs Westcott a ring and take you over.'

'*Would* you? Really?' Already Claire could feel the familiar surge of elation as the coach rattled along secretive Suffolk lanes, past wind-hunched trees, deserted barns, the wink of a sly stream. Mr Carter would meet her in the Land-Rover, a frolic of dogs at his heels. His handshake was iron, in contrast to his soft hesitant voice. In spite of having five daughters he seemed shy with little girls.

The woman was writing something in her diary. She tore the page out and handed it to Claire. 'Here's my address and phone number. Do give me a ring.'

Fortunately she'd added her name, which Claire hadn't caught when they were introduced – Janice Hetherington, Ivy Cottage. She couldn't remember an Ivy Cottage, but Gambledown stood a good two miles from the clutch of houses that, with the church, made up Norton Ashberry. You drove out of the village along a meandering road fringed by unkempt hedgerows, rustling and astir, and turned off on to a cart-track with fields on either side. Sensing they were nearly home, the dogs would begin to ripple with excitement, and as the Land-Rover bumped into the drive a synod of rooks would startle the sky with a jubilant welcoming anthem.

'I mean it,' Janice insisted. 'I'm not just being polite. I don't have many visitors, so it would be a treat for me to have you to stay.'

'Well, thank you . . . It's so kind . . . I don't know what to say . . .' She folded the paper and put it carefully in her bag. She would phone first thing tomorrow. Suddenly, incredibly, Gambledown was within reach again.

The role of guest at Ivy Cottage proved arduous. Actually it wasn't a cottage at all but a constipated modern bungalow. Nor was there any ivy. Indeed, anything as straggling as ivy would never have been tolerated within fifty yards of the house. Janice was wedded to Tidiness, and the pair of them laboured to keep every room clinically neat. Back and front gardens were paved, debarring any blade of grass or – horrors – weed from unfurling its green flag of revolution. Trees were anathema: leaf-shedding miscreants that must be rigorously trimmed, if not scalped.

'What a marvellous view,' Claire observed, as she sat by the window the first evening of her stay, sipping coffee from a dainty porcelain cup. At least the surrounding countryside was beyond her hostess's control.

'Yes, lovely, isn't it?' Janice's frown suggested otherwise, as if she longed to seize the rumpled counterpane of fields and shake it back into place. 'I moved here after Harold died. Our other house was too big.'

Claire nodded politely, wondering if she could propose an early night without it seeming ungracious. A widow and a divorcée ought perhaps to have more in common, but whereas Janice still mourned Harold, *she* had consigned Anthony to the metaphorical scrap-heap. She was lucky to have found any sort of husband, and the fact it hadn't lasted was no reason to keep harking back to the past. If anything was worth revisiting it was her early girlhood at Gambledown, when the only men were fathers, and sex was something the dogs did, not sensible, vertical grown-ups.

'Look, Janice, about tomorrow . . . please don't take this the wrong way, but . . . would you mind awfully if I went to the farm on my own?'

Janice couldn't quite conceal the disappointment that flickered across her impeccably made-up face. 'No, not at all, if that's what you prefer.'

Claire struggled to find words, although she could hardly explain that she had come to see the visit as a sort of pilgrimage, to be undertaken with reverence, not in the company of a chitchatting acquaintance. She wanted to savour it in silence, pausing at every bend in the road to remember and rejoice; picking the flowers she had gathered as a child: pout-lipped vetch, lace parasols of cow parsley, the forbidden thrill of deadly nightshade. Janice, tottering in her smart cream shoes, would have no desire to penetrate the spongy damp of copses or crunch dry grey cowpats underfoot, nor could Claire imagine her lying hidden in long grass, listening to the chirruping of grasshoppers or sucking the tubed pink sweetness from wild clover. 'I'd hate you to think I'm being unfriendly, Janice. It's just that . . .'

'Don't worry. I understand.'

No one could understand the miracle of finding a substitute home and parents. Delhi could never be home – too hot, too bright, too foreign – and her father's lofty rank meant that she was constantly chaperoned or spied on by his minions. Yet he himself was invisible, except rarely at weekends. She had been quick to realize he had wanted a son and that nothing about a daughter could engage his interest for long. Mr Carter, on the other hand, was present at every meal and seemed bashfully content with his six females. He would pad into the kitchen in his thick, green, woolly socks (muddy boots must be left outside the door) and take his place at the head of the table. Sitting beside him, she soon became accustomed to the faint tang of tractor oil or fertilizer that lingered on his clothes and somehow blended reassuringly with the smells of frying bacon or steak and kidney pie. Mrs Carter served him first and he would work through his food with the stolid determination of one of his herd of Friesians cropping new spring grass.

'Tell you what,' she said, aware that Janice still looked piqued, 'when I get back from my reconnoitre tomorrow why don't I take you out to dinner? We could go to the Swan in Lavenham.' She hated fancy dinners – food braised in pretension, servile waiters salaaming – but her offer had the desired result of mollifying her hostess. 'I'll book in the morning,' she added, rearranging herself in the chair: head up, back straight, feet neatly side by side. Having won a major concession she must conform to the house rules.

Her favourite time at Gambledown was just before harvest, when the farm itself seemed to share her anticipation of eight blissful weeks' release from the prison-camp of school. The undulating cornfields would quiver with excitement; the clouds push against their blue restraining lid, as if, exulting in their freedom, they sought to widen the dimensions of the sky. Everything was ripening to a peak of readiness, like the taut-stretched, bulging udders of the cows. She would sit by the stile, deliciously idle – no need of an improving book to justify her existence here: it was enough to simply *be*. She could loll, unmonitored, inside the gateway of a field and do nothing more productive than marvel at the contrast between the stiff bewhiskered regiment of barley and the frail red fluttery poppies it sheltered in its midst like exotic émigrés. Peering into the coarse brown forest, she'd watch tiny enamelled beetles toiling up the towering stalks; hear the dart and scuttle of harvest-mice or maybe more mysterious feet bustling about their private business. A rabbit might appear, or the long ears of a hare, only to vanish again and become a shudder in the corn.

Yes, the stile was still there, as lopsided as ever; the barley richly ripe, its surface brooding grey or flashing golden as breeze and shadows played over it. And the sun was the courteous English kind, slipping tactfully behind the clouds every now and then to ensure it didn't outstay its welcome. She thought of the countless times she and Bridget had wandered down this lane in their scuffed Clark's sandals and skimpy summer dresses; she with ugly glasses and two thin mousebrown pigtails down her back. She hadn't known she was plain – not then. Only with puberty came the impossible desires: not to be the smallest in the class, and to have breasts and big blue eyes and ash-blond curls. Her hair was grey now, short and permed. She had achieved her curls, at last, along with a furrowed forehead and arthritis in her knees, but today she would stick at age ten, when her only dream was for a pony of her own and for Grange Park (and all other loathsome boarding schools) to be swept away in a hurricane.

She turned from the lane on to the narrow rutted cart-track, the pocket of her dress bulging with a package of Mrs Carter's flapjack – a perfect combination of the gritty and the gooey that left a comfortingly sweet sludge on your teeth. In those days sugar was good for you, just as Mr Carter's after-supper pipe was a harmless source of pleasure, not a danger to his lungs. At Gambledown everything was safe. God Himself lived in Norton Ashberry, up beyond the clouds; His special task to guard and bless the farm. There was no proper God in India, which was why it had such frightening things as cyclones and monsoons and a sun that glared and tyrannized.

The still-green knobbly blackberries in the hedgerow reminded her of Mrs Carter's bramble jelly – dark glossy jars of it, swanking beneath their mobcaps in the cavernous, cold-breathed larder with dozens of other preserves. She and

Bridget would creep down there for midnight feasts, munching cold, fat, blackened sausages, picking the crusty bits off a bread-and-butter pudding or stealing spoonfuls of trembly pink blancmange. Or they would lie awake for hours, discussing things like Heaven – would they be given wings there and, if so, could they fly? They decided early on that whoever died first would send the other blessings: ponies, of course, and also an everlasting supply of sherbet lemons. They had sworn to be best friends for ever, but 'for ever' had proved elusive, like love and faith and Anthony.

Such negative thoughts vanished as she rounded the next bend and there it suddenly was – the kindly red-brick farmhouse unseen for thirty years. At this distance the details were indistinct, but her mind supplied them instantly: the outcrops of green lichen on the roof, the inquisitive creeper poking dogged fingers across the blistered windowsills and into every room. Appearances didn't matter here: she, the house, the Carters, were all free to be themselves. Mrs Carter wore pinafores, not tea-gowns like her mother, and you could glimpse pink bits of knee through the holes in Mr Carter's trousers. (Her own father didn't have knees. The only visible parts of his flesh were his shuttered face, his restless hands and the angry back of his neck. She assumed he went to bed fully clothed, too exalted for pyjamas.)

She broke into a run, impatient to see inside the house: the attic bedroom she and Bridget had shared, whose sloping roof and uneven floor made her imagine some capricious giant had wrenched it out of shape; the comfortably cluttered sitting-room, where the chairs had lost their bones so you squashed down deep inside them or – better still – lay outstretched on the rug, which smelt of dog and wood-smoke.

The gates stood open, as always, their weather-bleached wood furred with moss. And the pungent smell of the pigsties caught at her throat in the same obnoxiously enticing way. And coming to greet her was a strutting despot of a cockerel, with half a dozen drab brown hens subservient in his wake. Unlike Mr Carter, he bossed his harem rudely, marshalling and parading them, crowing his importance to the world.

Having watched the procession pass, she went up to the front door. Mrs Westcott was expecting her at three o'clock and it was just a minute past. She used the knocker rather than the bell, simply for the pleasure of grasping its big brass nose. The rat-tat-tat echoed in the silence. Silence was strange for Gambledown – a houseful of girls produced a constant hubbub. Tentatively she rang the bell and heard its jangle resounding through the hall, followed by the barking of a dog. Then the door was flung open by an angry-looking man, his eyes dark slits beneath black brows. His hand gripped the studded collar of a huge wolf-like creature that bared its teeth and emitted a low gargling growl.

'M . . . Mr Westcott?' she stammered.

He nodded curtly

'I believe your wife's expecting me. I'm a friend of Janice Hetherington, and she phoned last night to ask if –'

'My wife's not here.'

'But Janice said –'

'I'm sorry, she had to change her plans. You'll have to make it some other time.'

'Would tomorrow be any good? I'm only here for the weekend, you see, and . . .'

'No, she won't be back tomorrow.'

The dog twisted in his grip, showing the whites of its eyes. The dogs at Gambledown had been friends, not dangerous traitors. One had shared her bed, a lollopy mongrel whose solid, snoring weight on her feet kept away the prison dreams.

'Mr Westcott,' she pleaded, seeing he was about to close the door, 'all I want is to have a quick look round. I used to stay here as a child. It was like my second home.' First home; only home. 'Would you mind? I won't be any bother.'

'Yes, I would mind. I'm busy.'

'But there's no need for you to –'

'Look, I haven't time to argue. I've lost the whole morning as it is. And you can tell your friend Mrs Nosy-Parker Hetherington that we're not a stately home, open to the public at her whim.'

With that, the door was slammed in her face.

She stood trembling on the step. She had disturbed him when he was busy – an unpardonable offence. Worse, she had answered back, although she knew full well he wouldn't tolerate defiance. He would cut her off in mid-sentence if ever she had the temerity to argue. She clutched her stomach, which was full of writhing snakes. It took only one harsh word from him and she couldn't eat for the rest of the day.

If she had been a boy he would have let her in. Or at least if she'd been pretty. He hated ugliness in anyone, which was why he'd married her mother. Sometimes she suspected that she wasn't her mother's child: there'd been a mix-up at the hospital and the blue-eyed, blond-curled princeling had been spirited away and *she* laid in his cot. A frail and beautiful lady like her mother should never have had a baby in the first place. Pregnancy was dangerous, and although a boy was worth the risk, a girl most certainly wasn't.

She ought to tell him she was sorry, apologize for being born. She reached up to the bell again. It clanged out impatiently, but no one came. Well, what did she expect? His work was terribly important and it was wicked to think she could just barge in and waste his time.

All at once another, even larger dog came prowling round the side of the house, ears laid back, tail down. It spotted her and lunged forward with a snarling trap of teeth. She turned and fled, her feeble brown Clark's sandals hurting on the pitted drive, her pigtails thumping against her back. The dog's maddened barking startled the rooks, which rose in a black tantrum from the tree beside the gate. They were no longer black-robed elders intoning a psalm of welcome but a vicious rabble screeching abuse. The noise was as loud as gunfire, pursuing her as she hurtled down the cart-track.

Desperate to escape, she tried to run still faster. The hedges were closing in; the spiteful ruts grabbing at her feet. Several times she stumbled, but managed to right herself and race on, ignoring the stitch in her side and the pain in her ears from the bombardment of the rooks. And then suddenly her ankle gave way and she tripped and sprawled full length on the ground.

Dazed, she lay listening to the silence. Absolute silence – no rooks, no ravening dogs. Had she imagined them? Imagined the farm itself? Was Gambledown a place she had invented as a solace in the long, hot Delhi nights?

She lifted her head and stared in shock at the fields. They were cutting the corn; vast waves of it buckling and breaking before the ruthless blades. Flung poppies spurted blood, wounding the earth with livid scarlet gashes. All the small and timid creatures that had found shelter in the miniature forest were being mutilated, mown down. She could see the broken corpse of a fieldmouse; the broken bells of convolvulus, flushed pink with fear. Yet still that steel-toothed monster went lumbering, charging on; guzzling everything in its path and farting clouds of dry brown chaff from its rump. Its gigantic belly rumbled for more as it felled homely groundsel and meek green chickweed, mangling them into the cowering corn.

She groped to her feet, her eyes smarting from the dust. Her glasses were broken; the lenses scattered fragments. Through a blur she watched the final swathes surrender; heard the death cries of the field. And now nothing remained but stubble; a parched wilderness of truncated stalks where once so much life had thrived. She could feel its pain throbbing in her grazed and bloodied palms. Picking up the empty frames of her glasses, she walked slowly, blindly away.

Childhood was gone.

Free Love

'I'm Hazel, by the way.'

Margaret shifted on her chair. She had never liked vegetative names: Cherry, Primrose, Iris. No class to them. No tradition. Her daughter was called Eleanor: the name of queens, historical and dignified. She had been christened in a French lace robe that had belonged to her great-grandmother and had behaved impeccably throughout. Not so much as a whimper from her.

'And you're Margaret.'

'I'm Mrs Carter-Hawtrey.' To strangers, she added silently.

'We're trained to use Christian names. It's friendlier.'

Trained? The girl had seemed barely proficient, shoving her head between her legs in that graceless fashion and then producing a so-called sick-bag – an ordinary brown paper bag, so crumpled and tatty it could have been discarded in a sandwich bar. Being sick was humiliating, especially in front of other people. She must put the incident out of her mind. She had felt a little poorly, that's all. It had happened several times before, but she was none the worse, in the long run. 'What training do you do?' she asked.

'Essential Care Skills, Life-Saver and Life-Saver Plus.' The girl rattled them off at top speed. 'Oh, and Life-Saver for Babies and Children. I done that in the summer.'

Her grandson had twin boys. Not that she'd ever seen them. Nor much of her grandson either. Zachary. What sort of name was that, for goodness' sake? She had suggested James, or Alexander, but Eleanor had always been headstrong – since her christening, anyway. She would have liked a son herself, one who lived in England, visited on Sundays. Sundays were the worst. 'And how long are these courses?'

'A weekend each. Less for Babies and Children.'

'A weekend? Is that all?' Margaret looked up sharply at the girl, standing beside her in the dim, low-ceilinged corridor outside the lecture hall. *She* had the only chair. Seating appeared to be rationed, except in the hall itself, where a veritable battalion of chairs – the wooden stacking variety – were ranged in front of the stage. Strange there wasn't also a first-aid room in a big public place like this.

'It might not sound much, but it's dead intensive, I can tell you! Nine to five, Saturday and Sunday. My head was spinning by the end. I passed, though, just about.'

If she'd been taken seriously ill, this girl wouldn't have had a clue. Life-Saver Plus, indeed.

'Well, if you're feeling better, Margaret, let's go back in the hall. I'm meant to stay there, in case . . .'

'I'm not feeling better.'

'Still sick? I've got another bag if you . . .'

'No. Dizzy.'

'You need some fresh air. It's stuffy in these basements. That's probably half the trouble. Here, I'll give you a hand upstairs.'

Hazel linked her arm through hers. The girl's hands were small and sallow. She wore one narrow silver ring, although not on her wedding finger. Girls didn't marry nowadays. No need.

They made their way upstairs, step by step, step by step,

haltingly like toddlers. The lecturer's voice was a faint drone from below. She wasn't sorry to miss the talk. Most of it had gone over her head. A one-day conference on 'Europe at the Millennium' was only another way of disposing of a weekend. Like last month's workshop in Elementary French, or the Saturday School on Ceramics, back in February. Saturdays and Sundays contained more hours than weekdays. Besides, there were big reductions for senior citizens and subsidized food in the canteen. She'd had a tolerable beef casserole for only £2.95 and apple sponge to follow. Well, it had seemed tolerable at the time. Now all she could remember were the globules of fat floating in the gravy and dampish brown-stained sponge submerged in phlegmy custard.

Hazel led her across the foyer and out through the glass doors. The wind pounced viciously, slapping their faces, clawing at their hair. 'Aren't you cold?' asked Margaret, as they stood huddled in the shelter of one of the grime-encrusted columns flanking the main entrance. The girl looked scrawny under her uniform and was wearing tights with so little substance to them her legs might as well have been bare. *She* still had her coat on, although it was spattered with flecks of vomit and would need dry-cleaning now. Cleaning cost a fortune. 'I said, aren't you cold?' she repeated. The girl had been distracted by a workman on a ladder, repairing a broken window in an office block. People rarely listened. Or not for long.

'No. The uniform's quite warm.'

Margaret glanced at it approvingly. The jacket was neat no-nonsense black, with the St John Ambulance badge embroidered on each shoulder. Which St John, she wondered? Johns were ten a penny, saints or otherwise. John the Apostle was her favourite. He could teach Eleanor a thing or two. He had been devoted to the Blessed Virgin, and she wasn't even his real mother. After Jesus' death he had never left her side.

'You get it free,' Hazel remarked. 'Well, all except the shoes. Some divisions charge you, but ours is good like that. They pay for the training, too. It works out pricey otherwise. Thirty quid each for Life-Saver and Life-Saver Plus. Babies and Children is cheaper – only seven fifty.'

Babies and children were never cheap, in her experience. She was constantly shelling out for her grandsons – not that they knew who she was. And airmail postage on top. You couldn't trust surface mail. Things got delayed or lost. 'So how long have you been a . . . ?' As she spoke, she heard her voice skidding out of control and then felt her body crumpling. Hazel's black serge arm grabbed her, eased her down to the base of the pillar, pushed her head between her legs again.

'You're all right, Margaret. I've got you.'

The girl's hand was warm against her neck. She tried to shake it off. You could get germs from strangers' hands.

'How you feeling? Better?'

The words came from somewhere far away, where people spoke a different language. 'I . . . I . . .'

'It's OK. No need to talk.'

Minutes passed. Bit by bit, the sounds grew more distinct. Voices – coming closer. Hazel's, closest of all.

'Just take a deep breath, Margaret, and relax.'

How could she relax, sitting on a cold stone ledge, making an exhibition of herself? People were probably staring. She couldn't see anything; only feel her coat rough against her cheek, smell its putrid smell.

'OK now?'

'Mm.'

'Not too cold?'

There had been a frost this morning. The first of the year. She had noticed the nasturtiums in Mrs Baxter's flower-bed, their leaves limp and flopping over; a faint white dusting on their undersides. She had never liked nasturtiums. They barged insolently all over the place, smothering better-mannered plants. And that vulgar, garish orange. She preferred black. Strange there were no black flowers.

Slowly she lifted her head. The buildings opposite stopped swaying; the street settled into focus. And the pounding in her head moved mercifully outside and was swallowed up in the barrage of traffic. Cars were rumbling past, red buses, motorbikes. One child in ten suffered from asthma. Or was it one in nine? Her grandsons lived in the Outback. No pollution there. And no postboxes, apparently. Zachary never acknowledged the parcels. And Eleanor hadn't written since last Christmas. Best not to think of Christmas. Not easy when it started in October.

Footsteps. A man in a white raincoat was walking towards them with a swinging, easy stride. He stopped and smiled at Hazel. 'Pardon me, ma'am. Could you direct me to the Strand?'

'This *is* the Strand.'

'I'm looking for Simpson's, ma'am. The restaurant.'

'It's further on – the other side of Lancaster Place. Just keep walking, past two or three sets of traffic lights and you'll see it on your left.'

'Much obliged, ma'am.'

Margaret stared at his retreating back. Hazel wasn't a tour guide, for heaven's sake. Americans were all the same. London was full of them, even in the winter.

A taxi coasted past, closely followed by another, both empty, with their 'For Hire' lights on.

'You could get a cab home,' Hazel suggested. She was crouching by the pillar, and her skirt had ridden up, exposing skinny thighs.

'A cab? I live in Northolt.'

'Where's that?'

'Too far for a cab. Anyway, I'm not well enough to go anywhere.'

'I just thought it might be better than freezing to death out here. At least let's go back to the hall.'

'But you said it was too stuffy.'

'I'm meant to *be* there, Margaret. In case anyone has a heart attack or . . .'

'That's hardly likely, is it? They all looked very young to me.'

'You can't ever tell. It's not a question of age.' Hazel clapped a hand to her mouth. 'Oh Lord!'

'What's wrong?' The girl *was* cold, Margaret realized. Her skirt was far too short – indecent for a uniform. You'd think there'd be a regulation length.

'I've forgotten the paperwork! D'you mind if I do it now?'

'Paperwork?'

Hazel rummaged in her black canvas bag and pulled out a form, as dog-eared as the sick-bag. 'I need your details – age, address, that sort of thing.'

'I'm sorry, dear. I never disclose my age.'

'But we have to put it. It's rules.'

Margaret juggled figures in her head. It was dangerous admitting your age. People made assumptions: that your memory was going. Or your mind. 'Well, put, er, seventy-five. No, seventy-three.'

Hazel looked dubious. She was trying to save the form from being snatched away by the wind and had it propped against the bag on her lap, one hand holding it down. 'But if you're not seventy-three . . .'

'I am.' She watched Hazel labour over the figures. The three came out like an eight. 'Seventy-*three*,' she said again, more sharply.

'Yeah, I've put that. And how do you spell your name?'

'The Carter or the Hawtrey?'

'Both.'

'C-A-R-T–'

'Hang on. You're going too fast.'

The girl's writing was all but illegible. That's how mistakes were made. Serious mistakes. It was the same with the parcels. You had no idea if they actually arrived.

'Excuse me, miss, could you tell me the way to . . .?'

Another tourist using Hazel as an unpaid guide. Who did these people think they were, interrupting the paperwork? She liked the thought of being included in the records. It gave her weight, importance.

Hazel dispensed more directions, then turned back to Margaret, grinning. 'It's the uniform,' she explained. 'I've been taken for all sorts. A policewoman, a traffic warden, even a prison officer.'

'In that case, they don't use their eyes.' Margaret shook her head impatiently. The 'St John' was perfectly clear, embroidered in neat white letters not only above the badge but on both epaulettes. In her youth, she'd had a weakness for uniforms, until her husband died in one.

Hazel got up from her crouching position. 'Shall we do the rest inside? It's perishing out here. Anyway, I must get back to the hall. Jim cried off sick this morning, so I'm covering on my own. I never done it before, and I must admit . . .'

'You go, dear. I'll stay.' She refused to share Hazel. If someone else was taken ill *she* would be abandoned. How could she compete with a heart attack?

'I can't leave you all alone. It's getting dark.'

Margaret peered up at the sky, which looked ashen rather than dark. It had been pitch black when she woke, at five. The hours till dawn seemed to crawl and limp. Even at seven the birds were eerily quiet. 'Let's stay together then.'

'I told you, Margaret, I'm meant to be in the hall. It's rules.'

'You said it was rules to do the paperwork.'

'Yeah, but . . .'

'Well, can't we finish it?'

'It's almost finished. I just need your address.'

'Flat five, Orchard Court.' Ridiculous, these names. There wasn't so much as an apple tree for miles, let alone an orchard. 'Orchard has another R.'

'What?'

'There.' Margaret pointed between the A and the D, then quickly withdrew her hand, ashamed of the swollen finger-joints. If ever she wanted to remove her wedding ring, the new GP had said, it would have to be cut off. Why should she want to remove it? Arthur had been shot down in 1944, but that didn't mean she'd forgotten him.

'And your postcode?' Hazel asked.

'UB5 . . .' Postcodes were a new-fangled thing, like kilograms and those fiddly 5p coins. She still missed threepenny bits.

Hazel's Biro was poised, waiting for the rest. Biros smudged, or ran out with no warning. Arthur had used a fountain pen, a black Sheaffer with a real gold nib. It still lay in its silk-lined box in the bottom bureau drawer. Arthur lay somewhere in France. She had never seen his body or knew how much of him they'd found. Orchard Court was full of widows. Women lived longer than men – seven years on average, according to *Saga* magazine. *She* had lived fifty-three years longer. Time healed, people said.

'UB5 . . . ?' Hazel prompted, tapping the Biro gently against the form.

'Er, 6LG,' she murmured, wishing she had an address for Arthur; a specific place she could visit or at least find on a map.

Hazel made a final squiggle on the bottom of the form and stuffed it in her bag. 'That's it, then. Off we go.'

'Don't you need my doctor's name?'

'Nope.' Hazel rammed her hat down over her ears. It covered most of her hair, but the curls escaping at the sides were a reddish sort of brown. Eleanor must be grey by now, although she was still dark in the photos. Such a comfort, the photos: Arthur was alive in them. Hazel had blue eyes, like his.

'Come on, Margaret. Let's help you up.'

'I'd rather stay here, thank you.' She braced her feet against the base of the pillar, noticing the crumbling stone. Everything crumbled, in the end.

'Well, at least come into the foyer. There's a seat there and it's warmer.'

Reluctantly she let herself be steered inside. Their footsteps echoed in the deserted foyer. The seat was a metal bench, rigid and unloving.

Hazel cleared off two empty crisp-packets and patted it encouragingly. 'Right, you sit here, and promise not to move, OK? I'll come back and see you in a while.'

Margaret perched on the edge. No one ever stayed. They'd be sorry when she died. She would enjoy her death – the flowers. Lilies, not nasturtiums. She had left everything to Eleanor, so the least the child could do was buy a decent wreath. And come over for the funeral, with Zachary and the twins. It was most important to give a good impression: the devoted daughter, the grieving family. They would only have the wreath to pay for. Her Funeral Plan should cover everything else. Except the fares, of course. *They* were astronomical. But every week she put aside a pound or two, and it was mounting up quite nicely. She didn't want Eleanor complaining about the cost of death, like Mrs Kendall's daughter. Even the plainest coffin set you back a hundred and ninety pounds.

'Margaret, are you all right? *Margaret?*'

She opened her eyes. She had died and gone to heaven.

Heaven was lovely and warm. They covered you with rugs; soft, fuzzy, scarlet rugs. They gave you cups of tea. They even held the cup for you. She took a sip. The tea was strong and sweet. She smiled. A face smiled back – a small, sallow face. Blue eyes, black uniform. 'Hazel!' she murmured. 'Are you still here?'

'I've been here all the time.'

'All the time?'

'Yeah.'

'But I thought they . . . they needed you in the hall?'

'No, it's over now. Everyone's gone home.'

'Home?' Margaret struggled to sit up.

'Don't worry. I can stay a bit if you're not feeling all that bright.'

Puzzled, she looked around. The room was small and warm, and she was lying on a sofa, with cushions behind her head. She wondered where she was. Not that it mattered – not if Hazel was here. 'What's the time?'

'Five to six.'

'Evening, do you mean? Or morning?'

Hazel laughed. 'Evening! It's OK, Margaret, you haven't been here all night.'

She nodded in relief. Over the years she had lost so many things, nights included. 'I hope they pay you overtime.'

'Oh, we don't get *paid*.'

'You mean you do all this for nothing?'

''Course. It's voluntary.'

'You give up your weekends?' The girl was pretty – well, prettyish. She probably had a boyfriend and planned to go out tonight.

'It's no big deal.'

How wrong. It was beyond rubies, beyond price.

'And what about the tea? Did you pay for that?'

'Yeah. I got it from the canteen. It's only 30p.'

'It's not the cost, my dear. It's the thought.' How often she had said that to her daughter. And to Zachary – on the rare occasions she'd seen him. 'You'd see him more, Mother, if you'd only fly, like everyone else.' Since 1944 she hadn't trusted planes. Besides, when you flew, you lost things – time, to start with. And dignity. She might be taken ill again, miles up in the sky. And there wouldn't be a Hazel. Someone willing to stay. Willing to stay for nothing. She recalled the reading last Sunday: *Love is patient, love is kind . . . Love is never selfish. There is no limit to its faith, its hope, its endurance.* Charity, it was called, in her day. But love was better – the best word in the dictionary. She fixed her attention on Hazel's shoes. They looked rather the worse for wear: scuff-marks on the front and a gash in the left heel. Yet she did all this for nothing. 'Tell me, dear, what . . . what happened?'

'You fainted again. In the street. You shouldn't have moved. You promised. We was worried sick about you.'

'*We?*'

'Me and the man who helped you up.'

'You were . . . worried?'

'Mm.'

She didn't remember a man. Perhaps an American, a tourist. Someone who cared enough to stop. To help a stranger – a foolish old woman who should have stayed at home. She stroked the rug: so soft. 'Eleanor never worries.'

'Who?'

'Oh, never mind.' Worried meant love. Worried meant concern. Hazel was concerned. Maybe concerned enough to stay with her all night. 'Where do you live, my dear?'

'Lewisham.'

'That's a long way. Did you come by car?'

'No, I haven't got one. Train and tube. We have to pay our own expenses – train tickets and stuff.'

'That doesn't seem quite fair.' Unfair, but wonderful. She was worth a day return from Lewisham; worth hours of over-time. 'Have you no family near by?' the new GP had asked. Hazel was her family. Lovely girl. So pretty. 'Is your mother still alive, dear?'

'My mother?'

'Yes. Or has she . . . passed away?'

'Oh, no. I live with her.'

'You live with her?' A devoted daughter. On duty, night and day. Worrying, concerned. Fetching blankets, making tea. If someone brought you tea, it meant you were special. Sacred tea for the shell-shocked, virtuous tea for blood donors, tri-umphant tea after giving birth. 'I wonder, dear, would it be an awful bother to, er . . . get me . . . another cup of tea?' She must use the dear girl's name. Hazel wasn't so bad. The name of a tree, a delicious little nut. She had even seen hazelnut spread, in Safeways, although it was a wicked price for only a small jar.

'No bother at all. So long as the canteen's still open. Fancy a bun as well?'

A bun. Astonishing. Perhaps hot, with butter and raspberry jam – the sort with little pips. Or did Hazel mean an iced bun? Pink icing glistening on the top, like the birthday cakes she had made for Eleanor. Six candles, seven, eight . . . flickering and shining. And a real fire in the grate. 'You're sure it's not a nuis-ance – Hazel?'

''Course not.'

'Don't be long – Hazel – will you?'

She closed her eyes while she waited, so she could see the girl in her mind. There would be room for two in the flat. Hazel could have the spare room. Except it was very small, barely more than a cubbyhole. Better if she moved in there, then Hazel could have her bedroom and the wardrobe. Young girls had so many clothes these days. Not like in the war. Her wedding dress had been made from a pair of curtains. Good-quality curtains, but all the same . . .

'Wakey-wakey, Margaret!'

'I wasn't asleep.'

'Here's your tea. No buns, I'm afraid, so I got some ginger nuts.'

She couldn't eat ginger nuts. The dentist had told her to avoid biting anything hard. He was new as well. Mr Khan had retired. '*You* have them, dear,' she smiled. 'And what do I owe you for the tea?' The least she could do was pay for that. *And* the biscuits, even if she couldn't eat them. They wouldn't cost much. There were only three, imprisoned in one of those stubborn cellophane packets. So many things were impossible to open these days. Milk cartons, sardines . . .

'Well, it's 90p altogether.'

'Right. Could you pass me my bag?'

'Leave it till you've had your tea. You're not about to do a bunk, are you!'

Margaret smiled again and took the cup, wishing Hazel would hold it for her – hold her morning cup of tea, her lunchtime glass of water, her mug of Bovril before she went to bed. 'And you mean to tell me they don't pay you anything?'

'Not a bean.'

'But they must have money, surely, an organization like that?'

'I expect they get grants and stuff. And some people give donations – you know, patients we've treated, and . . .'

'Donations?'

'Yeah.' The girl laughed. 'I s'pose they think it's worth it if we've saved their lives.'

'Donations,' Margaret said again, putting down her cup. Love is free, love is kind. Love never counts the cost.

'One bloke gave me fifty quid. And a woman gave me a bracelet. Real pearls, it was, she said.'

'So you *are* paid?'

'That's not pay.' Hazel ripped the cellophane off the biscuits and bit into two together. 'Anyway I handed in the fifty quid to Funds. It's against the rules to keep it.'

'And the bracelet?'

'That was different. She wanted me to have it. I told her it weren't allowed, but she insisted. She said nobody would know.'

'You didn't do it for love then?'

'Do what?' Hazel took another bite, spraying crumbs from her mouth.

'Help the lady with the bracelet.'

''Course I helped her. She had this dodgy heart and . . .'

'Yes, but not for love.'

'I'm sorry, Margaret, I don't know what you're on about.'

'Never mind.'

'Come on, drink your tea. You haven't touched it yet.'

'It's . . . cold.'

Hazel crunched the last of the biscuits, then tested the tea with a finger – a sallow, germy finger. 'It's not cold at all. Here, take a little sip.'

Margaret slumped back against the cushions, clamping her arms across her chest.

'Feeling rough again?'

Rough. Love was soft. Love was smooth. Love was freely given, showered forth, running over, expecting nothing in return. 'Pass me my handbag, would you.'

'What d'you want? I'll get it.'

'Just give it to me, please.'

'OK, keep your hair on.' Hazel handed it over, fingering the gold clasp. 'Nice bag.'

'It's old, but it's real leather.' The purse was older still, the stitching coming loose along one seam. She counted out a fifty-pence piece, a twenty and two tens. 'That's for the tea,' she said. She had collected her pension yesterday, thank heavens. The notes were new and clean. And there was the money from the heater – more than she had expected. She didn't really need a fire. A coat would keep her warm enough indoors. It wasn't advisable to leave money in the flats. Mrs Soames had been burgled twice already. And the man in number four had come back to find his windows smashed and his silver tankard missing.

She handed the notes over, one by one.

Hazel looked embarrassed. 'There's no need for this. Honest.'

Of course there was a need. She wouldn't have people saying she accepted things for nothing. Or Eleanor complaining about the cost of the fares when she came over for the funeral. One by one. One by one.

'That's plenty, Margaret. Really.'

She had always paid her way. It was no good expecting favours. One by one. One by one.

'Margaret, that's enough!'

Nowhere near enough. Love should never be rationed. *I may give away everything I have, or even give up my body to be burned, but if I have no love, I am nothing.*

One by one.

One by one by one.

'Margaret, stop! This is far too much.'

She shook her head, almost violently, adding the last crisp note to the pile on Hazel's palm.

How could you ever give too much?

Edgar H.W. – I Think He Said

I first found Edgar at three a.m. on a greyish sort of Wednesday in November. Three a.m. is not a good time. Quiet, unexceptional things like umbrella stands and bevelled-edged bookcases nag and mutter at that hour, and the moon takes bites out of the clouds.

It is the apogee of greyness, three o'clock. Grey sky, grey grass, grey moon, grey me. Occasionally I cry. I can't see my tears, but no doubt they, too, are grey. Nobody hears. Nobody's there. True, Charles lies beside me, in his maroon-striped silk pyjamas, but he is really somewhere else. At the Golf Club, I suspect, playing eighteen holes with God. Charles hates tears – they put him off his swing. You need discipline and silence on a golf course. So I've had to give up sobbing – one of the casualties of marriage, I suppose.

Before I met Edgar I resorted to death scenes instead. They are equally indulgent but quieter. I always start with Christ (*Consummatum Est*). That's a good one when the wind is snarling outside and rotten elms going down like skittles. I shut my eyes to blank out our Sleep-Eze orthopaedic bed and Charles's exercise machines pawing the ground beside his electric trouser press, and suddenly everything is Golgotha. The wall of the Temple is rent in twain. (Twain is just the right word for a death scene: a solid, old-fashioned, suffering sort of word. Words like that are rare these days.)

Sometimes I'm rent in twain myself. It's real grief, don't misunderstand me. I know all about Agonies in Gardens, although I don't think artists ever get it quite right. They concentrate on the sleeping apostles or the hushed and shadowy landscape, but the agony eludes them. Sweating blood is not pleasant. I studied it at night school and would recommend all artists to take a course in it.

Lord, let this chalice pass from me. I say it all the time. Not that the Lord listens. He's shining up His smile or accusing Charles of having made Him four-putt on the ninth.

When I'm not Christ I'm Nelson at Trafalgar. 'Kiss me, Hardy.' I hope Hardy did. There are records, no doubt – documents, biographies. Dead, dead, dead. 'Hardy,' I wheedle, 'talk to me.' (Charles has reached the twelfth and is fuming in a bunker.) Hardy sometimes does, sometimes doesn't. Depends on the sea conditions. Half an hour has passed, in any case.

I was deep in my death scenes when I first met Edgar. I'd done Thomas More, Little Nell and Marilyn Monroe and was frankly getting bored. It made a change to bump into someone living. Edgar had probably been hanging around here for years, only I'd never really seen him, everything being so grey. I spent an age deciding on his name. It had to be gentle and strong, like the toilet paper. I didn't want a bully or even a hero. He'd be the sort of good-natured, easy-going chap who didn't mind picking wild flowers or kissing another fellow on his death bed. He wouldn't need sleep and he didn't play golf. Purposely I didn't make him handsome. None of your ocean-deep blue eyes or rippling bronzed torsos. He was beige all over: eyes, skin, clothes, soul. He certainly wasn't passionate. No smouldering kisses and undying protestations. All far too obvious, and dangerous.

I threw out the romantic names – Romeo and Rudolf, Almaviva, Juan – and then the heroic ones: Alexander, Napoleon. Pretentious names like Jasper had no appeal whatever, nor cruel ones like Adolf. And I certainly didn't want the Formica-and-fish-finger sort like Kevin, Len or Wayne. There wasn't much left. Clive, Oliver, Malcolm, Edgar. When I said Edgar he came.

He was a pale, pleasant, unexceptional sort of fellow who sat in our brocaded bedroom chair, fiddling with hairpins and cracking his thumbs. The important thing is not to idealize people – just make them ordinary. Edgar has a skin-rash and an ingrowing toenail, but at three a.m. you can hardly see that sort of detail. He would sprawl there companionably, going on about blackfly on roses or repeats on Radio 4, and I'd wrap his voice round me like a duvet. Sometimes he would hold my hand, matter-of-factly, no frills. But his hand was a pillar, a mast, the fixed axis of the turning world. Charles never noticed. He was doing press-ups on the bathroom floor or practising his Colin Montgomerie scowl.

Edgar stayed around. When morning came he crouched in a cupboard or read Denis Wheatley in the wine cellar, while Charles and I creaked and shillied over the Cooper's Oxford Marmalade. Charles toyed with his free-range egg and his starch-reduced roll; Edgar gobbled Ready-Brek.

I waved Charles off with a starch-reduced kiss, and Edgar jumped out from the Chardonnay. We shelled peas together, and he held my hand while I vacuumed the bedroom. It took longer, of course, but it was worth it.

Living got easier all the time. If a bus conductor nagged me for not having change I no longer wept all the way from Clapham North to Muswell Hill. If someone killed a cockroach I didn't automatically wear black. I even lost interest in my Suicide Scrapbook, which up to then had been my favourite pastime. When Charles was delayed at the office I would spend contented hours browsing through the obituaries and messing about with scissors and glue.

'And what did you do, today, dear?' he'd burble, having eased himself out of his pinstripes into his low-cholesterol dinner.

'Boy makes noose out of nightdress,' I'd reply. 'Mayor flings himself under milk float. Stunt man drowns in paddling pool.'

'Fine, fine.' Charles speared a Brussels sprout on his silver-plated fork. 'Glad you're keeping busy.'

He never actually looked at it, although it was a very special scrapbook with shiny black covers, appropriately stiff, and purple Gothic script. I had arranged it meticulously and added an alphabetical index. Barbiturates came first, followed by drownings, hangings, hara-kiri, miscellaneous, Paracetamol, plastic bags and suttee. It was like my baby book, I suppose. Charles didn't believe in babies. Besides, there wasn't room for a cot, what with his treadmill and his rowing machine – he'd even annexed the spare room for his stereo equipment. Instead of baby's first words I lovingly recorded the details of deaths – pointed stakes up rectums, stately maulings by Longleat lions, lingering hemlock or lightning cyanide. The odd crucifixion was always a treat. One chap made a cross out of a draining-board and nailed himself to it on Camber Sands. It took him hours to die. A chicken-packer killed herself with Liquorice Allsorts – stuffed them non-stop through the forty days of Lent. They wanted to use her for a Bassetts TV commercial, but she died on day forty-one.

Edgar put an end to all that. With him in attendance there was no need to kill time in cemeteries or eat my sandwiches lying on a gravestone. We went to Madame Tussaud's instead and bought Jack the Ripper T-shirts and Henry VIII coffee mugs. Or took the train to Brighton and strolled along the pier. Edgar never held my hand in public, but our shadows embraced when it was sunny and we shared an umbrella in the rain.

Charles took up badminton and booked professional coaching. If it hadn't been for Edgar, I would have been very much alone. But as Charles's service strengthened, so did Edgar's. We began to fit together like a double-yolked egg. If only he'd had a surname I'd have taken it as my own. Marriage by deed poll. But he didn't have another name at all. I suppose it was safer really. None the less, I began to grow dissatisfied. One name seemed so little in a vast and shifting universe. A nice name, Edgar, but weak and insubstantial on its own – five frail letters pitted against the void. Sometimes I couldn't even find him. I'd take trains to every seaside resort and search the piers and beaches, or prowl through the house calling out his name; mouth full of chewed string, eyes tight and hard like marbles. (Charles was rubbing wintergreen into his quadriceps.)

'Edgar,' I'd shout. 'Edgar!'

He always turned up. 'I just popped down to Safeways for half a pound of lard.' Or 'I was up in the attic, riveting a swede.'

'I've got to nail you down,' I'd mutter, relishing the connotations of coffins and crucifixions. 'You need another name.'

Strangely enough, he resisted. He had never resisted anything before. If I decided we would read Wordsworth up to two a.m. and play rummy afterwards, he'd be rustling up the celandines and shuffling the cards before you could say 'Dove Cottage'. But he really put his foot down about the names.

'I'm Edgar,' he'd say, dunking a biscuit in his tea. 'No more, no less.'

I tried to reason with him, pointing out that Sir Thomas

Masterman Hardy had two surnames, *and* the Sir, whereas he didn't even have one. And our own Prince of Wales boasted at least four Christian names and a string of titles besides. And Marilyn Monroe was christened Norma Jean. I told him he was shadowy and only half there. There wasn't any meat on an Edgar – an extra name or two would build him up, flesh him out. Everybody else had a minimum of two names, to say nothing of pet names, patronyms, aliases and noms de plume.

'I'm not everybody else,' he said, impassively. 'I'm Edgar.'

'It's not enough,' I repeated. 'Edgar's too thin. Edgars get lost down crevices or slip between the fingers.'

I felt incalculably alarmed when he set his jaw like that, but somehow I couldn't drop the subject. It seemed absolutely essential.

I bought a book of babies' names and read it out loud to him, forwards and then backwards, with careful attention to the timbre. 'Boris, Leslie, Claude,' I intoned. 'Roger, Norman, Hugh.'

Edgar shook the crumbs from the biscuit packet directly into his mouth.

I changed to Italian names, revelling in all the o's: Mario, Carlo, Francesco, Roberto. Hebrew next: Abraham and Esau. Then I raided the classics – Ulysses, Ajax – and warbled through the world of opera: Tamino, Parsifal.

Edgar was making a battleship out of matches and a paper serviette.

I returned to the British Isles: Seamus, Llewellyn, Alistair.

Edgar crumpled up his dreadnought and threw it on the floor.

'All right,' I said, 'be English, if you insist. Harold William – both dignified and regal. Edgar Harold William. That'll have to do. I'll let you off a surname.'

I didn't feel as chirpy as I sounded. Edgar was kicking at

the shipwreck and his frown reminded me of Charles's. His trainers were dirty, I noticed, although, as I told him sharply, even trainers have names: Nike, Reebok, Adidas. And as for Charles's shoes, their names are incredibly fancy: Artiolie, Salvatore Ferragamo.

'Tell you what,' I ventured, 'how about a compromise – just initials. Edgar H.W. Would that suit?'

Charles returned from badminton. He didn't believe in Edgar, so Edgar slipped away. Charles ran a bath and put Band-Aid on his blisters. I offered him grilled organic lamb chops or a wholewheat, low-fat sandwich, but he said he'd already eaten at the club. He undressed and went to bed, first cleaning his teeth with his electric plaque-remover (which has a built-in timer to prevent skimping – something Charles would never do). Ten minutes later he was fast asleep. Badminton took it out of him.

I waited a decent interval, then got up.

'Edgar H.W.,' I whispered.

I heard the wind moaning through Charles's heavy-cropping Laxton Superb.

'Edgar Harold,' I called.

An owl screeched somewhere in the darkness, swooping on its prey.

'Edgar Harold William.' I wasn't whispering now. My palms were slimy with sweat and I was clawing feathers from the duvet.

'Edgar H.W.,' I repeated.

'H.W.,' mocked the wind.

I got out of bed and crawled on hands and knees across the carpet, banging my head up and down, up and down. 'Edgar, Edgar, Edgar . . .'

No reply.

The sheets were cold when I crept back into bed. I leaned

across and, with the tip of one scared finger, touched the curve of Charles's sternly closed eye. 'Charles?'

He didn't so much as stir. He was on the final set, so he needed every ounce of concentration.

'Charles,' I pleaded. 'I'll play, I promise. I'll learn. I'll take lessons. I won't hold you up. I'll buy my own shuttlecocks.'

Charles was smiling in his sleep. He had won, as usual, game, set and match. I slipped out of bed and opened the window. Grey, all grey. Grey sky, grey lawn, grey . . .

'Edgar?'

Silence.

I leaned out further. 'I know you're there, Edgar, so you may as well come out.'

Only the whisper of an owl's wing brushing against a cloud.

I thrust my whole body through the window frame and stretched up, up, trying to touch the stars with my bare hands.

'For God's sake, Edgar, it's not funny any more.'

Edgar didn't answer. I stood on the sill and peered down. The ground looked very far away.

'Edgar, please.' I was trembling now. 'Can't you see I need you.'

I stepped out into the sky. Cold grey ground came rushing, hurtling towards me. 'Edgar – Harold – William.' The words were smashed to pieces. I smiled.

I knew he wouldn't let me fall.

Glossy Daggers

Through the window everything looked black – walls, units, shelving, tables, chairs. That most hateful colour, black.

She turned away and began walking back to the tube. The whole thing was pointless, anyway. Fifty yards on, she stopped. Jo would be offended if she didn't keep the appointment. It would also be a shocking waste of money. Jo had paid already.

Retracing her steps, she stopped once more outside the expanse of smoky-tinged glass. In contrast to the black decor the staff wore clinical white, like nurses. The nurses at St Thomas's had been kind but matter-of-fact. Death for them was just part of the day's work.

She made herself walk in and stood waiting at the reception desk behind another customer, a girl of little more than twenty, in skin-tight silver trousers and a crop top. Staff and customers alike seemed young, glamorous and fashionably anorexic. Well, if nothing else she would serve as a reminder of age and mortality, like the skull in a Renaissance painting. At least there was flesh on her bones – too much, alas.

'May I help you?' The receptionist's nails were shiny scarlet talons sticking out a good inch beyond her fingertips – an advertisement, presumably, for the salon's name, 'Glossy Daggers'. She was dressed in a black pantsuit and her hair was dyed black to match. Behind her loomed a poster of another red-nailed vamp, crouching on a leopardskin rug above a naked man. The man's chest was scored with five livid, bloody claw-marks. 'Make your mark!' said the slogan.

'May I help you?' the girl repeated.

'Oh, sorry, yes.' She dragged her eyes from the poster. 'Mrs Groves. I'm here for a manicure.' It sounded absurd even as she said it. Why should she want a manicure?

A glossy scarlet dagger traced the list of names in the appointments book. 'Actually, we've got you down for nail enhancement.'

'I beg your pardon?'

'It's rather more than a manicure. We extend the nails.'

'*Extend* them?'

'Don't worry, it's quite painless. You're with Kelly – she'll explain. If you'd like to take a seat, she won't be long.'

Hannah eyed the chairs with some unease – extraordinary creations in the shape of giant black hands, with the same joltingly red fingernails as the receptionist's. Suppose those rigid black fingers closed around your back and squeezed . . .

Lowering herself warily on to the palm of the hand, she tried to take in her surroundings. There was a profusion of plants (black, tall, thin and fake, in keeping with the rest) and black artificial fruits in black steel bowls. She imagined biting into a cold black pear, squeezing a black lemon. Perhaps the apples in the Garden of Eden had turned black after the Fall. Whichever way she looked, she couldn't avoid the stare of the mirrors: black-framed mirrors reflecting the ravages of grief. Grief *did* ravage – her face was proof. Other clichés, too, had turned out to be true: time healing, for example – to some extent, at least. It was progress of a sort to be sitting in a beauty salon, dressed, dry-eyed, coherent.

A junior appeared, wearing the shortest possible white skirt and the highest possible black platform shoes; her lashes glossed barbed wire. 'Can I get you a tea or coffee? Or a fruit juice? There's orange, grapefruit and tropical nectar.'

'Er, tropical nectar, please.' At home, it would have been a tea-bag dunked in a mug. Or nothing. Often, tea for one didn't seem worth the effort.

Kelly arrived before the juice – a blonde this time and almost buxom. Her ample bosom was emphasized by a glittery brooch made of 3-D diamanté letters, proclaiming 'I DO NAILS'.

'Mrs Groves?'

'Yes, that's right.' Although Paul was gone, no one could take away his name.

'Happy birthday!'

She flushed. Fifty-two was a nothing sort of age – post-menopausal and pre-dementia; hardly cause for celebration.

'This way, please.' Kelly showed her to another giant-hand seat, flanked by a black pseudo-marble work-table with a black Anglepoise lamp built into it and a black rack containing hundreds of bottles and jars.

'Now, before I start' – Kelly laid a paper towel on the black padded hand-rest – 'I like to give clients my credentials. I've worked in the nail industry for more than fifteen years. I trained in California at the Da Silva Institute, and then taught Nail Art for three years in Santa Monica, and after that . . .' Her accent was south London, overlaid with a touch of Hollywood. 'And just last month I went back to LA to attend an advanced refresher seminar for nail technicians.'

Nail technician sounded odd. Odder still that a whole industry should be devoted to what, after all, were simply an accumulation of dead cells. 'Kelly, there seems to be some confusion. I thought I was booked for a manicure, but the receptionist said . . .'

'Ah, yes, nail enhancement,' Kelly smiled. 'When your

friend Jo came in to make the appointment, she and I had a little chat, and we decided that our aim today is for you to walk out of this salon feeling a totally new woman, as confident and glamorous as Catherine Zeta Jones. I'm afraid that may not be possible with just a manicure. But let's have a little look, shall we? Would you put your hands on here.' She indicated the hand-rest.

Hannah's nails were subjected to intense scrutiny. She had never given them much thought before, although they had served their purpose well enough, levering lids off tins, pinching out side-shoots on tomato plants, unpicking knots in string.

'Well, to be honest, Mrs Groves, they're not in peak condition. In fact if you'll forgive me being blunt, they're split, ridged and extremely dry and brittle. But with nail enhancement I can make them unbelievably long and beautiful.'

'In that case you should be called Miracles,' Hannah remarked tartly.

'You're right, we do achieve miracles – with these.' Kelly whisked the lid off a box to reveal row upon row of plastic strips: dead white and oblong-shaped, and slightly curved at each end.

'They're . . . *nails?*'

'Well, these are just the basic extensions, which we glue to the tips of your own nails. But after that we can achieve any length and any effect you choose. Let me show you.' Kelly laid a pile of brochures on the table and opened them at random. Hannah gazed in astonishment at scores and scores of nails, some attached to models, others disembodied; none bearing the slightest resemblance to the normal everyday variety. These were designer creations, sculpted in 3-D, with miniature multi-coloured feathers sprouting from their tips; or painted with all manner of designs – palm trees, strutting peacocks, spiders, snakes, Pooh Bears – or spangled gold and silver or set with minute jewels. Some had dangling charms attached: hearts or keys or ladybirds or tiny silver chains. The most bizarre of all had been built up into grotesquely twisted stalagmites and protruded a full two inches beyond the natural nails. And they weren't restricted to females. There were male models as well, proudly showing off their talons decorated with sporting trophies or football club logos or even naked women.

Hannah didn't know whether to laugh or cry. In a world where people died of heart attacks could such frivolity be justified?

'Your fruit juice, madam.'

More frivolity. The glass was black (of course), with two gold-striped straws and a dinky paper parasol, and piled high with chunks of kiwi, mango and pineapple. She wondered about the etiquette of tackling such a concoction. Did one eat the fruit or leave it genteelly in the glass?

Kelly was still leafing through the brochures. 'Of course, some of these are obviously not suitable. For instance . . .' She pointed to a model in an elaborate white lace wedding gown, with white lace nails to match. A second bride sported ten madonna lilies, diminutive but perfect copies of the lilies in her bouquet.

Hannah thought back to her own wedding. She had worn a simple cream two-piece and unobtrusive hat. When you were marrying for the first time at the age of forty-three you avoided ostentation.

'Aren't the bridesmaids cute?'

She nodded. A brace of under-tens in candyfloss pink tulle, with pink bunnies on their nails. It had been Paul's first marriage, too – at fifty-eight. She hadn't minded the age gap; she had regarded him as immortal.

'Anyway, these are just to give you a few ideas. Although of course we can do you a plainer look, if you prefer.'

'Yes, I do prefer.' Widows' nails should be brutally plain.

'In fact the nail extensions are so gorgeous in themselves you don't even need to have them varnished. But actually I *would* suggest a polish today. Your friend was insistent you have the full works, and we don't want to disappoint her, do we?' Kelly gave her tinkling laugh. 'I wish *I* had such a generous friend!'

'Yes, I'm very lucky.' Never mind the manicure – a birthday gift she would never in a thousand years have chosen for herself – without Jo's support she might not have survived at all.

'I ought to warn you, Mrs Groves,' Kelly added teasingly, 'nails like these are as addictive as drugs. Once you start you'll keep coming back for more!'

On a widow's pension? No.

'Anyway, there's a lot to do before we reach the polish stage, so let's get started, shall we? Make yourself comfortable and just sit back and enjoy.'

Unlikely. Enjoyment had died with Paul.

'First I'm going to sterilize your hands.'

Hannah jumped as the cold blue gel spurted on to her hands. She *needed* sterilizing. Death made you unclean in other people's eyes. Less courageous friends than Jo tended to avoid her now.

'Then we apply "Rescue" to the cuticles. This is a really brilliant product, Mrs Groves. It contains aloe vera, tea-tree oil and vitamins A and E.'

If only there were a similar product for grief, guaranteed fast-acting. Even with Jo, and even after seven months, she was still in need of rescue.

She watched Kelly wield the nail file, which was the regulation black with an exotic zebra pattern on one side. Kelly's own nails were less than perfect, Hannah noted with interest. Although they were long and nicely shaped, the polish was chipped in places. Perhaps she had to juggle job and children and never had time for herself.

Paul would have loved a child. They had tried, to no avail. As the doctor said, forty-three was late to start a family.

She was suddenly conscious of the background music – not the schmaltzy pop songs one might have expected in a beauty salon but surprisingly solemn music, reminiscent of a church. Maybe it wasn't so surprising, though, in this Shrine to Nails, where staff expended as much care on nails as medieval prelates gave to souls. The whole atmosphere was hushed and reverential – no raised voices, no vulgar laughter. Even the juniors, gliding back and forth with coffees, teas or various implements, seemed velvet-voiced, silken-shod.

'And now,' said Kelly, putting down the long black file and picking up a squat white object, 'we buff the nails to reduce their thickness slightly. It's a bit like crowning a tooth. We need to pare away before we add, if you follow what I mean.'

Hannah submitted, although privately she was beginning to think that ten nails was far too many if each process was as protracted as this. Doing her nails at home involved a couple of minutes with the clippers. But then what did time matter? There was nothing to go home for.

She winced as the buffer caught on a ragged cuticle. Pain was a peculiar thing – sometimes almost welcome as a distraction from grief. Given the choice of losing a limb or having to watch Paul's just-dead body manhandled by ambulance staff, she would lose the limb, no question.

'Your hands seem very tense, Mrs Groves. Try to let them flop, OK? Remember, this is your own special time for a little peace and pampering. We're all so busy these days we need to let go when we can.'

She wasn't busy, unfortunately. However, she did her best to relax, feeling strangely moved by Kelly's words and by the devotion she was lavishing on ten dry, discoloured growths. Each finger was held in turn and given a meticulous succouring. It was a long time since she'd been touched or had another person's fingers locked in hers. She and Paul used to walk hand in hand, even just out shopping – soppy at their age. Kelly, she observed, wore three sets of double rings – wedding and engagement – two on the left hand, one on the right. Had the poor girl been widowed twice? The thought was terrifying.

'That's the preparation finished. And now we're ready for the nail tips.'

Tips was an understatement for the dauntingly long acrylic shields. Hannah's index finger was firmly clamped as a 'tip' was fitted on to it and then secured with glue. The painstaking procedure was repeated ten times, until she had ten white shiny claws sticking out from the ends of her fingers. The effect was more Edward Scissorhands than Catherine Zeta Jones.

Kelly noticed her expression. 'Don't worry, we're nowhere near finished yet. First I'm going to trim them for you, then we build up the tip and the natural nail with a special acrylic substance. It's a sensational new line, this' – she picked up a small bottle and unscrewed the ornate gold lid – 'the number one enhancement product in the States, guaranteed not to age, discolour, deteriorate or crack . . .'

In that case, Hannah surmised, it was a pity it couldn't be applied to her whole body (mind and soul, as well).

'Now what I need to know, Mrs Groves, is how long you'd like your nails.'

'*Very* long,' she said, startled at the words, as if someone else had uttered them.

'Mm . . .' Kelly looked dubious. 'As this is your first time I wouldn't recommend them to be *too* long.'

'Well, as long as possible.' It suddenly seemed pointless, if not perverse, to sit brooding on her problems when she had the chance to forget them for a while. She must enter into the spirit of the thing, for Jo's sake, if nothing else. 'And I *do* want polish, I've decided. Something nice and bright.'

'Good for you! We've got some stunning colours this season, including a brand new range from California, all named after films – Casablanca, From Here to Eternity, Some Like It Hot. How about Brief Encounter? That's really zingy!'

Hannah appraised the hectic orange. No brief encounter, theirs, but a marriage lasting eight and a quarter years. She ought to be grateful – as indeed she was. Eight and a quarter years with Paul was worth eighty on her own. Maybe she'd choose a varnish in his honour, something horticultural to reflect his love of gardening. There was bound to be a Peony or Rose.

'The names are such fun, don't you think? Look at these from L'Oréal: Feisty, Frisky, Saucy, Trouble, Pout. Pout might suit you, actually. It's a shade to die for.'

Hardly.

'Or Dragon's Blood, which is all the rage at the moment. But, as I said, we're not at that stage yet.'

'It's a lengthy business, isn't it? I hadn't realized there'd be all these different stages.'

'But it's time well spent, I assure you, Mrs Groves. You see, nails are absolutely basic to our sense of ourselves as women. There's no way we can feel feminine if they aren't up to the mark. I'm sure your friend Jo would agree. And think how thrilled she'll be when she sees the transformation!'

Transformation it was. Hannah couldn't stop staring at her new nails. They were unbelievably, dramatically long and an electric shade of purplish-red called Fuchsia. Paul had been proud of his fuchsias and they, too, had exuberant names:

Venus Victrix, *Enfant Prodigue,* Whiteknight's Amethyst. If only he were here, to witness the miracle. It did truly seem a miracle to feel a scintilla of hope after seven despairing months. If nails could be transformed, then why not lives? For the first time since the funeral she could actually envisage returning to work.

Kelly ran an admiring hand along her index finger. 'They look so fantastic, Mrs Groves, I'd love to enhance them even further with some nail art. I know you said you'd prefer them fairly plain, but why don't I just show you the effect. Have you a bit of time in hand?'

Hannah hesitated. She had all the time in the world; only money was short. Had Jo paid for nail art or would it be an extra?

'You owe it to your friend, you know, to make this experience memorable, otherwise you're going to disappoint her.'

Hannah could recognize a hard sell when she heard it. On the other hand, she was reluctant to leave the salon. Being cosseted was so rare, and during the last two hours she had been treated not as a leftover wife but with deference and respect. As well as Kelly's attentions, a junior had brought Orange Dazzler tea; another offered chocolate wafers (long, thin, dark, delicious); a third had given her a back-rub. Most days she saw no one at all. And the rhythmic music, combined with Kelly's soothing voice, had lulled her into a most agreeable inertia. 'All right,' she said, 'why not?'

'Wonderful! But will you let me have carte blanche?' Kelly gazed into her eyes with an intense blue-laser stare. 'You see, working on someone's nails is such an intimate procedure, it can open up new channels of communication. I have this intuition, Mrs Groves, that part of you is ready for change, ready for brightness and beauty in your life. Am I making sense?'

'Well, no – yes . . .'

'Sometimes we don't like to admit these things. They're too private and deep-seated. But nail art can act as a release. It's very therapeutic in that way. So I want you to sit back and trust me to do what I think best.'

The carriage was almost empty, so Hannah was free to spread her hands on her lap and exult in them, without fear of being stared at. Other people might criticize the designs as outrageous, if not ludicrous. Only she and Kelly understood their symbolism: the two entwined hearts a reminder that no one could take away the loving years with Paul; the rising sun to represent a new start every day; the starburst for joy, the mini-rainbow for hope. Each nail was dusted with glitter to add sparkle to her life. Today that didn't seem a callous joke. In fact she had left the salon in high spirits, after asking, with some embarrassment, what she owed for the nail art.

'Nothing,' Kelly had smiled. 'It's all been taken care of.'

She repeated the consoling phrase in her head, feeling she had received not one present but two – from two people 'taking care': Jo, whose generosity had made the whole thing possible, and Kelly for her incredible artistry: painting the intricate designs with tiny tiny brushes, cutting gold tape into hair-fine strips, tweezing doll-size diamonds into place and finally drilling a hole in the top of her right thumbnail to hold the butterfly charm.

She was so busy twirling the butterfly she nearly missed her station, and then she tripped at the top of the escalator, still engrossed in her nails. She emerged from the gloom of the Underground to a glorious June day, as if Kelly had also worked her magic on the weather. The morning had been drizzly, with a sky the colour of cold porridge.

Arriving home, she found the house shrouded in its miasma of grief, like *her*, until today. That must change. Before checking the Jobs Vacant columns she would heal and comfort each neglected room. But first the washing-up – a shameful accumulation when once she had been so houseproud. She seized a saucepan lid, only to drop it instantly as her nail tips clanged against the metal. Horrified, she examined them for damage. None, thank God. Kelly had assured her that the extensions were strong but hadn't warned her how unwieldly they would be.

She tried gingerly to turn on the tap, but again the nails got in the way and prevented her fingers from functioning. Well, that was the price of glamour, and if Kelly's other clients managed to combine a normal life with nail extensions, then so must she. All it needed was practice, and then presumably she would get accustomed to the peculiar feel of the new length.

She went upstairs to change – the navy suit was too smart for housework and too warm for a sunny afternoon. She unbuttoned her jacket, or tried to, with fingers as clumsy as spatulas. The square ends of the nails only exacerbated the difficulties. (Kelly had recommended square as the 'in' shape for the summer.) Removing her tights was no less fraught. The butterfly charm kept snagging on them and then got entangled in her hair. In fact every smallest action posed a challenge, especially undoing her bra, which involved repeated fumbling at unseen fiddly hooks. Although finally succeeding, she was left with weals and scratches across her back. Daggers did seem a worryingly apt description: she, a peaceable type, was now armed with ten lethal weapons.

Eventually she returned to the kitchen wearing a loose sundress and slip-on shoes (buckles and laces were out of the question). She was actually hungry, for a change – not that there was much food in the place. Since Paul's death she had lived on soup, salad and Mars Bars. She found a can of oxtail in the cupboard, but operating the tin-opener required a basic co-ordination between her fingers, impossible with such cumbersome nails. She replaced the soup on the shelf – it would have to be salad.

The fridge yielded only a cucumber stub, a couple of tomatoes and half a wilted lettuce. Washing them was comparatively simple; chopping was another matter. Several times she almost sliced through a talon instead of a tomato. She licked tomato pulp off her finger. Another mistake: the nail tasted of chemicals and felt hard and obtrusive in her mouth. She abandoned the knife and began shredding the lettuce by hand – also a struggle because the dangly charm kept getting in the way. If only she were a dog or cat and could eat directly from the plate, instead of having to wield a fork or use Struwwelpeter fingers to pick up squashy pieces of tomato. At least her teeth weren't varnished and extended.

Over lunch she read the salon's aftercare leaflet, which explained that it might take several days to learn new ways of doing up zips and buttons, opening drawers and car doors. 'Although awkward at first, it will soon become second nature. Just be patient and cherish your beautiful nails . . .'

Patience was her forte – waiting decades for marriage, trying every fertility drug available, until foiled by the menopause. She had been patient even with the process of grief, accepting sleepless nights, unravelled days and sudden shameful fits of weeping in shops or on the bus. Having survived so much, she refused to be defeated by a frivolous thing like false nails. After all, they were intended as a source of inspiration (not annoyance and aggression), the butterfly charm in particular. A butterfly was doubly symbolic: a creature that had emerged to beauty from a drab grey chrysalis, and another reminder of Paul. His favourite part of the garden was the butterfly patch they'd created with buddleia, wild violets, nasturtiums, honeysuckle. On summer evenings they would sit together, breathing in the scents and watching yellow brimstones and tortoiseshells flit from flower to flower. It was a jungle now, like the rest of the garden; an unkempt, weed-choked graveyard. Jo had offered help, and Mr Phelps next door, but she couldn't bear the thought of anyone, however well intentioned, disturbing the place where he had died. Safer to keep it sacrosanct, regard it as a shrine. Doubtless people thought it odd that she herself hadn't set foot there since the death. The truth was, she couldn't face the laurel bush – a loathsome thing, crouching squat and misshapen, yet with powers beyond its size.

Deliberately she turned her back to the window and examined the butterfly charm. Its very intrusiveness – dangling in her tea, catching in her clothes – would serve as a constant reminder that she, too, must escape her drab confining chrysalis.

With a cry of frustration she slumped down on the sofa. The nails were shackles, thwarting her every move. It was like foot-binding in China: a way of keeping women passive. Kelly had fired her with enthusiasm to kickstart her life again, yet it was Kelly's very handiwork that made any task impossible. All she could do was sit idle, listening to the ticking of the clock. She had been severely tempted to grab a kitchen knife and hack the damned things off, but Jo was expecting to see them when they met for lunch next week. Besides, Kelly had warned her on no account to try to remove the extensions herself – it could damage the natural nails or even rip the nail-bed. In fact clients were expected to return to Glossy Daggers every couple of weeks for what Kelly called rebalancing and maintenance. The whole thing was a scam – she had become the salon's prisoner, a role she had neither sought nor could afford.

She pulled angrily at the charm, but that, too, was immovable without the aid of pliers and another pair of hands with normal, unextended nails. The clock-hands seemed as inoperative as hers. Time was suspended; the sun refused to set. She ought to ring Jo and thank her, but suppose she let slip some hint of her irritation? It would be terribly rude and ungrateful when the bill must have reached three figures. She could have bought a new wardrobe for that; spent a weekend in Paris. Except she didn't want clothes or holidays. All she wanted was to be rid of these alien growths and have her own blessedly short and functional nails restored.

The television was playing to itself – the news again, a rerun of the bombing in Armagh. It was hard to escape from death, especially with Paul's ashes on the mantelpiece. Another rip-off, that – the Royal Crown Derby urn from the so-called Fine Art Collection. There were certain similarities between funeral parlours and nail salons: the same pretentiousness (coffins with names like Balmoral, Emperor, Sapphire); the same inflated prices for services you didn't want; empty packaging for bodies. It seemed a travesty that a big, no-nonsense man like Paul should be cooped up in a china pot decorated with prissy little turtle doves. She had let herself be swayed by the funeral director's spiel that choosing the most expensive in the range was proof you really cared. Cared! She had imprisoned a man who loved to be outdoors in a cramped and airtight container. On a sultry evening like this he would never stay inside, but busy himself till dusk, mowing the lawn, watering the hanging baskets, dead-heading the roses and fuchsias.

Impetuously, she jumped up from the sofa and unbolted the french windows – the first time in seven months – and, despite the hindrance of her nails, somehow managed to force them open. Seizing the urn from the mantelpiece, she hurled it on to the patio, listening to it shatter.

Then she ran across the lawn to the laurel bush, grasped its central stem and started tugging at it with all her strength, as Paul had in December. 'Die!' she shouted, '*Die!* How dare you live when you killed him!'

Sweating and straining, she kept heaving at the bush, but it resisted her with the same contempt it had shown him. Maddened, she redoubled her efforts, summoning up super-human reserves, as if Paul himself had joined his strength to hers, in death as he had in life.

There was an ominous crack, a shudder, and all at once the root came free. She fell backwards with the force of it, but struggled to her feet at once, whereas the bush lay prostrate, vanquished. She began wrenching off its branches, trampling on them, smashing them, tears streaming down her face. 'You killed him,' she sobbed. 'You destroyed us both.'

The toughest branches refused to break, defiantly springing back and lunging at her eyes, as if even now it was intent on wreaking havoc. But she continued furiously wrestling with it, determined to avenge Paul's death, defeat his murderer.

Soon dismembered limbs lay strewn around, their splin-tered ends exposing raw white flesh. Next she attacked the pockmarked leaves, slashing at them, ripping them, mangling them to a slimy pulp. If it took all night, she didn't care. This bush must die, every cell and shred of it.

At last, surrounded by a pile of debris, she sank exhausted to the ground. The earth felt hard and lumpy under her bare legs as she sat gazing at the carnage. Gradually her breathing slowed and the trembling in her arms abated. How quiet it was, how still. Glancing up, she saw a drift of fine grey dust wafting across the grass.

Mesmerized, she watched it gently lift and float. *Paul* – free again, hers again, back in his beloved garden. She had released him from his cage; the two of them together once more on an enchanted summer evening.

She walked slowly to the butterfly patch and the rustic double seat he had built. The air was warm, the sky unclouded. She sat motionless, breathing in the fondant scent of honeysuckle; watching a red admiral alight on a flower and spread its wings, displaying bands of lustrous scarlet across deep velvet brown.

Suddenly, she heard a noise – a shrilling sound, jangling on and on. She dashed into the house and picked up the receiver. 'Paul?' she said breathlessly.

'*Paul?*'

'Who . . . who is it?'

'It's me – Jo. What on earth's the matter, Hannah?'

'Nothing.'

'But you said . . . Paul.'

Hannah didn't answer. She was thinking about the garden, planning for next spring: narcissi, wallflowers, marigolds, new exotic fuchsia plants.

'You sound so odd. What's happened? I was ringing to ask how the manicure went.'

Hannah glanced at her hands. They were raw in places; scratched and bruised all over. The nail extensions had broken off, leaving jagged edges, easy to file short. She was no longer paralysed or shackled. Tomorrow she could clear the jungle, burn the wreckage of the laurel bush, weed out the convolvulus, hack the nettles down.

'Oh, Hannah, was *that* what upset you? I'm sorry, honestly. I should never have booked the appointment. It was too soon to expect . . .'

'Jo,' she said, still looking at her hands: ravaged, bleeding, miraculously functional hands, 'you couldn't have given me a more perfect present.'

Cloudburst

'I made a Spanish omelette,' Stuart said.

'An *omelette*?'

'They're nice for picnics, cold.'

Yvonne watched in silence as he unwrapped the grease-proof paper. The top was freckled brown; beneath, the moistly quivering flesh was studded with vegetable jewels: emerald peas, kernels of sweetcorn, shreds of red and orange pepper, translucent onion strips. She hadn't even known that he could cook.

'And look!' he said, unveiling with a flourish a large if somewhat misshapen cake, iced lavishly in white. 'Carrot cake – your favourite. I'm afraid the icing's a bit runny, but otherwise it seems to have turned out rather well.'

'Oh, Stuart, thanks. How sweet of you.' It made her still more guilty that he should have gone to so much trouble. Iced cakes were for celebrations, not for wakes. She had only suggested a picnic because it would be easier to break the news on neutral ground and somewhere they'd have space to themselves. He shared his flat with three old college friends – big, bluff, sporty types whose noise and bulk made it claustrophobic. And her place would be impossible. He might never leave, spend half the night trying to change her mind.

She unpacked the food she had brought – all supermarket fare: pâté, coleslaw, quiche. 'I'm sorry, Stuart, I didn't have time to cook.' Not quite true. She could have rustled up a quiche last night instead of working late.

'Don't worry, darling. I know how busy you are.'

The 'darlings' made it worse. Distractedly she swatted at a wasp hovering over the cake. Another landed on the sticky icing and was instantly ensnared: a tiny, stripy saboteur in the expanse of pristine white. She dislodged its flailing body with a knife.

'I guessed we'd be plagued by them today,' Stuart said, rooting in his duffel-bag. '*Voilà* – a wasp-trap!' He brought out a tin of golden syrup and levered off the lid.

Mesmerized, she stared at the tin, remembered from her childhood: the elaborate livery of green and gold; the picture of a recumbent lion surrounded by a swarm of bees and, underneath, in diminutive print, 'Out of the strong came forth sweetness.'

A line from the Bible, so her father had told her. Judges, he'd said, which she hadn't understood. There were other puzzling things on the tin – 'partially inverted refiners' syrup' and 'By appointment to Her Majesty the Queen'. 'Partially inverted' sounded strange, and did Queens eat golden syrup? Her parents never touched it (her father said it set his teeth on edge), but she and her brother would cut doorsteps of white bread, spread them with condensed milk, then drizzle syrup initials on the top. Y for Yvonne, N for Neil. Yes and No, she'd sometimes thought, ungenerously.

She reached for the tin and read aloud, 'Out of the strong came forth sweetness.' A statement disproved, unfortunately, by life. Even her father's bouts of sweetness had been rare and unpredictable.

'What, darling?' Stuart was preoccupied, slicing the omelette.

The eggy bit had collapsed, and stray peas and bits of corn were rolling out on the ground. 'What did you say?' he repeated, picking a piece of onion off the knife.

'Oh, nothing.' It was too complicated to explain. When she had eventually got round to reading the story in Judges (14: 14), she was appalled at what she found: murder, carnage, revenge, a blameless wife burned to death. 'Don't kill the wasps,' she said suddenly. 'They haven't done any harm.' She put the lid back on the tin and placed it in her own bag, wondering what had happened to her brother. He, too, had been ill-tempered, like her father.

'Damn!' said Stuart. 'I've left the rug in the car.'

'It doesn't matter. The ground's bone dry.' She ran her hand across the springy grass, peering at the miniature world it harboured: enamelled insects going about their solemn little business; beechnut bombs left over from last year; the semi-transparent fragments of a snail shell. She sat cross-legged, trying to get comfortable – although not too comfortable. This wasn't a pleasure trip; it was a mission to be accomplished. Despite days of rehearsal she hadn't got the words right. It was important not to hurt him.

'Wine?' he asked. 'Or Perrier?'

'Perrier, please.' *She* should be taking charge – pouring drinks, setting out the food – but her mind was still elsewhere. However tactfully she put it, it was bound to come as a shock. Stuart *loved* her – he'd told her so, more than once – and she couldn't reciprocate. Besides, she was becoming dependent on him, and dependency was dangerous.

She watched the bubbles fizzing up in the glass. Just last month *Which?* had reported that many brands of bottled water were not only low in minerals but swarming with bacteria. She wished she hadn't read it – better not to know. It was like losing trust in something sacrosanct: the family, the Church.

Stuart clinked his glass against hers. 'To us,' he said, gazing into her eyes.

Without answering, she took a sip. The water was warm and slightly bitter. Was it the bacteria she could taste, seething at the bottom?

'Shall we start with the omelette, darling?'

'If you like.' She wondered how many 'darlings' they must have exchanged. Thousands; maybe hundreds of thousands. They popped out from force of habit now, each so light, so casual, yet, strung together, they formed a leaden chain.

'Darling, are you all right?'

'Why shouldn't I be?'

'You seem tired.'

'Well, I suppose I am, a bit.'

'Relax. Enjoy the picnic.' He handed her a slice of omelette, swathed in a holly-printed paper napkin. 'Sorry about these,' he laughed. 'A left-over from Christmas.'

Snow-sprinkled holly *was* incongruous in a heat wave. She hadn't known Stuart at Christmas – they had met soon after, at a New Year's party. It was as if she had acquired him with a six-month guarantee and the guarantee was nearly up. If she didn't send him back within the week, the relationship might become permanent. And permanence was like bottled water: its reputation tarnished by the facts.

She bit a piece off the omelette and held it in her mouth. It felt damp and smooth and solid, as his penis had last Sunday. When he came that way she couldn't bring herself to swallow; somehow queasy at the thought of a million million sperm wriggling in her stomach all night or torpedoing their way into her bowel.

'Don't you like it, darling?' As always he was noting her every reaction.

'Yes, it's . . . good.' She swallowed. Had her mother

swallowed her father's come? Unlikely in the extreme. If only semen tasted like golden syrup or had a different consistency . . .

'That skirt's pretty. Is it new?'

'No. Ages old. You must have seen it before.'

He shook his head. 'I'd have remembered the buttons.' Unfastening the bottom two, he laid his hand on her naked thigh. 'Easy access,' he smiled.

Involuntarily she tensed her leg. On Sunday, he'd come twice; she not at all. Perhaps it was just as well she lived alone – at least on weekdays she had the bed to herself.

He ran his hand across her knee, and down her calf to the ankle, which he held in a padlock-clasp. 'You'll burn in this heat. I brought a tube of sunscreen. Want me to rub some in for you?'

'No thanks. You're the one who needs it.' His fair, frail, English skin reacted at the first hint of sun.

He rummaged in his bag, found the Factor 25 and squeezed a dollop on to each cheek. Once he had smeared it on, his face gleamed ghostly white, in contrast to his weather-roughened hands. 'Sure you wouldn't like some, darling?'

'No.' She couldn't be bothered with sunscreens. Diseases, including cancer, were mostly a matter of genes. Divorce, as well, probably – which was worrying because both her parents were on their second marriage. Her mother's new husband worked in the City; her father's new wife (a mere four years her senior) was exuberantly pregnant.

Stuart leaned back on his elbows and gazed up at the sky. 'Isn't this glorious? We couldn't have picked a better day.'

She watched a huge white Soft-Whip cloud change shape before her eyes; pieces breaking off and drifting away. The same happened with relationships.

'Is anything the matter, Yvonne? You're so . . . quiet.'

'I'm hot, that's all.'

'We're lucky, though. They forecast rain.'

Forecasts could be wrong. Her friends had unanimously agreed that she and Mark were made for each other – until he left her for another woman. 'Want some quiche?' she offered, feeling ashamed as she unwrapped it. It was much smaller without the packaging and nothing like the picture on the lid. The child slices looked pathetic on the oversized paper plates and were oozing greyish phlegm. She spooned a coleslaw dam on top of each grey pool, wishing she'd brought tomatoes. Everything was so pallid, a jolt of red would have livened it up. But the only red was the berries on the paper napkins.

'What happened about your new job, by the way?' Stuart was eating with his fingers, even the coleslaw. 'Did they agree to honour your holiday dates?'

'Yes, after a bit of a tussle.'

'We could go away together, if you like.'

Now she must tell him, before he started collecting brochures or rushing off to pay deposits. Romantic Venice, Paris for lovers. She cleared her throat, but the words refused to come.

'Paris is always fun.'

As he spoke, she glimpsed his tongue, eager-pink and thatched with brownish sludge. 'Mm,' she murmured. 'A bit crowded in the summer, though.'

A leaf fluttered from a branch overhead. She caught it in mid-air. It was dry and yellowed already, although it was only early July. The seasons seemed mixed up: summer, autumn, winter holly. She wondered where she'd be by the winter. In another flat? On her own still?

'Or Vienna might be nice.'

Tourist snapshots sprang to mind: baroque churches, *Sachertorte*, Lippizaner horses. It would be unfair to go away with him. Like embarking on a honeymoon when it was time for a divorce.

There was a sound of frantic buzzing. Another wasp had braved the icing swamp and was convulsed in ecstatic death-throes. It might have been kinder to kill them outright. 'Stuart,' she said abruptly, 'there's something I need to . . .'

All at once a drop of rain spattered on her head, falling as if from nowhere. A few further drops flurried down, then suddenly, dramatically, the whole shimmering azure arc was engulfed in ominous grey.

'Oh, Lord!' cried Stuart. 'We'll be drenched.' Hardly had he spoken when the rain began in earnest. Frantically they rushed around, covering the food and stuffing it into the bags.

'Quick! Shelter under here.' He steered her up against the trunk of the tree, trying to shield her from the onslaught with his body. She was aware of the bark, scratchy-hard through her flimsy summer skirt. His hands, greasy from the sunscreen, seemed glued to her arms. His breath smelt of quiche and Chardonnay, and its warmth against her face felt disquietingly intimate, as if she were being sucked into his digestive processes.

'Let's hope it's only a shower,' he said, although the relentless noise of the downpour belied his optimism.

She remained silent in the enforced embrace. Sometimes they had sex in this position in her flat: clamped together, standing up. In fact she could feel the urgent nudge of his erection. And the rain was on his side, driving them even closer, providing sensational sound-effects. She envied it its histrionics, the way it had simply let rip, sheeting down in torrents with no warning or preliminaries, discharging its pent-up anger on any hapless victims. It took confidence to do that, an audacity quite beyond her scope. *She* was always holding back; always wary, fearful. Even now, she was in two minds: part of her responding as Stuart slipped his hand inside her T-shirt and rubbed his thumb against her nipple; part of her resentful, yet unable to protest.

Confused, she pulled away. It was wrong to lead him on when she was morally bound to tell him how she felt. She must set herself a deadline – as soon as they'd reached the car. At least it would still be private. There couldn't be anyone left in the park. 'Why don't we make a run for it?' she suggested.

'But, darling, we'll get soaked.'

'We'll get soaked anyway.'

'I'm sorry, Yvonne,' he whispered, using his finger to trace the outline of her lips.

She forced a smile. 'The weather's hardly your fault.' Nothing was his fault. It was her – she'd been uptight even as a child. She and her brother were two of a kind. She shivered.

'You're cold, darling. Maybe we *ought* to make a dash for it.'

Neither moved.

'It's a pity we can't pick up the tree and use it as an umbrella, then we'd keep dry on the way back.'

She was charmed by his idea, although it would be an umbrella full of holes. Great drops of rain had already penetrated the canopy of leaves. The tiny blue and pink forget-me-nots on her skirt had turned a purplish black.

His hand was groping between her legs, negotiating the barrier of her skimpy bikini pants. She closed her eyes as his nails grazed her burning bush. 'Burning bush' was Mark's term. Even down there her hair was distinctly red – rare, according to Mark, and he should know. She'd had no words for her sexual bits and pieces until various men had christened them. It was rather like being colonized.

She waited till his finger reached Sophia (Mark's term again, not Stuart's), then placed her hand on top of his and guided it gently away. Men's pride was massive, and fragile – you had to be so careful not to wound it. She kissed the hand in apology, catching a disturbing whiff of Sophia combined with the chemicals in the sunscreen.

'Let's go,' she said, seizing the bags. She slung one across her shoulder, pushed the other into Stuart's arms, then struck out along the path, stumbling and practically blinded by the rain. Within minutes her clothes were saturated, clinging to her breasts and thighs; her hair clumped in snaking strands. Her white sandals squelched with every step; mud from the path splashed up on her legs.

She was aware of Stuart behind her, yet she could hear nothing but the thunderous squall. Normally, summer rain was gently beneficial; reviving flower-beds and parched lawns, assuaging city dust. This destructive cataclysm was in a different league entirely. The whole five-hundred-acre park might be swept away in a tidal wave of mud, leaving only a churning crater dotted with a few picnic plates.

Suddenly she tripped and fell, and her bag went flying, disgorging half its contents. Needle-sharp jets assailed her prostrate body, reduced the quiche to a pathetic slush, hammered on the golden syrup tin.

Stuart panted up and squatted at her side. 'Darling, are you OK?'

Of course she wasn't OK: her hands were bleeding, her T-shirt covered in mud. But she must get up or she'd be swept away with the park. She pictured her bones, discovered centuries later – satisfyingly clean bones, purged of blood and slime.

Slipping and slithering, he helped her to her feet, then rescued the remnants of food. The cake lay shattered in the mud, its icing no longer white but glutinous brown. They hadn't even cut it, she realized with a stab of guilt – all Stuart's time and effort gone to waste. *Her* fault again for being clumsy, although he should have put it in a tin. Cakes, like people, needed protection.

He repacked the bag with difficulty – in these conditions the simplest action was a challenge. His hair was plastered to his head; his once-baggy chinos were sheets of clingfilm moulded round his legs. 'We'd better slow down. You don't want to hurt yourself.'

Instead she speeded up. The slower they went, the longer they would be subjected to the barrage. Already it had changed everything: solids into liquids, June into November, landmarks into blurs. She was genuinely cold now; the sodden skirt chafing against the insides of her thighs; gooseflesh prickling her arms. The short stroll in the sunshine from car to picnic site had become a gruelling forced march.

Stuart caught up with her and took her hand, and they ran side by side, the bags clunking on their shoulders. Sometimes she had run like this with her brother (before he'd grown big and bad-tempered), but never in such ferocious rain. It was stripping her naked, the vicious little needles piercing her skin.

'Nearly there,' Stuart puffed, making a final spurt towards the car. With a struggle he unlocked the passenger door and, having helped her in, groped his way to the boot, head bowed. Wrenching it open, he grabbed the picnic rug and bundled it on to her lap. 'Wrap that round you, darling.'

'But what about you?' she asked, as he plumped into the driver's seat and slammed the door.

'Don't worry about me. I'm weatherproof!'

True, he never seemed to feel the cold. Even now there was a healthy glow to his skin, despite the fact he was wringing wet. His tough brown lace-ups, she noticed, had survived the assault course far better than her helpless sandals. The only sensation in her feet was a sort of lumpen sogginess. 'Actually,' she said through chattering teeth, 'my clothes are so wet I doubt if it'll make much difference.'

'Well, take them off.'

'Oh, Stuart, I can't! Not in public.'

'Hardly public.' He peered through the misted-up window at the tarmac wasteland. 'It's crazy to sit in wet things. You'll catch pneumonia.'

Don't fuss, she wanted to snap. But he was only being kind. He was always kind. That was part of the trouble. 'Couldn't you put the heater on?'

'It's broken. I was going to get it fixed, but it didn't seem a priority in June!'

His laugh annoyed her, which was mean. At the moment, though, everything annoyed her – including her own inability to speak out. Practising at home, it hadn't seemed so difficult, but then she hadn't been wedged in a fuggy car, with the elements in turmoil outside. Trying to ignore the furore, she ran through various openings in her head. A simple statement might be best – they were fundamentally wrong for each other and that was the end of the matter. If she didn't make the position clear, he'd expect to be with her next weekend again, and the weekend after and . . . 'Stuart, I know this might sound . . .'

He wasn't listening, his whole attention given over to the unbuttoning of her skirt. 'This is absolutely sopping, darling. Let's get you out of it.'

How could she stop him when he meant well? (People invariably meant well, which was why she got landed so often with foods or jobs or friends she didn't want.) 'It's OK, I can do it, Stuart.' The skirt felt waterlogged and heavy, like a piece of washing taken from the machine before it had spun. Blue dye had stained her pants. Reluctantly she wriggled out of them, banging her knee on the dashboard. Stuart's hand pounced on her naked crotch.

Removing the hand – with a friendly squeeze, so as not to offend him – she wrapped the rug tightly round her lower half.

'What about your T-shirt? Better take that off, too.'

Instinctively she crossed her arms over her chest, but he prised them away and peeled the dripping garment off, then began to fumble with the hooks of her bra. This shouldn't be happening – it wasn't part of the plan at all. His hands were already roving over her breasts: proprietorial, clammy-hot.

'No, darling. Not here.' The 'darling' was a peace offering, although he didn't appear to have heard. She raised her voice above the uproar – rain was pounding on the window and bludgeoning the car roof, as if conspiring with him to stifle her resistance. 'Not here, Stuart, OK?' Not anywhere, she should be saying – it's *over*. Instead, she pulled the rug up to her chin and sat like a swaddled Egyptian mummy, staring straight ahead.

'Spoilsport,' he teased.

'I'm sorry but this rain . . .'

'I find it rather exciting. And it means no one can see in.' Again, his prowling fingers negotiated the folds of the rug.

She tried to close her own secret folds against him. 'I'd prefer to wait till we get back.' Except when they did get back she must speak her mind with no more ifs and buts. She couldn't have a showdown now, stark naked under a rug. Stupidly, she felt close to tears – as usual, she wasn't in control. There was so much one couldn't control: weather, fathers, men. The car had become a cage, marooned in a wilderness of grey, she its blindfolded prisoner. 'Let's go, Stuart, please.'

Water was dripping from his hair on to the steering wheel. He brushed it off. 'I really don't think it's safe to drive.'

'We'll be all right. The park's deserted.' She should have brought *her* car. Male pride again: Stuart hated being driven. '*Please*,' she begged, withdrawing her arm from the rug and fondling the back of his neck: a caress for a concession.

'Mm. That's nice.'

'Why don't we just creep along? Take it at a snail's pace.'

'OK.' He turned the engine on and they edged cautiously out of the car park. The windscreen wipers, in farcical contrast, whirred frantically back and forth. She clenched her fists under cover of the rug. They would never get back at this rate.

Huge puddles straddled the road and despite Stuart's torturously slow advance, the water formed a heaving wash behind them. She craned her neck to look at it, recalling a long-ago boat trip: the powerful, foam-flecked wash stretching back and back. 'If you fell in there you'd drown,' her brother had taunted, pushing her perilously close to the rail.

Stuart, though, was enjoying himself. This was he-man stuff: battling against the elements, risking life and limb.

She shut her eyes, which made the rain sound louder still. There was a malevolence about it, a vengeful personal spite. Then, as she listened, she heard it start to abate; the savage bombardment changing key to a steady muted drammer. It was a relief, of course, yet at the same time disconcerting, like people with unaccountable mood-swings who left you struggling to adjust.

'Wow-ee!' cried Stuart. 'The worst is over.'

If only . . . She wiped her window with a corner of the rug and stared out at flattened grass, bedraggled trees. Even when they *were* back home she could hardly say her piece until he'd changed his clothes. It was all very well for her, warm and dry in the rug – *he* must be horribly uncomfortable and deserved a large Scotch and a hot bath as soon as they got in. Except that would throw things even further off-course: alcohol made him amorous and he'd want her to share the bath.

She shifted her knees well clear of the gearstick. 'Do you think we could go faster, Stuart?'

'No, I don't want to get water in the brakes. It'll be OK once we're out of the park.'

He had spoken too soon. As they approached the wrought-iron gates they could see a row of stationary cars, nose to tail, blocking the road in both directions. And, judging by the impatient bouts of hooting, they had been stranded here a long while. The less irascible drivers had struck up conversations or were commiserating with each other through wound-down windows. Somewhere a baby was screaming, on and on and on.

'Bloody hell!'

She glanced at Stuart anxiously. He very rarely swore. But she saw from his face that once again he was relishing the situation. She envied the way he could enjoy even a traffic jam instead of anticipating another Noah's Flood. 'Oh, look!' she said. 'I think there's a bit of movement ahead.'

After observing the stop-start progress for some minutes, Stuart was waved on by a kindly driver and edged out to join the queue. But, having crawled forward a scant fifty yards, he was forced to stop again. Trapped in the long a line of cars, she felt her individuality drain away. They had become a mere statistic, an item in a travel bulletin: a tailback stretching five, ten, fifteen miles.

The two children in the car in front turned round to stare at them. She was suddenly conscious of her odd appearance: the Egyptian mummy in the tartan rug. And still more conscious of her nakedness beneath. What if there were an accident or she had to get out for some reason? She should never have agreed to take off her clothes. Although in fact she hadn't agreed. It had been Stuart's persuasiveness, as usual, overcoming her prevarication. Even when she was born, she'd been a fortnight overdue, as if uncertain whether to brave the world or not. Stuart always knew what he wanted. *He'd* been born premature – raring to go.

'I expect the road's flooded further on. Unless there's been an accident. Whatever, we'll just have to sit tight.'

'Yes,' she said miserably, avoiding the curious eye of the two little boys in front. It was probably her hair as much as the rug. Red hair was too blatant and didn't suit her character. She preferred to blend in with the crowd, not stick out like a beacon. Her parents both had decently run-of-the-mill brown hair, but some rogue gene had doubtless invaded her DNA. Genes were like bacteria: invisible but lethal. Which was why she didn't want children herself. Stuart had never broached the subject, thank God.

The boys in front were giggling now, waving at her cheekily as they bounced up and down on the seat. Their parents were only heads; one dark, one bottle-blonde. Were they happy, she wondered? Compatible? Had their children been mistakes?

'Cheer up, darling! It's not the end of the world.'

'No.'

'Want to play I-Spy?'

Surely he couldn't be serious. 'All I can spy is traffic, Stuart. And more traffic.'

'*I* can spy a shapely ankle.'

Hastily she concealed it under the rug.

'You know, it's a tremendous turn-on, darling, having you sitting there beside me starkers.'

'I do wish you'd stop going on about it. It's not a turn-on for *me*.'

'There's no need to be so ratty.'

'I'm not ratty. I'm just hot.'

'You were cold a minute ago.'

'Well, I'm boiling now.' The fuzzy wool had become a suit of armour, immobilizing and uncomfortable, yet a protective necessity. Sweat was beading between her breasts, trickling down her back. She hated sweat – its slimy feel, its smell.

'There's no pleasing you today, Yvonne. What's got into you, for God's sake? I can't do anything right.'

No, she thought. You can't.

'OK, we've been unlucky with the weather, but you needn't take it out on me. Frankly, I'm getting sick of all your –'

'Stuart,' she cut in, 'I know this may not be the ideal time, but there's something important I want to say.'

'And there's something important *I* want to say.'

Blood rushed to her cheeks. He was about to round on her. Already he sounded aggressive, which had never happened before. But then she was the one who had started it by being so ungracious, repulsing his advances all day. His patience had finally snapped. And no wonder. She *was* uptight and unresponsive. Mark had said so. And Roger. Even her father used to complain when she was only eight or nine that she could never relax and had no feelings. (But feelings didn't show, so how could he tell?) She couldn't bear to hear the whole depressing litany again. Kicking one leg free of the rug, she clutched her ankle with a grimace. 'Stuart, I . . . I've got cramp.'

'Yvonne, this is serious.'

'I'm sorry. It . . . it hurts.'

'Well, give it a rub. That may help.'

She massaged her leg violently, hoping the action would forestall his words. She knew what was coming: she was narrow-minded, prudish, far too introspective. When Mark went off with Laura, she *had* become withdrawn, brooding on the rights and wrongs for months. And she did find it distasteful imagining them in bed together (Laura an avid swallower, she guessed). But she hadn't made a scene or tried to stop him going. She even stood by impassively when he walked off with all the china and the books. At this very moment the pair of them might be drinking from her fragile gold-rimmed cups.

The sudden blare of a siren made her jump. A police car,

blue lights flashing, was trying to muscle its way past. At least it had prevented Stuart speaking, yet the horrendous wail only seemed to reinforce the criticism, as if all the haranguing voices were now granted official sanction.

Several cars lurched up on to the pavement to allow the patrol car through. Stuart watched with interest, but he was not to be distracted from finishing what he'd begun to say. As the siren faded to an echo, he looked at her unsmilingly. 'I'm not sure how you'll take this . . .'

Badly, she knew. She would be devastated. Crushed.

The driver in front suddenly got out of his car and strode towards them. Oh, God, she thought, he must have noticed her hostile reaction to his sons. Instead of being amused by their antics, or responding when they'd waved and giggled (as any normal woman would), she had sat there poker-faced. If you didn't like children there was something wrong with you. You were squeamish about dirty nappies or sticky little fingers. Stuart probably *did* want babies but couldn't say, because of her fastidiousness.

The man bent down, level with Stuart's window. She held her breath, anticipating the diatribe: 'Unnatural . . . selfish . . . supercilious . . .'

'Sorry to trouble you, mate, but I wondered if by any chance you had a mobile phone I could borrow?'

She breathed again – one castigation less, thank God. Although Stuart's strictures were still to come.

'Wish I could help,' he was saying to the man, 'but I'm afraid I haven't got it with me.'

She sat, embarrassed, in her cocoon, while the pair exchanged pleasantries. Her grazed hands were throbbing painfully, as if pieces of grit had lodged beneath the skin. It was like the grit of criticism, which could work its way deep into your system, poisoning and infecting . . .

'Poor devils!' Stuart remarked as the man returned to his car. 'Those boys look quite a handful. They'll be screaming blue murder soon!'

Or *she* would.

Now they were alone once more, he turned in his seat to face her. 'Yvonne . . .'

Even the way he had said her name was unnerving. He didn't use it often and never with such vehemence. It was she who'd made him angry. It always happened in the end – she drove people away.

She kept her eyes down, studying the pattern on her tartan lap: red outshouting green; faint yellow lines forming smaller squares.

'I've been wanting to say this all day . . .'

She bit her lip, awaiting the attack.

'The lease on my flat is up, and the landlord won't renew it. Jim's already found another place and suggested I share with him. But I wondered if . . .'

'If what?' she asked, bewildered. This wasn't what she expected.

'If we should look for somewhere together.'

'I'm sorry, Stuart, I . . . I don't quite . . .' A driver behind was leaning on his horn, which had set off a chorus of hooting. With all the din she couldn't have heard him right.

'Buy our own flat. Shack up together.'

'Sh . . . shack up?' The anonymous baby was crying again, a hopeless sort of sound.

'I'm crazy about you, Yvonne, and I want to make things permanent. Oh, I know this is hardly the right time or place. I should be on my knees at home, with red roses and a ring. But you know me, darling, I've never been much cop at all the romantic stuff.'

True.

'What I'm really trying to say – ask – is . . . is, darling, will you marry me?'

'*Marry?*' One of the boys in front was sticking out his tongue at her. Marriage meant children. Possibly. Probably. Broken nights, rogue genes. Marriage meant binding vows. Marriage meant bad temper.

No. She'd got it wrong. Stuart was always decent, always kind and sweet.

He reached across and groped for her hand beneath the rug. 'Yes, *will* you darling? Make me a happy man?'

She listened to the baby's screams and the thrumming of the rain. Was it sneering at her? Criticizing? She wasn't sure, as usual. She peered out of the window, wishing she had some idea what had happened on the road ahead. Of course, nothing might have happened. It didn't have to be a catastrophe – an accident or flood. Maybe just a bit of congestion caused by a freak shower. All things considered, though, it wasn't easy to be optimistic.

'Well?' said Stuart, feeling for her wedding finger and giving it a playful tweak.

She continued examining the tartan; there were black lines she hadn't noticed before, intersecting the red. Carefully, deliberately, she put her leg back under the rug and enveloped herself still tighter.

'Yvonne?' A hint of impatience had crept into his voice. 'Is it yes or no?'

She swallowed, tasting sperm, bacteria.

'It's . . . yes, darling,' she said.

The Hat

'What size is your daughter, madam?'

'She's, er, petite.'

'A ten, d'you think? An eight?'

'I . . . I'm not sure.' Since the wedding, Kate had become a stranger. New name, new country, new job. And quite possibly a different dress size, too.

'These sweaters are designed to fit any size, madam. And they're beautifully soft. Eighty per cent mohair.'

'They do look rather . . . large.' Kate must feel dwarfed in America: the Land of the Outsize. People, houses, cars, beds – even oranges and apples – were bigger there and boastful. Weddings, too. Three hundred guests, almost none of whom she'd known. She had hated California on sight. Too much of everything, including sun and sea and sky.

'That's the style this season, madam. Sweaters are worn loose.'

Hardly down to your knees, though. Olive moved to another rail: négligé and nightie sets.

'Gorgeous, aren't they, madam?' The saleswoman was stalking her: a jangle of bracelets, a waft of cloying scent.

'Mm. Too long, I'm afraid. My daughter's barely five foot.'

'Well, perhaps clothes are best avoided. How about a hand-bag? You can't go wrong with a handbag.'

But that was just the trouble. She *could* go wrong. Kate had married money.

'Or a piece of jewellery. A necklace or a ring.'

Wouldn't Joel buy her those? Joel Schultz. A foreign-sounding name. Names with z's in were never to be trusted – she knew that to her cost. 'Kate's not a great one for jewellery,' she said, peering at the price-tags on the necklaces.

'Shall I leave you to look round on your own?' The tone was slightly sharper, the 'madams' petering out. 'Obviously you know your daughter's taste.'

No, she didn't – not now. Once, it had been easy: Sindy dolls, roller-skates, Duran Duran T-shirts. Although not easy to find the money. Her own clothes she bought at jumble sales. Secretly, of course. Kate disapproved of second-hand.

In this boutique she felt distinctly second-hand. She should have gone to a department store, somewhere anonymous, with no hard sell. The saleswoman's determined glamour – taut, unjowly cheekbones, bosom hoisted high, unfeasibly blonde hair swept up in swags and scallops – accentuated her own submission to gravity and time. She always said appearances didn't matter – a painless way of accepting she was plain.

She picked up an emerald silk scarf, put it down again; stroked the purple plush of a high-heeled velvet slipper. Colours were a minefield. After the fiasco of her wedding outfit she was frightened of making another mistake.

Besides, the present would have to be sent by post and might get damaged in transit. She ought to be there in *person* for Kate's birthday. A thirtieth was important, a milestone in a daughter's life. But Joel paid the air fares, and she wasn't due to go again till June. Joel was six foot four, with broad shoulders and great hairy arms. She tried not to think of him and Kate in bed: a gorilla grappling with a gazelle.

'Lucy, darling, how lovely to see you! How *are* you?'

Olive peered round the rail of feather boas, wondering who could merit such an effusive welcome. Someone rich, presumably. She stared at the girl in the doorway. *Kate!* A younger version (nineteen, perhaps, or twenty) but the same trim figure; dark, straight, glossy hair; imperiously blue eyes. She had to restrain herself from rushing over and embracing her.

'Any sign of the hats yet, Diane?'

'Yes, they came in last night. I was going to phone you.'

'Well, I've saved you a call, then. Can I try one on?'

'Of course. They're still in the stockroom, but I'll fetch you a couple. What colour would you like?'

'Something sort of damsony – to match that dress I bought last week.'

'I've got just the thing! Won't be a tick.'

Olive continued staring, edging towards the girl. Come home with me, she pleaded silently. Back where you belong.

The blue eyes met hers, evidently intrigued at the close scrutiny. Then the perfect mouth parted in a smile. 'Are you after a hat, too?' she asked.

'Well, no, I . . .'

'I shouldn't be here really.' The girl tapped her car keys impatiently on the counter. 'I'm playing truant from work!'

'What work do you do?'

'I'm in marketing.'

Incredible. The same as Kate.

She herself had never had a career. Her career was Kate: bringing her up, creating a work of art, taking her to ballet lessons, deportment, elocution. And after Kate left home she'd still made herself indispensable, running up curtains and cushions for the flat, doing the shopping, baking cakes. She wasn't in the way – Kate's friends all accepted her, even the boyfriends. Nice safe English boys who lived nearby, not halfway across the world, and with names you could trust, like Charles and Paul, Smith and Brown.

The girl screwed up her eyes against the sun. 'Amazing weather, isn't it? More like June than October.'

In June she would see Kate again. Eight whole months to wait. Before Joel carted her off they'd meet at least twice a week. Every Saturday morning they'd have coffee at the Copper Kettle, share a Danish pastry; most Thursdays they went late-night shopping, and of course they saw each other often at the flat. 'You two are more like sisters,' people would remark. 'How marvellous to be that close.' And never would they miss each other's birthdays. Birthdays were sacrosanct.

Go away! Olive hissed, as the saleswoman returned with two hats. Leave us on our own.

But the cajoling voice purred on. 'This one's just the colour – a glorious rich plum. And the shape's inspired, isn't it, with that jaunty little brim. They frame the face to perfection.' She placed it on the girl's head and stood back to appraise the effect. 'Fabulous! It's *made* for you! And velvet's so wonderfully flattering.'

The girl was in no need of flattering – she was pretty enough as it was. But yes, Olive had to agree, the sumptuous damson velvet did intensify the darkness of her eyes; accentuate the translucence of her skin. Kate's skin, too, was flawless – a tribute to the healthy regime enforced since early childhood: no sweets, no soap and water, no exposure to the sun, and the most expensive face creams from the age of seventeen. She didn't begrudge the cost; her devotion had paid off. Of course Ian had played his part in providing the right genes in the first place. Kate was her father's daughter when it came to looks and physique. The fact that he'd returned to his wife in Scotland before Kate was actually born had been a sort of death. She hadn't known the wife existed. (Lizzie. Fatal: two z's.) But somehow she had struggled back to life and tried to make the best of things.

'They're all the rage this winter, Lucy. They'll be walking out of the shop.'

The girl was studying herself in the mirror. Olive admired her confidence, the way she refused to be swayed by sales talk. Kate had similar poise. Even as a tot she'd known exactly what she wanted.

'It's brilliant, Diane! Can you put it on my account? No, don't bother to wrap it. I'm in a tearing rush.' And blowing a kiss she swept out, the hat still on her head.

Wait! Olive shouted voicelessly. Don't go. I need you. I miss you.

The door banged shut, causing the feather boas to tremble in the draught.

Why was it so difficult to stop people from leaving? They all went in the end. Joel had a gun. He'd shown it to her when she went over for the wedding; he'd even let her hold it. She should have shot him there and then.

'How are you getting on, madam? Have you found something suitable?'

'Er, no. Yes . . . The hat that girl tried on – do you have another just like it?'

'The same style, madam, but not that particular colour, I'm afraid. I only ordered one of each shade.'

The disappointment seared. It *had* to be the damson. A subtle, understated colour she knew Kate would approve of. Kate's approval was so rare.

'Although, wait a minute, let me go and check. You just might be in luck – they do occasionally get the orders wrong.'

Olive prayed. 'Please, God . . .' God would surely side with mothers who'd had their daughters kidnapped.

'Well, would you believe, they *did* send two of the damson. Isn't that extraordinary?'

Not extraordinary at all; simply the power of prayer. 'Thank you,' she said, 'I'll take it.' She didn't ask the price. She could economize on other things.

She watched the saleswoman swathe the hat in tissue paper, layer after layer after layer. Not just any old tissue paper – this was satin-textured, superior stuff, embossed with the name of the shop.

'And how about a hat box, madam? They really are an essential, to protect your beautiful hat. And a snip at ten pounds.'

Ten pounds! A fortune. And it would more than double the postage. But the box was almost a present in itself: regal black and gold and fastened with two tasselled cords. She pictured Kate's delight as she unwrapped it.

'Yes, please,' she said, after only another moment's hesitation. If she asked for a deferment on the rent, she could manage, just about.

She caressed the silky tassels. What mattered was pleasing Kate, and for once she'd got it absolutely right.

'You do understand, Mum, don't you?'

'Yes, of course.'

'We'd take you if we could, but it's to do with work, you see. And the guys in Joel's office are frightfully boring, anyway. You'd hate it.'

'Don't worry. I'll be all right.'

'Joel's hired you a couple of videos. Comedies – nothing heavy. And he's just gone to get you a pizza, so you won't starve!'

'He shouldn't have bothered, Kate. I can cook for myself.'

'No one *cooks*, Mum – not out here. There isn't time.'

Time was something she had plenty of. Her first evening in La Jolla, and Kate was off to a party. La Jolla: foreign again. It was nothing to do with jolly. You were supposed to pronounce it 'La Hoya', with a kind of snort in your throat. She couldn't get the hang of it. Or of the money. One dollar sixty-five to the pound. Although it kept changing, Joel said. There should be a law against change.

'I expect you're feeling jet-lagged, so it'll do you good to have an early night. Don't wait up for us, for goodness' sake! And help yourself to anything you want. There's wine in the fridge and fruit there on the table.'

Olive glanced at the apples. Monstrous great maroon things, polished to a mirror-shine.

Alone, she couldn't relax. The house felt too new, and vast. Space for a whole tribe. Last June, when it was being built, she had stayed in a motel. That had been lonely, too, but at least there'd been the man on the desk and odd noises from the other rooms. Here, the only near neighbours were trees, and even they were foreign. An oak or a beech would have reminded her of home, but these sinister-looking palms seemed to emphasize the vast distance she had travelled. Flying wasn't natural.

She shivered. Ninety-six degrees outside and inside like a morgue. She imagined the dead bodies stacked in rows. At least they would be company. After her mother died she had talked to the corpse night and day. Until it was removed.

Joel might be offended if she didn't watch his films. But she had no idea how the video worked – any more than she could adjust the air conditioning. Even opening a window was beyond her, what with all the locks and security alarms.

A magazine lay open on the sofa – *Brides*, the current issue.

Odd, she thought, considering the wedding was a year ago. There was no escaping brides. In front of her on the bureau stood Kate and Joel's wedding photo in an ornate silver frame: Joel's rubber lips slurping towards the dainty rosebud mouth.

Revolted, she looked away and began leafing through the magazine. It frothed with lacy dresses, bubbled with champagne receptions, gushed and throbbed with ideas for honeymoons. Shouldn't Kate be reading *Mother and Baby* by now? Neither she nor Joel ever mentioned children. Too busy, presumably. Children were hard work.

There was a lot to be said for hard work, though. It stopped you brooding, or feeling nervous in an empty house. She needed a job to keep her busy, like the old days. 'Olive, you're a miracle!' Kate's flatmates would exclaim when they returned to find every surface gleaming. A miracle. Imagine!

Well, she could hoover this room, for a start. Admittedly the maid (as Kate called her) had been here this afternoon – an amazing creature who wore designer clothes and drove a Cadillac. But since she'd left, Joel had dropped crumbs on the carpet as he shambled about munching biscuits ('cookies').

The broom cupboard was enormous – more of a walk-in room; indeed bigger than her kitchen at home. Its size was rivalled only by its untidiness: a jumble of mops, buckets, brushes, rags; every type of polish, cleaner, aerosol and spray (all giant-sized, needless to say); even a half-dismembered radio and an ancient sewing machine and, right at the back, she noticed suddenly, a distinctive black and gold hat box.

She froze. Kate had written a thank-you letter all those months ago, in raptures about the hat – she had worn it loads of times; it was so warm in winter, yet elegant enough for parties; she adored the colour and the box itself was fab: she was using it to keep her tights in, so she could admire it every day. Kate was good at letters.

Picking her way through the lumber, she managed to retrieve the box, wiped the dust off the top with a rag, and carefully lifted the lid. Layers and layers and layers of tissue paper – not just any old tissue paper: satin-textured, superior stuff, embossed with the name of the shop. The hat was still inside. Perhaps Kate had stored it here for the summer, although it seemed a peculiar place to choose.

Tenderly she unwrapped it, then stared aghast at the care-instruction label still dangling from its string, which was itself attached to the lining with a small gold safety pin. The hat had never been worn. But, no, that couldn't be right. Kate had said specifically how versatile it was and how it went with almost everything in her wardrobe.

She examined it in detail, praying she was mistaken. But God was deaf this time. There wasn't the slightest mark on it; no thumb-print on the velvet where Kate might have adjusted the brim; no smell of her hair or perfume. The dearly bought present had simply been dumped the day it arrived.

She sprang to her feet, disbelief giving way to fury. Joel was behind this. *He* was the one who had done it; shoved Kate's hat in here with the trash, as a deliberate affront. He resented their close mother–daughter bond and was determined to keep them apart. That's why he'd insisted on going to some stupid party the very night she'd arrived. To show that Kate was *his*, and so that he wouldn't be offended by the sight of someone second-rate defiling his perfect house. It was a crime in California to be middle-aged, or shabby.

She marched into his study and went over to the desk. Jerking open the bottom drawer, she lifted out the gun. Joel had told her to use it if ever she was startled by an intruder and needed to defend herself. Well, now that time had come.

Holding the gun the way he'd shown her, she walked back to the sitting-room. Her legs were trembling under her, but she remembered his advice. 'However shit-scared you are, don't rush. Your aim will be truer if you keep cool.'

Cool. She was burning hot – even in this ice-box of a house. And her innards had seized up, like a boiled-dry kettle whose element had blown. She must mend the kettle; show her snobbish son-in-law she wasn't as dumb as he thought. Dumb was a word he used a lot.

She leaned against the sofa to try to stop the shaking in her legs. Holding a gun was terrifying. It changed the way your lungs worked, so you could only breathe in, not out. Ragged breaths, like gasps.

She counted up to ten. Then twenty. Thirty. Kate was thirty and eight months. That birthday card she'd sent – a 'daughter' card, with a big red heart – had Joel torn it up, tossed it in the bin?

Forty-five. Fifty. *She* was fifty-one. Not too old to fire a gun. Joel had said you had to line up the gun-sight with the target. Which she'd done already. Almost. The gun-sight was watching Kate – Kate resplendent in her wedding dress. The dress had cost thirteen thousand dollars. Joel had paid: his bride-price. Thirteen was unlucky.

Fifty-seven, fifty-eight . . . She closed her right eye, squinted through the left.

Fifty-nine, sixty. Her mother had died at sixty. Suddenly. One night.

Sixty-two . . . The house was very quiet. She could hear the hum of the air-conditioning. It spoke Spanish, like the maid.

Seventy-nine.

Eighty-nine.

Ninety.

She took a deep breath in; let it slowly out to the count of ten.

One, two, three, four . . .

She tightened her grip on the gun.

. . . eight, nine, ten.

'A hundred,' she said, out loud. And squeezed the trigger.

The glass shattered into pieces as the bullet pierced the bridegroom's heart, blasting him to oblivion. The silver frame was unscathed; the exquisite bride still smiling in her thirteen-thousand-dollar dress; her rosebud mouth no longer under threat.

Olive laid the gun down. It was over, at last, the marriage. She had her daughter back. Any minute, Kate would come home. And they would settle down for a nice cosy evening together. Just the two of them. Again.

Going Down

'Take the escalator,' they pleaded. 'Wait for the lift.'

I didn't listen. The stairs spiralled down down down; cracked brown tiles butting against cold black balustrade; drops of water oozing through the walls.

'Take the lift!'

It had come now – iron gates screeching, clanging to a halt. My foot was already on the second stair, nudging the chipped stone like a tongue caressing a cavity in a tooth. All the steps were crumbling. I tripped against their rupture and scathe, hearing the stone rhythm of their heartbeat.

'Hello – ooo – ooo,' I called. (Just testing.)

'. . . ooo . . . ooo . . .' replied the stairs.

There was nobody else. That was one of conditions of the stairs: no one. You get used to it in time. You can occupy a life-time puzzling out the patterns on one broken step. Or stand staring at a stain on the wall, a patch of damp, perhaps, and watch the tide seep in and out of it. Sometimes I ransacked every step for its faint powdering of dust; collected enough to make the dungeons of a sandcastle. I never got as far as the battlements. Dust was scarce, like people.

Or I would spit out cherry-stone words and send them bobbing down the stairs. Tisk, fadget, gryre, heil. They all went their own independent ways. When you hatch a word, it soon leaves the nest, forgets you. Often I ran after a word all day, without succeeding in pinning it down. 'Blimp,' I'd shout. 'Canisterial, goatworthy.' But the word only wriggled or turned over on its back, exposing all its vowels.

I never counted stairs. It is fatal to order your universe. Although sometimes I was tempted. Counting is soothing and addictive. Rosaries, abacuses. *Eins, zwei, drei.* Even if you make a mistake, it still proves something. Sixty-three, sixty-four, sixty-six, sixty-seven. You could spend a whole lifetime proving sixty-five didn't exist. You could even reach sixty-five yourself and have your pension book stamped at the post office and you'd still be an Old Age Atheist. Then you'd lift up the covering in your coffin and find sixty-five grinning underneath. OK, Einstein, so where's your system now? Proofs of the existence of a glossary, genealogical index to a staircase, errata, bibliography, footnotes to footnotes to appendices. The Balustrade Theory. The Foam Rubber Underlay Hypothesis. Proof of the Existence of Death. Cogito, ergo staircase.

On Sundays I sang, usually halfway down the stairs where the acoustics were marginally better. I had already turned sections of Plato's *Republic* into plainchant; other times I intoned 'Lead Kindly Light' in a sombre baritone. Even before I knew he wrote it, I'd been a fan of Cardinal Newman. His bust stood on the piano of my childhood home. He had bulgy white marble eyes and my father's red woollen scarf tied round his neck. He glared at me when I sang out of tune. Every year, we gathered round the piano, me and the seven brothers I probably never had, and sang Schubert *Lieder* for my mother's birthday treat. Newman hated Schubert and my mother hated treats. I called her sometimes from the stairs.

'Mother – rrrr – rrr,' I whimpered, from the seventh stair

or the twenty-seventh or the one thousand and seventh. (I never counted.)

'Rrrrr – rrrrr – rrrrr,' growled the stairs.

'Are you proud of your boy? Your doover little fish-eyed curly boy? Your bread-and-dripping image-of-his-favourite-father boy? He's made it, Mother, just as you said he would. He's gone far-rrrrrr. He's descended thousands and thousands of stair-rrrrs and not yet reached the depths. Mother-rrrr! HE'S STILL GOING DOWN.'

My God, how she did go on! Worked my plundits to the bone, real home-made nurture, none of your instant; cold teat Monday, boiled tid Tuesday; try feeding a forkarse on what he brings home; scoured the streets scriming for cut-offs, turned sheets side to muddle, eking out grisket with crimplings; it's all nothing, leave you soon as look at you, thirty years slaving over a . . . split apart having you, twenty-six hours in labour and then the plumber didn't come; midwife gave me up for dead; don't put your feet on the birdcage, little boys should be clean and not . . . don't walk across the midwife don't touch the don't think of don't love you don't . . .

That was one advantage of the stairs. No one. No sons, no mothers, no seventeen brothers. If you say no one for long enough, someone always turns up. Often I couldn't tell where nobody ended and somebody began. There weren't any mirrors and my shadow was resting. I was born at home (thirty-six hours of labour), so I didn't even have an identity bracelet. Perhaps I wasn't anyone at all. It was hard to tell. I tried jumping out at myself from corners or treading on one foot with the other. Proof of the existence of foot.

I'm rambling, wasting time. I can hear Mother flidgeting up by the lift. Call that stuff work? Don't make me shark! All chuff and no gringe. Pretending you're a writer and then fobbing me off with words. Hurling sentences about without so much as a midwife. You promised me a story. Well, I want one with meat on, a decent, hard-working, headucated story, with a beginning and an ending and a three-course moral.

She didn't understand. I'd been looking for an ending ever since I missed the beginning. You don't always find one. It takes a lifetime sometimes, reaching your end. But Mother never listened.

Don't you schmuck me! What d'you know about ends, when you couldn't pass your CPGs? Bone idle, even as a baby. Didn't love your mother after all she did for you. Forty-six hours in labour and then you got entangled in the cord. Couldn't even fill in your own birth certificate. And not a thank you for your mother's milk. Always been ungrateful, even as a midget. Addicted to dictionaries, stoned on staircases, leaving all the lights on. Never finished anything. *And* I put six eggs in . . .

Look, I *will* finish, Mother, I promise you I will. I crawled all the way to the bottom of the staircase, to see if I could find an ending, but there wasn't any bottom, let alone conclusion. I groiled right back to the beginning again, but, because I hadn't counted, the stairs were all the same. No beginning and no end. Number one might just as well have been a hundred, except for the noughts, and number sixty-five was still refusing to exist. I'm trying, Mother, honestly I am. Right, Mother? Fine, Mother. Yes, Mother. YES, MOTHER . . . ?

Oh, God Almighty – except He wasn't there. I grovelled to Cardinal Newman as the Next Best Thing, crawling on my belly down the stairs.

'Help me,' I pleaded. 'I'm desperate for an ending, a climax, consummation, dénouement, epilogue. Proof of the Existence of a Story. For God's sake. For Mother's sake. She's getting furious out there. Wants her mother's worth. Fourteen stitches and then I was a runt. Can't you give her recompense?

A guarantee it's all been birthwhile? Proof of the existence of the persistence of a son?'

'Ssh,' barked Newman, flicking a comma from his cold marble brow. 'I'm putting the x in the Oxford Movement, and I need every why I've got.'

I panted up again, found Schubert killing crotchets. Surely he could help. He knew all about cadences and codas, dying falls, final chords, finales, curtain calls.

'I need help myself,' he frowned. 'I'm finishing the Unfinished and it may well take for Ever.'

There was only Plato left. He was sitting in a cave watching a shadow shadow-play.

'How d'you end?' I begged.

'Socrates chose hemlock,' he said sadly. 'But please don't interrupt me. I deal only in Ideas.'

I backed away. 'Sorry,' I whispered, then stopped in sudden shock. I *had* my ending – that was it – it must be. I'd been saying it my entire life, one way or another. And mother would be thrilled.

Sorry.

Cuckoo

'Oh, listen!' Bev stopped on the overgrown path and clutched my arm. 'A cuckoo!'

The sound was so faint I thought she was mistaken. Twelve days into April is ridiculously early for a cuckoo. But then I heard it, too: a distinct 'Cuckoo, cuckoo . . .'

'The first,' she said in triumph. 'Which means we get a wish.'

Bev is strong on wishes. We had already wished on our first strawberry at lunch. I'd brought a couple of punnets from London, where seasons count for little – asparagus in January, roses in December.

Bev stood motionless, fists clenched, eyes screwed up. So much hope and energy was being poured into that wish I felt sure it must be granted. Although, knowing my friend, it would be some small-scale, innocuous wish: that her thirteen-year-old labrador would see another spring or the brood of baby ducklings survive.

At last she opened her eyes. 'Zoë, have you wished?'

I nodded. The same as my strawberry wish – to see Theo dead. Or, better, kill him myself.

'Shall we turn back?' Bev suggested. 'You seem tired.'

I was. Not tired of the walk but tired of my resentment;

furious with the cuckoo for reminding me of him. Theodoros Koukoulis. The name had a threatening edge now, although when I heard it first it sounded mysteriously exotic as I rolled it round my tongue. I never discovered whether Koukoulis was a common name in Crete – his halting English wouldn't stretch to that. Although little else was halting about him. Eating, drinking, walking, screwing, Theo was always in a spitfire rush. We communicated best in bed, where cries and grunts supplanted words.

'Now it's started, it won't stop!' Bev laughed, as we retraced our steps through the wood. The bird's endless, self-important call seemed to follow us home. Cuckoos are obsessional. Like Theo, they go on and on and on. I could hear his voice in each haranguing repetition: it was my fault that he'd left me; I didn't understand him; how could I expect him, an artist and an anarchist, to commit to just one woman?

I hadn't answered. Cuckoos neither expect nor welcome answers – they know it all.

When we got back to the cottage Bev settled me on the sofa with tea and home-made cake – her way of sympathizing. Not that I'd told her anything, either today or during the last six months. Normally we share our troubles, but Theo had come between us. I had kept him secret from everyone, and Bev especially would have hated him on sight. The men *she* knows are simple kindly souls, the sort who mend broken china or feed motherless lambs with babies' bottles. Now she lives alone, not counting the cats and dogs.

'How's work?' she asked.

'Fine.'

'And Paula?'

'OK, considering.' My sister had also been dumped. Maybe it was in our genes, to love and lose. Our parents had stayed together, although from necessity, not love.

'Shall we have supper right away, then you can have an early night? After all, you're here for a bit of a rest.'

'Mm, that would be lovely.' Everything I said sounded forced and false. Theo's fault again. I carried on an unceasing interior dialogue with him, which meant I couldn't really concentrate on Bev. His face was even superimposed on hers: olive skin and coarse black stubble in place of her fair freckled cheeks. I knew he was wrong for me the minute he picked me up in the bar. Wrong and wildly desirable.

After supper we sat in the conservatory, crowded by geraniums and ferns. Bev likes to be close to nature, even when it's dark. There was a strange musky smell – a hint of something tropical and rank, as if Theo's alien otherness had penetrated even here. Duke lay on my foot, snuffling and dribbling in his sleep. The cats, disdaining sleep, watched us through narrowed eyes. Cats make me uneasy; they rarely fawn, like dogs, or think humans are infallible or even of much consequence. George, the tabby, seemed to be peering into my very soul, comparing my murderous impulses with his. His prey were birds and fieldmice, whereas I burned to kill not just Theo but all his fellow Cretans (Ireni in particular); plunge the entire island into the sea.

'Anything you want, Zoë? A hot-water bottle? A warm drink?'

'No thanks.' I was hot enough already. Jealousy makes you feverish. If someone had taken my temperature, it would have been 104 at least.

Bev gave me a goodnight kiss. Since Theo left, my nights have not been good. I either rerun our marathons in bed (again, things I can't share, since friends would think them dangerous and perverse) or get trapped in horrific nightmares where he tries to choke me to death.

Upstairs, a sharp-lipped moon was grinning in the window-pane, and a cat I hadn't seen before had already taken up sly residence in my room. '*Out*, moggy,' I said, shooing him towards the door. I like to share my bed but not with cats.

I gulped down a sleeping pill, seeking oblivion from both inner turmoil and outer. It's a myth that the countryside is quiet. Bev's cottage is actually noisier than my flat in Kentish Town. Foxes fight, rabbits squeal, the electric fence on the adjacent farm keeps up a maddening humming sound. Mornings are worse still: cockerels outcrowing rooks, the boisterous clank of buckets as bullocks snort and jostle, every bird exultant at the dawn, and those soppy wooing wood pigeons assuring their mates that they're in love, in love, in love. Theo never mentioned love, although *I* told him I loved him our very first night together. Bev would have called it lust, but I defy a compiler of dictionaries to disentangle the two.

I lay in bed, listening to Bev downstairs – locking doors, stacking dishes, settling elderly dogs, and then her stealthy creaking on the staircase. Did *she* have trouble sleeping? Even with best friends there's so much you never know.

I tried to get comfortable in her ancient spare bed, which dips in the middle like the old pony she once rescued from the knacker's yard. She's forever taking in stray animals or stricken friends. Tomorrow, I vowed, I'd earn my keep. I'd laugh, I'd chat, I'd groom the dogs. Theo had ruled my life quite long enough.

When I woke, it was dark. At first I couldn't remember where I was. The duvet lay huddled on the floor and I was clutching a pillow hard enough to throttle it. I switched on the bedside light and the room settled back into place: daisy-sprigged walls, warped, arthritic floorboards, broad-shouldered wardrobe with a dent in its right flank. A breeze from the open window was fidgeting the curtains, flittering over my face. And then I heard it – the same treacherous call. Or was I dreaming? Surely it couldn't be a cuckoo at this hour. No other bird was singing; no other creature awake.

I sat up and strained my ears. There was no mistake: 'cuckoo, cuckoo, cuckoo', encroaching on the silence, bringing back my nightmare: a Theo, made of marble and so tall he touched the sky, and I, a diminutive sculptress chipping vainly at his foot.

Still torpid from the sleeping-pill, I dragged myself out of bed. How dare he follow me here, ruin not only my sleep and sanity but my precious week with Bev. I limped over to the window and looked out. The first fingers of light were poking through the dark gauze; bruise-coloured smudges trembling into shape. Beyond the farm, the hills curved like the rumps of giant black labradors. The sky seemed ill, and troubled; bolsters of cloud convulsing as they smothered the thin moon. The poisonous bird was invisible, as always, yet its disembodied voice insisted and insisted that it was master here, unchallengeable. 'Cuckoo, cuckoo, Koukoulis.'

I crept downstairs, threw my coat over my nightdress, scribbled a note for Bev and left it on the kitchen table. Duke stirred but didn't bark. The cats watched me with cool insolence, and as I lifted the latch I was aware of their green gimlet eyes boring into my back. Outside, the cuckoo's call was louder, again stating its case over and over and over, allowing me no chance to put my side of the story. The whole sleeping earth was in thrall to it. Even the electric fence, taut and twitching, held its breath, subdued.

I drove, fast, along the lane, through the grey ghost of the village and up the shadowed hill, pursued by that unchanging contempt: 'cuckoooo'. Even on the motorway the echo of its echo drowned the roar of lorries and the angry hooting of cars. My only excuse for reckless driving was Theo. He was my excuse for everything, including genocide.

I reached the flat in record time: two hours. Without pausing to lock the car I ran upstairs and dragged the case from under the bed. There he was – all I had of him: the matted sweater he'd left behind, his six scrawled and misspelt letters, the beer glass stolen from Ed's bar the night we met, a scrap of his hair, also stolen (snipped off as he slept). And, wrapped in tissue, the only present he had ever bought me – chosen for his own titillation – a tarty G-string in scarlet satin, trimmed with scratchy black lace. It was cheap and badly made, and when I washed it the first time it bled all over my other, plain white underwear. I didn't mind – it gave me more of Theo. Red was his colour: aggression, danger, fire. He even wrote to me in red ink. His letters incited mine. Sometimes I would stay up all night, hurling meteors and starbursts on to the page; my pen reeling across the paper, ejaculating frenzied spurts of passion. I would quote whole chunks of poetry – Petrarch, Shakespeare, Donne – although no poet in the canon could match my Theo-induced bewitchment. The letters were wasted on him, of course. He knew only two words: yes and no. Yes for bed; no for love, commitment.

I bundled the mementoes into a black dustbin bag and humped it down the five flights of stairs. I was out of breath by the time I reached the street, but the dustmen were still there, thank God. One of them reminded me of Theo – swarthy, lean, snake-hipped, with the same heart-stopping clash of blackest hair and bluest eyes. He probably took me for a halfwit, with my Ophelia-style nightie trailing below a duffel coat. I ignored him though, even when he yelled. He didn't seem to like me throwing my own bag on to the cart. Enraged, I shook off his hand. There was no way I would let a stranger have any part in this rite. It *was* a rite – a marriage and a funeral rite. The dustmen were our ushers and our pall-bearers, suitably barbaric in fluorescent jerkins and heavy rubber boots.

I stood close to the back of the cart, watching the steel shutters clamp slowly, slowly down, pressing us together: Theo's sweater against my G-string, his thick horse-mane hair startling my naked skin, our red-ink juices merging. It was our wedding night, our honeymoon. He even told me he loved me, in perfect English, so he couldn't say afterwards that I hadn't understood. Elated, I listened to the clatter as we were compacted to one flesh by the remorselessly efficient blades; crushed and ground so fine no one could ever part us again. I imagined our funeral pyre: an incinerator somewhere in the country; our mingled ashes nurturing the soil as we were finally laid to rest. Theo could never rest in life, but I had granted him eternal rest in death.

With a judder of gears, the dustcart pulled away. Time for me, too, to leave. I drove slowly out of London – no need for reckless haste now. Majestic music was playing in my head; weighty words like consummation, immolation, sounded their sad chords. It was a fitting end. For all his faults Theodoros Koukoulis deserved due reverence.

Despite my cautious driving it was still not quite eleven when I drew up at Bev's again. I found her in the kitchen, chopping carrots. She didn't ask me where I'd been or what was going on. Bev accepts. Which is why we're such good friends.

'Sit down,' she said, flicking me a brief but searching glance; the sort she gives Duke to make sure he's breathing still.

I sat, watching the gleaming discs of carrot frolic from her knife.

'Oh, listen!' she said, corralling them back on the board and tipping them into a pan of water. 'The cuckoo again! Hear it, Zoë?'

I gazed towards the wood. Of course I could hear it, loud and clear: 'cuckoo, cuckoo, cuckoo'. But I felt no pain. Felt nothing.

Theo was dust.

Crucifixus

Have you ever noticed how flowers flourish in graveyards? It was the same with Beechwood House. Despite the dead hand of authority, the stifling shroud of religion in excess, the daffodils bloomed themselves silly and the azaleas were famed for miles around. The site itself was an idyll. Beeches are queenly trees: slender silvery trunks, tenderly veined leaves that gleam fox-red in autumn. And their nuts are precious miniatures: smooth and highly polished, yet spitting from barbed husks. Beyond the wood stretched fields, cradled by the strong arms of blue hills. In summer, the wind sighed through the rippling wheat in paroxysms of pleasure (although pleasure never dared intrude within the convent walls).

Beechwood House attracted that section of Roman Catholic girlhood blessed with low intelligence and high parentage; the latter willing to pay exorbitant fees to alleviate the former. Part of the cost was danger money. The nuns left us in no doubt that our presence among them jeopardized their peace, their peace of mind and possibly their chance of eternal salvation. We were all of us aware, after Reverend Mother's first alabaster handshake, that Beechwood House was primarily a forcing-house for God and only marginally a school. Religion with a capital R far outweighed the 'three Rs'.

The Holy Souls in Purgatory and the Eight Beatitudes loomed larger in our minds than any king or general in a history book.

The nuns cut off their lives from ours to a degree that invited constant speculation. Did they feast on caviar or air, whip themselves bloody or tune in to heavenly choirs? Their quarters were underground, in the basement of the austere Georgian mansion they shared with us. We watched them gliding up and down for services and lessons, their faces inscrutable, their gait measured and serene. Nuns are like snakes: all sinuous grace, disguising the venom inside.

The only time we mere girls were allowed – indeed compelled – to set foot in the basement was when one of the Holy Sisters died (returned to her Maker was the preferred expression). It was a rare occurrence, in fact. Nuns have uncanny powers: they live longer than ordinary mortals, building up their strength on flimsy communion wafers. But those few girls who had experienced the ordeal spoke of it with terror and disgust. The corpse would lie in state in a dim, black-curtained room, while the entire school processed past, intoning the *Dies Irae*. Each girl was obliged to pause by the open coffin, make the sign of the cross, then stoop to kiss the stiff white hand. We all feigned nonchalance, but even the boldest among us dreaded such a summons. We might wish secretly for the death of a nun, a particular tormentor, but how then could we face her, cold dead in her winding-sheet?

I had been at Beechwood House exactly four years when Mother Mary Basil 'returned to her Maker'. We knew her only as a name. Having long since retired from teaching, she divided her time between basement and chapel, making ready for death. Sometimes we caught a glimpse of her frail form shuffling into a pew, bent double with age and religion. Her face was a pale parchment inscribed by ninety-seven years of life; her eyes we never saw.

The announcement was duly made: every girl must pay her respects to the body on Sunday March 14. I went shivery with fear. Death for me was still a romantic concept, awash with silver lilies and golden epitaphs – Shelley drowned off Viareggio, not Mother Mary Basil mouldering in a basement.

The 14th came too quickly. I concealed my cowardice behind the brown serge prickle of a Sunday frock; matching knickers itchy on my nether parts. We girls wore earthy brown; the nuns celestial white. My rebelliously red hair was confined beneath a black lace veil – black for pain and death. At ten o'clock sharp we assembled in the Great Hall, grouped in rows of three. (Twos were considered dangerous: they might lead to 'unhealthy' friendships.) Hands joined and eyes cast down, we filed in slow procession past the chapel and along the corridor; the sad plaint of the *Dies Irae* rising like a wounded bird.

As we reached the narrow staircase leading to the basement, we were forced to go in single file. Nervously, I descended the first steps. The light began to dwindle and my nose twitched to a waft of smells: cabbage, polish, death. I pictured decaying flesh, a white seethe of bloated maggots. The dark walls imprisoned; the ceiling seemed to press down on my head. We grouped in threes again, although the girl beside me was little more than another clash of smells: hot feet, cough-sweets, menstrual blood. She was snuffling rather than singing, but no cough nor cold nor period pain could excuse a pupil from this solemn rite.

We turned a corner and I noticed another, narrower passage, leading off. Swift as the thought, I darted out of line into its merciful escape. The ranks closed in. The nuns, heads bowed, saw nothing. I squeezed myself against the wall until the last of the girls had passed. I would rejoin them when they returned, forewarned by their singing. Meanwhile, I was safe.

Every nun, as every girl, was committed to homage at the corpse. I edged a little further down the passage, fear still chafing like the serge knickers. The passage turned again sharply, before branching into two. It astonished me that so stately a mansion as Beechwood House should shelter this crude warren beneath its skirts. I took the left-hand fork and froze. Across the passage fell a shaft of light from an open door. Strange creakings and mutterings were coming from the room – human sounds. Torn between fear and curiosity, I took a hesitant step forward, glimpsed a stretch of lino, a strip of beige rug. Another step – an empty fireplace, a stiff-backed wooden chair and, sitting on the chair, Mother Mary Aloysius, hardly recognizable.

She had removed her veil and wimple, and her head was bare save for a growth of coarse grey stubble. An old blue curtain was draped loosely round her shoulders, still bristling with its fringe of curtain hooks. In her arms she cradled a rag doll, one of those made by the older nuns and sold for charity. Normally the dolls were clothed in prim, high-necked floral dresses, with bloomers underneath, but this one was joltingly naked, its limp pink legs dangling in her lap.

More shocking still was Mother Aloysius's breast – that, too, was bare, and unlike any breast I had seen: a thin, fawn, flabby thing that flopped on to her stomach like a growth. As I watched, she scooped it up and forced the nipple against the embroidered red-wool mouth. The doll's face was choked by a muffler of withered flesh as the nun pressed her baby closer, rocking back and forth. Her face was as ugly as a gargoyle's, yet her eyes had swallowed heaven. The mouth hung open, spilling out faint sounds like scraps of food.

I strained to hear. She was reciting the Hail Mary, repeating the words over and over again. 'Hail Mary, full of grace, full of grace, full of grace, the Lord is with thee, with thee, with thee . . .'

Then suddenly the voice changed timbre and became a cry of triumph: 'The Lord is with *me*. With *me*. With *me*.' The blue curtain flared like a sail as she rocked faster, faster, in her chair, the doll's feet swinging wildly to and fro. The inscrutable nun who taught us maths had disappeared; in her place a crazed and frightening creature, quivering with the Holy Ghost.

I stood, transfixed, while the normal world somersaulted, smashed to pieces. The shock-waves must have reached her, for all at once she dropped the doll and sat bolt upright, looking round. I shall never forget the scalding gaze she fixed on me – a Gorgon-stare, which, had I lingered, would have turned me there and then to stone. Panicking, I scuttled like a small brown vermin back the way I'd come, along the maze of passages, up the narrow stairs, regardless of the other girls who might also be returning. All I could see was a shaved grey head, a sagging breast, a murderous eye.

'The Lord is with me,' I whispered.

But He was not.

Monday passed in a clammy writhe of fear. What punishment could be severe enough for having seen a nun exposed? Nuns had no bodies – only their hands were ever visible and the haloed semi-circle of their faces. Indeed, I imagined them as having been *born* into their habits, every button fastened from birth; a rosary attached to their waists like a second umbilical cord. To have seen one half-undressed was gross impiety. And in the enclosed world of Beechwood House the nuns' power was absolute. However harsh the judgement, we had no appeal, no redress. Our parents were as distant as eternity, and in any case parents inevitably sided with the nuns.

Tuesday dragged into Wednesday. I dared to hope. No guillotine had fallen on my neck, so perhaps Mother Aloysius had decided to barter her silence for mine.

On Wednesday afternoon I came face to face with her for the first time since our encounter in the basement. She sailed into our classroom for the maths lesson, as aloof and dignified as ever; her head-dress starched to perfection, not a whisker of hair escaping the neat white veil. Her granite features wore their normal impenetrable expression, and she was, of course, breastless; her silver cross hanging against a demurely swaddled chest. We opened our books, and the familiar flow of question and answer began. Chalk scraped on board, a pencil dropped and rolled, a bird flew past the window. I fixed my whole attention on the blackboard, seeking comfort in equations. Algebra is soothing, a closed world in itself, pure, abstract and analytical. The compassionate classroom clock ticked out second after second of reprieve. If the lesson ended without incident I knew I would be safe.

Five minutes to go. My breathing gradually calmed; the pencil no longer shook in my hand. But then, without warning, Mother Aloysius swung away from the blackboard and swooped towards my desk. She bent so close I could smell her prayer-and-incense breath exhaling in my face.

'Thérèse,' she said sharply. My name was plain Teresa, but the nuns preferred to give it the full Lisieux treatment. 'You seem thoroughly distracted. Have you heard a single word I've been saying?'

'Yes, Mother. Every word.'

'Don't be impertinent! It's perfectly clear to me that you have not been paying attention. I have been wasting my time, Thérèse, as far as you are concerned.'

I swallowed. Not for one stray second had my eye wavered from the chalk stare of the blackboard. The stolid clock could vouch for that.

'In fact you have *never* paid attention.' She sounded incalculably sad. Could she have forgotten that I was the best pupil in the class and that I had won the form mathematics prize four years in succession?

'We have given you so many chances' – the 'we' signified her and God: nuns always work in partnership – 'made every allowance, reasoned with you, prayed for you, yet you still refuse to make the slightest effort.'

Her voice was wired to heaven; the angels must be weeping as they listened. 'It's not just a question of laziness, you are obstinate into the bargain.' A small, regretful smile lifted the grey caterpillar lips. A nun was never vindictive or unfair. I glanced down at my exercise-book: red ticks on every page, A-pluses in profusion, 'Well done' and 'Excellent' written in her own neat hand. The other girls were silent; they knew injustice, but they feared the whip.

'And this is the final indignity.' The voice was divinely, sweetly patient. 'Complete inattention, total lack of interest. I have no choice, Thérèse. I cannot presume to punish you myself. I must send you to our Holy Mother.'

The class rippled like a cornfield. 'Our Holy Mother' was Queen and Empress in the hierarchy of nuns; their guide, their leader, their interlocutor with God. Upon her lay the sanctity of divine revelation; from her emanated holy wrath. No girl faced her without spasm of the gut, softening of the brain.

'And I'm afraid I shall have to tell Our Holy Mother that you might in fact do better in a different sort of school – one with lower standards, where less is expected of the pupils and where, alas, the teaching staff don't have the same sense of vocation.'

This time there were audible gasps from the class. Expulsion was for *crimes*. Only one girl had ever been expelled in the history of Beechwood House: an out-and-out thief, caught red-handed. I pressed my fists into my eyes to prevent myself from howling like a dog.

When I dared look up, Mother Aloysius had gone again, as silently as she had come, and was drawing perfect circles on the board. Minutes later, the bell rang, but I continued staring at the board, mesmerized no longer by white chalk but by the blackest of black forebodings.

Our Holy Mother saw no girl until the evening. She spent the day in communication with God, then at eight o'clock she glided to her study, where portraits of twenty-seven Popes glared from the walls. Her face was so thin God must be pinching it between His fingers; her mouth was set in an eternal no. But as I stood before her, all I saw were the toecaps of my terrified brown shoes.

'Come here, child,' she commanded.

Trembling, I approached her desk. I could almost hear all twenty-seven Popes drawing in their breath in contempt.

'Mother Mary Aloysius has reported your distressing lack of progress in mathematics.'

'Yes, Reverend Mother.' To contradict a Superior was insubordination.

'I have telephoned your parents . . .'

A wave of nausea surged up in my throat. Were they already on their way to fetch me, scandalized, enraged? In my parents' view nuns were not just good but holy, and invariably right. My father's sister *was* a nun, and my mother had been brought up by the Ursulines from the age of four and regarded them as saints. Neither of my parents would ever recover from the shame if I were cast out into some common, low-grade school (Beechwood House was a listed building and stood in thirty acres), nor ever forgive me for letting them down.

'I'm sorry to say, Thérèse, that they are bitterly disappointed in you . . .'

My nails dug into the palms of my hands. I could see my father's face, implacable and shuttered, his eyebrows two black lines. Just to send me here cost thousands. I wasn't worth it; probably never had been. How would I look them in the eye?

I struggled to find a voice. 'Reverend Mother, did they . . . ? Are they . . . *coming?*'

She didn't answer, deliberately keeping me in suspense. Perhaps no other school would take me, not even a low-grade one. I would be a pariah, with no future and no friends.

'Thérèse, before we discuss your parents and any decision they may or may not have made, there is something extremely important you appear to have forgotten. It's not just Mother Aloysius you have offended, and the other girls, whose precious time you have wasted. And myself, of course. No, infinitely more serious, you have offended *God.*'

The word God rang out like a rallying cry, as if she were alerting Him to my crimes. And, thus invoked, might He not respond with some unspeakable retribution?

'Thus it is to God,' she pronounced, 'that you must make your reparation.'

She rose to her feet and swept towards the door, her white robe swishing imperiously. 'Follow me.'

I stumbled after her, assuming that we were going to the chapel, to pray, to confess my sins, but we walked on past the door and continued along the passageway, making for a narrow staircase – one I recognized.

No, I thought, as my legs seemed to lose their bones and become wobbly like the rag doll's – not that gruesome basement. But Reverend Mother was already descending the steps, and I had no choice save to follow, wondering in terror whether Mother Aloysius would be sitting in that room again, ready, like God, to wreak some monstrous vengeance. But we turned the opposite way, along a claustrophobic passage that seemed to lead only into darkness. I had always feared the dark, although it was just about bearable at night in a dormitory of twelve solid girls and a nun as chaperone. Here, I felt utterly alone, despite Reverend Mother's ghostly form ahead.

Then, a flicker of light began to eat into the gloom, almost more sinister than the darkness it replaced, since its eerie shadows made the passage tremble. Reverend Mother stopped, and I realized that the light was coming from a votive candle, set in front of a gigantic crucifix – the largest I had ever seen. No expense or labour had been spared to depict the torments of the dying Christ. Crimson paint gushed from the gaping holes in His hands and feet and side. His head lolled sideways, twisted out of alignment with the body. The yellow tongue bulged. And along the pinioned limbs darted the restless, hungry light, making them squirm and shudder in pain.

'Kneel there, my child.' Her voice was steel, muffled in a cloud. 'Kneel before your Saviour, gaze upon His wounds and see what your sins have done to Him. Weep for those sins, which have nailed Him there. Only when you are moved to tears can we – and He – forgive you.'

Suddenly I remembered Mother Basil's corpse. The funeral was tomorrow. Had they already closed her coffin, or was she still lying exposed, the vacant eyes filmed over, the body decomposing? In either case, she was hideously near.

'I beg you, Reverend Mother' – it was all I could do not to cling on to her physically, except it was forbidden to touch a nun – 'don't make me stay down here. It's so frightening and . . .'

She raised her hand to silence my entreaties. 'Kneel,' she repeated icily.

I knelt, the cold stone floor hurting my bare knees. To disobey would bring further retribution, maybe even extinction. Our Holy Mother's wrath could snuff me out like a candle, reduce me to a crippled stump of wax.

As her steps grew fainter, my fear increased. My eyes were empty sockets, my mind a heaving blank. Death stalked so close I could smell its carrion breath. Yet waves of injustice began rolling through the fear and broke upon the shore of my head in cascades of crashing spray. The neat red ticks in my exercise-book darkened to an indignant scarlet. The four form prizes flaunted their tooled inscriptions and their smart blue leather spines. Was God always on the nuns' side?

Defiantly I looked up, almost tempted to do the unthinkable and answer the Almighty back, but the shock of the crucifix cauterized my thoughts. I stared at the bony feet, each toe sculpted in its last tiny detail and protuberance. My gaze travelled along the plaster legs stretched taut beyond their length, blue veins as thick as ropes; then on to the wounded side, which was gouged out like a crater, streaks of blood daubed across the chest. The arms were pulled cruelly tight, twelve-inch nails tearing through the flesh. And finally the head – thorn-crowned, sweat-beaded; eyes protruding from the sockets in a last wrenching agony. This was their living Lord.

The candle had lost its nerve and reached out quaking fingers to clutch at its own shadows as they panted up and down the walls. In the quavering light, Christ seemed to be toppling from His cross and falling right towards me. Terror slithered down my spine like a rat. I could hear the worms in Mother Mary Basil munching on her body while her soul soared up to God.

See what your sins have done to Him.

How could I not see? I was the crucifier, the spear-thruster, the callous pagan soldier who had hammered in the nails. I was Herod, Pilate, Judas, all in one. A shame so deep convulsed me, I fell forward on the floor and heard my head strike against the stone.

And now at last the tears came, hot and desperate tears,

streaming down my face as I sprawled there prostrate with my rude red hair and shapeless uniform, in place of shaven head and flowing robes. I had not been breathed upon, wedded to Christ with a silver ring, sanctified with rituals. What a profane and piddling thing I was, with my with barley-sugar breath and sinful buds of breasts, presuming to defy the Brides of Christ! How could I compete with them, those sinless, breastless Mouthpieces of God, who fed their cold white strength on His body and blood? While they sipped manna and bathed in martyrs' tears, I scrubbed with coal tar and guzzled penny buns.

'Forgive me,' I sobbed, with new guilt and even sharper desolation. And it was they I was imploring, not their God.

He, like Mother Basil, was cold stinking dead in the basement.

Toffee Apple

'Mm! Naan bread – delicious!' Colin tore a large piece off, without offering the plate to her. His teeth clamped down, leaving marks in the pale flesh. Predator's teeth.

'Don't you want any?' he asked, still chewing.

'Yes.'

'Well, eat it while it's hot then.'

She had to lean across to reach. The bread was blistered in places; shiny black weals contrasting with the matt softness of the rest. Like life.

'I reckon this is the best Indian place in Streatham.'

'Yes,' she said again. Dull this evening, he must think; why can't she make an effort? Her mind was still on bread – whether it related to national character. Baguettes in France: crusty yet soft inside. German pumpernickel: bitter, black, severe. The sweetish elasticity of naan.

'Ah, here's our nosh at last. I was beginning to think they'd forgotten.'

The fiercest curry for Colin, as usual. It was a matter of pride with him, as if the hotter the spices the more macho he became. Later, she would taste it on his breath; have to share a bed with Chicken Vindaloo. If he cleaned his teeth it was worse: mint mixed with fenugreek.

The waiter spooned rice on to her plate: immaculately white and impeccably cooked, each grain separate, no glutinous little clots. He left a hollow in the centre for the Lamb Khorma. A perfect hollow to curl up in at night, caressed by gentle heat, protected by a white encircling wall. Colin tended to sweat and thrash about.

'Did I tell you about my bonus this month?'

'Yes.' She had congratulated him twice already.

'Pretty damned good, eh?'

'Yes. Congratulations.'

He gave a modest shrug. 'Come on, let's get stuck in.'

She imagined all the food he had ever eaten taking up permanent residence in his body; curries swelling out his stomach, *frites* like sinews in his legs, apple pie and clotted cream pudging round his neck.

'Mm, this is good, Suzanne. How's yours?'

'Fine.'

'Can I try some?'

'Help yourself.' He always did.

'A bit bland for me. But nice.' Fork poised, he surveyed the half-empty restaurant. 'I'm surprised this place isn't busier.'

'I suppose it's rather out of the way.' And claustrophobic, with oppressive ceiling and ponderous blood-red walls. There were no seasons in the Shahee Mahal. The scented breath of spring couldn't penetrate its gloom, nor the bite of winter pierce the blinkered fug. It was how she pictured the after-life: a dim maroon solemnity, timeless and unchanging, with silent-footed attendants bringing manna. 'And the parking isn't easy,' she added, knowing Colin had no interest in the after-life.

'*You'll* drive back, won't you, Suzanne?'

Why ask? She drove; he drank.

'More wine?'

'No thanks.' She watched the couple at the corner table.

Late fifties, at a guess. And married, definitely. Perhaps conversation didn't matter so much when you had reached your silver wedding. You had probably said it all by then and silence was a relief. She pinched her ringless finger, hard, as if in rebuke. Too fussy, her mother said; about food, as well as men. But in fairy tales the girls were invariably fussy – always waiting for their prince to come, even if it meant sleeping for a thousand years. She couldn't spare that long. Thirty-five was old.

Colin forked in more rice. It was no longer white but a dirty yellow-brown colour and greasy like his lips. 'The only down side to Indian food is the puddings. They're useless at puddings. It's always fucking lychees.'

Weren't lychees more Chinese? Moist, white, naked eyeballs; too inoffensive, surely, to be sworn at.

He spattered sauce on the tablecloth and tried to rub it off, smearing it into a tawny stain. 'Although didn't we have toffee apples once?'

'Toffee apples?'

'Not the English sort. These were more like fritters, as far as I recall. Disgustingly sweet.'

All at once a memory from childhood lit up in her mind: her brother Tim buying a toffee apple at the fair. Just the one. She had only tuppence left and watched with envy as he unwrapped the cellophane. Then, slowly, almost reluctantly, he took out his pocket knife and hacked the thing in half. No, not exactly half. One piece was substantially larger and less of the toffee coating had cracked off. More important, it was the piece attached to the stick, and of course it was the stick that made a toffee apple special – removed it from the province of food on the one hand and everyday sweets on the other and elevated it to an Experience.

He must have stood a full minute looking at the two pieces,

debating which to give her. Even now she could recall the taut, choked feeling in her throat.

'*Suzanne!*'

'What?'

'I asked you if you'd thought any more about the Bank Holiday weekend.'

'No, I haven't.'

'Well, we must decide. I promised Jack I'd call him.'

'OK.'

'What do you mean, OK?'

'I mean OK I'll think about it.' She was thinking about her brother. Finally he had given her the bigger piece. She could taste it now as she bit into the brittle shell: the tooth-twinge-ing sweetness of the toffee countered by tart apple flesh. Without swallowing, she had held it in her mouth, savouring the contrasts: hard, shiny snap and crunch; juicy, yielding pap. And for the rest of that day her tongue encountered tiny fragments of toffee lodged between her teeth, and continued sucking out their dark, burnt, fervent flavour. She had kept the stick for ever.

'When?'

'When what?'

'When will you think about it?'

'Tonight.'

Colin reached forward and squeezed her hand. 'We'll have better things to do tonight.'

Mechanically she returned his smile.

'I love you, darling,' he whispered.

Love was the stick in the toffee apple – perfect love, selfless love, giving away what you wanted for yourself. It had forged a bond between her and Tim. The stick was her ring, she realized with a jolt. Eternity ring.

Colin's pale eyes were fixed on hers, but she was gazing

into Tim's – lustrous black, long-lashed. Tim was dark, like her. Thin like her. Tall and lean. Reserved.

'I don't tell you often enough, do I, Suzanne?'

Things were better left unsaid. The waiters here knew that. They never gushed, as Italian waiters did, or assumed a bogus bonhomie and insisted you 'enjoy your meal'.

'I like that dress you're wearing.' Colin was still whispering. Men couldn't seem to get the hang of whispering – she had noticed it before. Instead they sounded breathy or even hoarse. 'It shows off your tits.'

Life had been easier without tits. Those carefree years when she and Tim had been dressed the same in shorts and baggy T-shirts. She never saw him naked, so there were no differences, no gender. Twin bodies and twin souls.

'Christ, I feel randy tonight! Curry gives me the hots.'

She picked up two spilt grains of rice from the table. Tim hadn't married either, and he was thirty-seven. After university, he'd gone to Kenya with VSO. And stayed there. His pupils in Mombasa were his family. Three hundred of them, a large proportion orphaned. His letters hummed and glowed with their achievements: the new reading scheme, the drama club, their triumph in a football match or courage on a camping trip. It made her jealous sometimes.

'What's wrong, Suzanne. You're not eating. Aren't you hungry?'

'Not very, no.'

Tim lived on his own, in a tiny flat with temperamental plumbing. Despite his busy round at the school he might be lonely, too. Occasionally, she detected in the letters a note of sadness behind the buzz and verve, as if he were aware of something lacking. Certainly he couldn't have forgotten how close they'd been as children. Such intimacy was rare. And non-existent in adulthood – in her experience, anyway.

'Well, it's a shame to waste good food.' Colin hoicked her plate towards him and started eating from each in turn.

She let the twin seed-pearls of rice dissolve slowly on her tongue. Colin was too big for her. He crushed her when he lay on top. People's physique should match: fat with fat, thin with thin. And twins should be inseparable.

'Lychees for you?' he asked. A joke, of course.

Dutifully she laughed.

'Or coffee? No, on second thoughts, let's not be too long.' Under the table, his fingers groped for her thigh, attached themselves like a sucking insect.

'I'm just going to the loo,' she said, dislodging his hand by standing up. 'Won't be a sec.'

She walked towards the toilets, then doubled back and slipped out of the door, careful not to let him see. But he was still busy eating, using the last of the naan bread to mop up the sauce from both plates.

It was cold without her coat, but she ran full tilt down the road. There was a travel agent's on Streatham Hill that stayed open till half past nine.

They would know about flights to Mombasa.

Three-Minute Egg

'George,' she said, aloud, 'I'm going to scream.'

No answer. Only his dogged breathing: in, out, in, out, in, out. Unwavering. Polite. She nudged his blue-pyjamaed arm, hoping to break the complacent rhythm, but there was not a moment's interruption in the measured inhalations, the monotonous rising and falling of his chest.

She tugged at her nightdress, which, bunched up round her neck, appeared to be trying to throttle her. Should she wake him, she debated, just to hear another voice? No, that would be unfair. George worked long and hard and relied on these rare weekends away to catch up on his sleep.

Disentangling her limbs from his, she crept out of bed and over to the window. Beyond the heavy curtains, a full-frontal moon was throbbing in the sky; the waves below ejaculating in a whoosh of shimmering foam. She pressed her palms flat against the pane, as if willing it to break and let her float free to join the wild convulsion.

'George,' she murmured. 'You don't know what you're missing.'

She laid her forehead against the cool kiss of the glass, imagining herself a wave, surging up up up up, then plunging, seething down. So unlike George's rhythm.

She peered over at his recumbent form. In, out, in, out, as regular as a metronome. A courteous sleeper, George. He never snored or snuffled or erupted in technicolour nightmares that might disturb the repose of others.

On a sudden impulse, she began fumbling in the darkness for her clothes, which lay in a heap where she had dropped them late last night. (George, of course, had hung his in the wardrobe; placed shoe-trees in his brogues.) Her blouse felt slimy-cold against her skin; the tweed skirt seemed to clamp her thighs together. She needed different clothes: unrestricting, flowing.

Tiptoeing out, she closed the door with a barely perceptible click. There was no sound from any other room, no laughter or raised voices. The lift's arthritic creaking seemed an affront to the clotted silence as it shuddered its slow way to the ground floor. That, too, was hushed and dim. The ballroom stretched ghostly and deserted; the empty restaurant smelled of stale cigar smoke; the bar reflected only darkness in its mirrors. In her head, however, she could hear the strains of a tango, taste the peacock fizz of a cocktail, smell the brandied buttery whiff of crêpes Suzette. According to George, there was too much in her head. 'You must live in the *real* world, darling,' he'd exhort.

The night porter stared at her accusingly from his cubbyhole, as if she were a naughty child breaking the rules. Guests should not have the temerity to get up before the day staff arrived, nor venture out in March without a coat.

Too bad. She wasn't going back for it. It was a shock, though, to emerge from the stifling hotel lobby and collide head-on with the wind. It knifed lewdly through her blouse, thrust impertinent fingers up her skirt. Determined to outrun it, she set off at a jog, only slowing as she reached the bottom of the hill.

The town looked elegant, even in the anaemic pre-dawn

light. George liked it for its architecture (Regency, in part) and its tasteful pleasure-gardens, and the local council's vigilance about such eyesores as obtrusive billboards or overflowing litter-bins. He insisted on coming here out of season, before the summer razzmatazz encrusted the place with 'trippers'. *She* had a sneaking preference for more vulgar seaside resorts, where the spun-pink sugar smell of candyfloss clashed gloriously with the greasy reek of chips, and bodies bared themselves on the beach: pale and paunchy rolls of flesh offered naked to the sun.

It was too early for the sun just now. The moon lounged on in the sky, although fading and effete; the explosive thrill of black and gold dimmed to sober grey. Dawn doesn't break, she thought: it seeps. Sunrise was too active a word, suggesting a burst of brilliance beyond this stifled monochrome.

She turned right, along the promenade, where she and George had walked arm in arm yesterday afternoon, admiring the fierce yellow of the gorse flowers and the cliff-top's damasked green. The sharp colour photo had become a blurred grey negative. Shapes emerged from the gloom and assembled themselves into beach-huts, benches, a bandstand. The moon grew steadily paler, as if a celestial hand were rubbing it out, leaving smeary marks across the sky. It was no longer night but not yet morning. Nothing-time.

She continued walking briskly, her steps echoed by the thwack-thwack of the waves. It was a relief to be free of George's protective arm, his improving conversation. George was a tireless educator, correcting her if she muddled gorse with broom, or used the vague word 'gull' for an Arctic tern. And they were *groynes*, he'd said, those concrete structures jutting out from the promenade; like the breakwaters they held the beach firm against erosion. In fifteen years she had learned a lot from George.

Jumping down from the promenade she crunched across the shingle, feeling she could carry on all round the coast and still have energy to spare. The tide was high; the waves frolicking towards her, as if in need of company. And the stalker wind pursued her with its low, insistent whine.

She clambered over a breakwater, cursing as the rough wood snagged her tights. Up ahead reared the grey bulk of a groyne, with a hazy figure sitting on the top. Drawing nearer, she saw it was a lad of seventeen or so, shrouded in a duffel coat and holding a fishing rod. (Long ago, George used to fish, although only in good weather.) Curious, she picked her way up the green-slimed steps and along the slippery concrete.

She smiled a greeting. He wasn't unattractive: tall and skinny, with strong, dark, wilful hair contrasting with a peaky face.

He responded with a curt nod, not looking up from his line. Fishing paraphernalia was marshalled all around him – a canvas bag, a tackle box, a tin of bait, a clasp-knife. At his feet were two flounder and a bass, their mouths opening and shutting in pathetic little gasps, as their gills flapped in and out.

She nudged them with the tip of her shoe. 'Isn't it early for bass?'

'Easterly wind. Brings 'em in closer.' He spoke as if he begrudged the words, his expression wary, even suspicious. She had expected pleased surprise. Not every woman could recognize a bass or tell a dab from a flounder. George was a human encyclopaedia.

'Is that lugworm?' she asked, watching him bait the hook.

'No, king rag.' His tone was barely civil. The words seemed to struggle up from the region of his feet and emerge rusty and reluctant.

Undeterred, she sat beside him, glancing down at her damp Kurt Geiger shoes, their soft beige skin stained darker from the sand. *He* wore rugged combat boots with broken knotted laces. His hands were long and lean, like the rest of him, although the thick coat bulked him out. One of his front teeth was slightly buckled, which gave him a touching vulnerability. His features were undefined in the pallid morning light; only his eyes alive, narrowed watchful eyes, following every flicker of the rod tip. He tightened the line an inch or two, against the play of the waves. His body, too, was rigid, as if held taut on a string by an unseen puppet-master. Spray from the incoming tide spattered both their faces as the angry water slammed against the concrete, then swirled and fretted back.

'You must get lonely on your own.'

The wind pounced on her words and whipped them away. Her hands and feet were numb, and she wished she could snuggle up inside his coat and share his body-heat. George would be warm in bed, ensconced against the pillows reading the business news, or perhaps just getting up to shave. Did this boy shave? she wondered. His cheek looked smooth and virgin like a child's.

He changed position, as if embarrassed by her scrutiny, then put his rod down and shambled to the side of the groyne, turning his back to the wind. She saw his feet brace themselves, knees bend, shoulders hunch, and realized with a shock that he was peeing over the edge. Torn between distaste and fascination, she took in the intimate details: the tensed and powerful legs, the buttocks thrusting forward, the intense concentration on a private ritual. She couldn't help but stare, mesmerized by the stream of urine jetting into the sea – its sheer unstoppable force and robust colour: brimstone or English mustard, not George's insipid Chardonnay. (George had become a dribbler of late.)

The boy re-zipped his flies and, eyes cast down, slouched back to his rod. She ought to move – she was trespassing on his space – but he seemed to possess some peculiar power compelling her to look at him: his slender hands with their grimy, bitten nails, his shuttered, almost girlish face, the fine blond down on his upper lip. No, he didn't shave.

Irritably he reached for his thermos, unscrewed its dented cap and drained the contents at a gulp, his throat pulsing as he swallowed, like the gills of a hooked fish. When he put the flask down she noticed greasy fingermarks blotching the red plastic. She longed for a drink herself, something hot and strong.

Next he rummaged in his canvas bag and pulled out a newspaper package, which he unwrapped to reveal a pair of hardboiled eggs. He cracked one against the tackle box and, stripping off its shell, devoured the naked egg in two swift bites. She could feel on her tongue the flabby shiny texture of the white; smell the stubborn odour of the yielding crumbly yolk. She swallowed with him, licking invisible crumbs from her lips. And now he attacked the second egg, his grubby fingers picking at the shell, scattering flakes on his coat. He took a bite and paused, glancing again at the rod tip. She saw his toothmarks imprinted on the egg – tiny little gouges, flanking a horizontal ridge where his upper and lower teeth had come together. Unsettling. Intimate. He took another bite, exposing the yolk, off-centre and black-edged, as if it had begun to putrefy.

Just one mouthful left. She pictured that last piece of egg mingling with his saliva, becoming moist and soft, slipping down his throat, down further to his belly. She could almost hear the ferment in his stomach, the magnificent orchestration of churning food and gurgling, flowing juices. She yearned to be a part of it, swirled around with the spasms and secretions.

Leave him alone, she told herself. He doesn't want you here.

He wiped his mouth. She wiped hers. A tiny fragment of

egg still clung to his upper lip amidst the soft, blond, fledgling hairs. She just had to remove that minute fleck of yellow, feel the downy texture of those hairs. Slowly, very slowly, she moved her hand towards his face, dislodged the crumb and gently stroked the not-quite-yet moustache.

His knuckles tautened like a row of marbles along his tight-clenched fist. He was shy, of course, embarrassed, but she could help him, teach him, as George was always teaching her.

Closing her eyes, she traced the outline of his lips, then, coaxing them apart with a fingertip, let the teasing finger explore the soft red plush inside his cheeks; glide up and down the contours of his teeth. He seemed to have lost all power of movement, unable either to rebuff her or respond. She lapped her hand across his Adam's apple, feeling the provocative little bulge quicken to her touch. Encouraged, she unfastened the first two buttons of his shirt and nuzzled her lips against his hairless skin. Still he didn't move, just let her heave his coat off, like a young child being undressed. His jeans were tattered and revealed patches of pale flesh through the largest of the holes. She struggled with the buckle of his belt which, obstinately stiff, seemed unwilling to release him. No matter. She had time.

She squinted through her eyelids. He was sitting exactly as before, hunched in his coat, his undivided attention on the rod tip. A minute passed. Another.

Then suddenly he sprang forward, seized the rod and, yanking it back in one violent movement, scrambled to his feet. The line lunged furiously as he reeled it in, pressing the butt hard against his stomach. His eyes were blazing blue now, and his face had hatched from its chrysalis stare; every nerve and muscle strained as he fought the flailing fish.

No, *she* was the fish – his hands fighting her flailing body as he yanked at her skirt, wrenched off her blouse, pushed her to her knees against the groyne. The wind thrust between her legs, its icy blast displaced by solid warmth as he covered her like a dog. The thing inside her jerked and threshed, a rising salmon, plunging home to spawn.

'*Yes!*' she shouted, relishing the scarlet pain in her knees as he kept grinding them and grinding them against the barnacled surface of the groyne. She arched against him, picking up his rhythm – an angry, breathless rhythm, as he slammed and thrust against her, his barbarous nails clawing her bare back. The sea was joining in: slavering towards her; panting, foaming, gathering speed; one headstrong wave swelling up and up, sweeping her to treacherous heights before crashing, pounding down.

There was a last frantic spasm, followed by a cry. His voice or hers? She couldn't tell.

Opening her eyes, she glimpsed a bulging eye, a spiky fin; felt the shock in her own body as the boy hauled in a sea bream. He dropped it on the concrete, trying to hold it still with a piece of dirty sacking. It squirmed beneath his hands, zigzagging and writhing in streaks of silver fury. He grabbed a pair of pliers and with a flick of his wrist removed the savage hook. Although blood was oozing from its gills it continued to twitch and flap until he struck it on the head.

Reeling from the blow, she rose shakily to her feet. Her clothes were damp, her legs stiff and cramped, and there was a trail of greenish slime on her skirt. Head down, steps slow, she limped towards the promenade, turning back once only. The boy was on his knees still, fussing with the fish. He probably hadn't even noticed that she'd gone.

It was lighter now but overcast; the sky bloated with dyspeptic clouds that had extinguished any glint of sun or sparkle on the waves, leaving dull, censorious grey. Trudging on, she passed the skeleton of a deck-chair and a gull's decaying corpse. No, an Arctic tern. George would have finished shaving by now and be pressing down his cuticles with the ivory-handled hoof-stick; Scarlatti on the radio, Old Spice on his chin.

She stopped, trying to erase his image from her mind. Away to the left, the white chalk of the cliff-face was stained and streaked with tear-marks. The gulls, too, seemed to grieve; their shrill tormented cries outkeening the wind as they circled overhead.

The first locals were appearing – a stout matron with a snuffly Pekinese; a jogger in a lurid purple tracksuit thudding along the pavement. Both looked through her as if she wasn't there.

She plodded up the hill, her ears aching in the wind. It was a relief to reach the hotel entrance and step from lecherous cold to welcoming warmth. There were reassuring smells of coffee and fried bacon. And the receptionist was at her desk, smiling and well groomed.

'Good morning, Mrs Harrington.'

George's name. It had never seemed quite right for her.

The lift was waiting, empty. It juddered to the second floor, where George was also waiting, anxiously patrolling the corridor.

'Darling, where on earth have you been? I was beginning to imagine the worst. I know you like your morning constitutional but not at this ungodly hour! And where's your coat, for heaven's sake? You'll catch your death, going out in all weathers with next to nothing on.'

'I'm not cold,' she lied, letting him lead her back to the room. The radio was playing. Haydn, not Scarlatti.

'And look at your shoes. They're soaked! Shall I run you a hot bath?'

'No, I . . .'

There was a soft tap at the door. The *boy*, she thought . . .

'Come in,' George called.

She froze.

An elderly black-coated waiter entered with a tray. 'Your breakfast, sir, madam.' He placed the silver coffee pot on the table, bone china cups and saucers in a dainty rosebud pattern, and finally two matching egg-cups, holding large brown speckled eggs.

George was a creature of habit. Boiled eggs for Sunday breakfast, roast beef for Sunday lunch. The pattern never varied, even when they were away and he could choose anything from Loch Fyne kippers to Cumberland sausage. He was fussy about his eggs – they must be soft-boiled, he insisted, with the whites just barely firm. At home she timed them to the dot, she and the pinger counting down the exact three minutes. They could almost measure out their marriage in three-minute eggs; Sunday after endless Sunday, dipping wholemeal soldiers into runny free-range yolks.

The waiter cast his eye over the table, checking everything was there: toast shorn of its crusts, scallop-curls of butter, marmalade thick with chunks of peel. A single pink-blush rose floated in a crystal bowl. George chose hotels for just such attention to detail, and he was right in that respect. Bone china did enhance an egg, and of course they should be soft. They smelt different then, not tainted.

'Is there anything else you require?' The waiter hovered obsequiously at the door.

Yes, she thought, I . . .

'No,' said George, 'thank you.'

Shivering, she sat down at the table. George was fussing with plates and spoons, pouring coffee, adding cream. His hair was carefully combed across the bald patch; his cheeks a self-righteous pink. He wore what he called his smoking-jacket, although he would no more dream of smoking than of having a flutter on a horse. George preferred life to be devoid of risk.

On her plate, with the eggcup, he had arranged three fingers of neatly buttered toast. 'Are you sure you're feeling all right, my dear? You don't seem quite yourself.'

'I'm . . . fine.' She watched him rap his egg, then slice off the top with a single brisk movement of the knife. The yolk spilled over and began to dribble down the shell. Fastidiously he scooped it back and took a first small mouthful, dabbing at his lips with the starched white napkin.

'Aren't you hungry, darling?'

'No . . . Yes . . .' She picked up her spoon, cracked the top of the egg and put a tiny blob of yolk to her lips. The smell was overpowering – the sulphurous stench of the boy's hard-boiled eggs penetrating every cell of her body and right down between her legs. She forced herself to swallow. Instantly her stomach distended, as if the tiny embryo of egg had swollen to grotesque proportions.

George glanced up at the window with a rueful shake of his head. 'The weather doesn't look very promising. I reckon we're in for a storm.'

'Yes, there's quite a wind already.'

'Perhaps we should stay safe indoors.'

'Mm. That might be best.' The stiff napkin slid off her lap and, bending to retrieve it, she suddenly saw the state of her legs. Her tights were lacerated and her knees scored with angry red weals. She stared aghast at the viscous ooze seeping from the broken skin. What on earth had she *done*?

George, thank God, hadn't noticed, and in any case was busy with his egg; his spoon deep inside, prising out the last warm curl of white. She clamped the napkin over her knees, aware all at once of pain – a fierce rush of pain in her legs, flar-

ing upwards to her thighs and breasts and increasing in inten-
sity until it was blazing through the room.

George frowned at her untouched egg and congealing cup
of coffee. 'What's wrong, my dear? It's not like you to be off
your food.'

Powerless in the thrill of pain, she watched the damp stain
impregnate the napkin, growing slowly larger, larger.
'George,' she said, with the ghost of a smile, 't . . . tell me
about catching bream.'

SOS

Here is an SOS message for Mr John Fraser, from Edgbaston, at present on holiday in Wales. It's about his mother . . .

He slammed on the brakes and turned up the volume on the radio.

Will Mr John Fraser from Edgbaston, who's on holiday in Powys, please get in touch immediately with St Mary's Hospital, Birmingham, where his mother, Mrs Gladys Fraser, is dangerously ill. The phone number is . . .

Hands shaking, he fumbled for a pen. 0121 63 . . . Christ! He'd missed the next digit. His brain wouldn't function. He could hardly grip the pen. This couldn't be happening. Not to him. His mother was never ill.

He looked despairingly at the numbers, petering out to nothing. No damned use at all. Anyway, how could he ring from one of the loneliest parts of Wales? He'd chosen it deliberately, to avoid other people and their pointless conversation. There hadn't been a house in miles, let alone a phone box.

In a daze he turned the car round. He had planned a trip to Builth Wells, to see the castle mound. His mother was built like a castle: stout, indomitable. Surely her ramparts couldn't fall? He must get to a village, phone the hospital from there.

He took the corner too fast. These roads weren't built for

speed: narrow, winding and shuttered by tall trees. The whole area was secretive and gloomy. Like him. 'A smile won't crack your face, John,' she used to say. He carried her sayings in his head, like a Bible forever putting him in the wrong. And this time he *was* in the wrong, for leaving her alone. But how could he have known that anything would happen? She had waved him off with her usual peevish vigour a mere six days ago. 'Go if you're going, John, and stop fiddle-faddling about. I'll be glad to see the back of you.'

He swerved to avoid a fox lying mangled in the road; a sac of bloodied intestines bulging from its stomach. Perhaps she'd had an accident, been knocked down by a car. But no, she never went out. Like royalty, people came to her.

. . . another incident in Portadown. A man was shot in the chest. A second man escaped with minor injuries.

His mother disliked the Irish. She had employed an Irish cleaner once, who had stolen toilet rolls and sugar. There was no actual proof, but his mother didn't need proof – not for anything, God and the after-life included. Her certainty was terrifying.

Reluctantly he slowed at a crossroads. No more trees, only barren hills; the glazed grey rock grimacing through its shabby coat of grass.

Dangerously ill . . . And in this oppressive heat. The countryside was simmering, as if a gigantic gas-flame had been turned on underground, leaving the earth to boil dry. The hottest July since records began, according to the news. . . . *Severn Trent Water are warning that rationing may be intro-duced . . .*

She often talked of the rationing in the war, how people made such a song and dance about it when all you had to do was grow your own vegetables or keep a hen or two. He remembered only queues and lying in bed hungry at night, not fresh eggs or home-grown parsnips. Their memories never tallied. Not just of the war but everything.

He wiped a collar of sweat from his neck. Would the hospital be air-conditioned? He hoped so, for her sake. Or was it too late for . . . ?

He put his foot down hard. Where *was* the wretched village? He had passed the sign ten minutes back, yet the roads were stretching themselves out on purpose, maliciously detaining him. In his mother's eyes, it was a crime to be late for anything, even breakfast: stewed tea and brittle toast; prunes on Sundays, for their bowels.

Ah, a sign of habitation at last – a clutch of sullen houses, a squat, unfriendly church and, thank God, a pub with a phone box outside.

The air felt stagnant and soupy as he got out of the car. Someone had used his stomach as a saucepan. It was full of choppy, curdled liquid, threatening to boil over, and there was a similar convulsion in his head. He stared at his fistful of coins: fiddly 5ps, pennies with the portcullis on. No escaping castles.

He picked out two fat pound coins and rang Directory Enquiries.

'What name, please?' asked a grotesquely cheerful female.

The recorded voice giving the number sounded just as exuberant, as if announcing lottery winners. They should train their operators to take their work more seriously, remind them of death and disasters.

He dialled the number. Engaged. A hospital engaged? There would be dozens of lines, surely. He tried again. Still engaged. Perhaps something was wrong with the phone. He banged down the receiver and strode into the pub, only to find its pay-phone was out of order. 'For God's *sake!*' he muttered, wincing as the jukebox suddenly pounded into life. In the old days phones used to work and you could hear yourself speak in public places.

No joy in the next village either. It took him ages even to locate a call box, and then it was occupied. Two mini-skirted girls were squashed together inside, surrounded by a gaggle of their friends, the whole crew of them giggling and smoking. If he asked them to give him priority he could imagine the response: 'Wait your turn, you boring old fart.'

In any case, every minute wasted meant that by the time he got to Birmingham his mother might be . . . No, he couldn't even think the word. She was immortal, indestructible.

'There's nothing wrong with *me*, John. You're the one that's feeble. For crying out loud, pull yourself together and get me out of this godforsaken place. I can't abide hospitals, you know that.'

Yes, he did know. Of course she wasn't ill – her voice was as forceful as ever, berating not only him but the brazen teenage girls as well. It was his duty as her son to drive straight to St Mary's and take her home, as she asked. No more dithering on phone calls.

He returned to the car, cursing the map for trembling in his hands. The A44 . . . Where was it? Could a main road disappear? He finally spotted the sly red line idling its way to Leominster, then meandering on to Worcester. His mother would never have tolerated such indolence – she'd have whipped it into action, got shot of those ridiculous cones and directed the traffic personally, if need be. Still, even without her intervention, he should make Birmingham by six.

At ten to seven he drew up in the hospital car park. His legs seemed to buckle under him as he stumbled into Reception and over to the desk. How could the girl be so impassive? Didn't she understand emergencies?

'Yes, that's OK. Your mother's in Grosvenor Ward. Take the lift to the third floor, turn left when you get out and it's straight ahead of you, just along the corridor.'

The corridor seemed longer than the eighty-odd miles he had driven; the floor wet concrete dragging at his feet. His back ached, his head throbbed, as he limped his way to another desk, another chirpy young girl. Were there no over-twenties left in the modern world?

'You'll have to speak to Sister.'

'Where is she?'

'I'm not sure.'

Incredible. The BBC poured its resources into alerting relatives, and then some flibbertigibbet of a nurse kept you hanging around while your mother . . .

'Hello, I'm Sister Lloyd. Would you like to come with me?'

She showed him into a windowless room that contained nothing but a few empty chairs and a vase of plastic flowers. It reminded him of a funeral parlour – reserved for hopeless situations. Even the carpet was ash-coloured and worn.

'Do sit down, Mr Fraser.'

Sit down? Surely there wasn't time for that?

'I'm sorry to have to tell you . . .'

No, he all but shouted, she can't be dead. Any more than God could die or the earth could die.

'. . . that your mother's had a major stroke. It's left her paralysed. I'm afraid she's unable to speak.'

A blatant lie. His mother never paused for breath. Her voice thundered from the mountaintops, clamoured in the rushing streams. He had heard it in Wales, all through his silent holiday.

'And I should warn you that she may not recognize you.'

Her only son? The man who had shared her life for sixty-seven years?

'But if you just sit and hold her hand I'm sure she'll find that a comfort.'

Wrong again. His mother disapproved of physical contact. Even as a toddler he couldn't remember ever sitting on her lap. The very thought unnerved him, to be that close to her under-clothes, her . . . her . . .

'I realize what a shock this must be, Mr Fraser. But let me take you into the ward.'

Why an ordinary ward? Shouldn't she be in Intensive Care or at least have a room to herself? He ought to complain, demand to see a doctor.

'Mr Fraser?' The nurse stopped – impatiently, he felt – to allow him to catch up.

'Y. . . yes, I'm coming.' He kept his eyes resolutely down, seeing only the beige vinyl and her brisk black lace-up shoes. The smells seemed wrong for a hospital: curry and cheap scent.

As they entered the ward he made himself look up. Eight beds, all a blur. The nurse approached the third on the left. 'Mrs Fraser?' she said loudly, as if addressing a deaf or witless person, 'your son's arrived.'

He stared at the wizened figure in the bed. He was reminded of a fledgling ousted from the nest to make room for the more sturdy birds; a pathetic runt of a creature. Her mouth was twisted to one side and hung open vacantly; a long string of saliva drooling on to her concave chest. Her skin was the colour of congealing porridge; her hair straggly and unwashed. Her pale blue eyes were glazed with fear, as if mesmerized by some unknown horror.

His mother had *brown* eyes, deep dark Bovril brown. And she was tall and stocky, with broad shoulders and large hands, and an imperious prow of a bosom. Even a major stroke couldn't alter someone's eye colour or anatomy. This Mrs

Fraser was different altogether: different features, different shape of face.

'Sit down,' urged Sister Lloyd, indicating the small arm-chair by the bed.

Unsteadily he groped towards it. He should be feeling relief; instead he was wrestling with new shock. The coincidence was uncanny: two Mrs Gladys Frasers, both elderly, both with sons called John who happened to be on holiday in Wales.

'I'll leave you with her, Mr Fraser, all right?'

'No, wait . . .' He must tell her there'd been a mistake, explain that . . .

'Although she can't speak, do feel free to talk to her. She's probably aware of what we're saying. *Aren't* you, Mrs Fraser?' Sister enunciated with tactless over-emphasis.

'But she's not . . . I mean . . .' The words were lumps of gristle stuck in his throat.

'And if you notice any change in her condition, ask one of the nurses to call me at once.'

What change did Sister envisage? The poor old thing already seemed beyond hope. One scrawny hand scrabbled at the sheet, but apart from that she was motionless. The few teeth she had left were stumpy and discoloured. Her hair, too, had a strange jaundiced tinge.

'Now I'd better run, if you'll forgive me. We've had several new admissions today, so I'm rushed off my feet.'

With a cheery wave she was gone. And he was still clearing his throat to speak. But it wasn't easy with strangers listening in; invisible eyes watching from the beds. And the noises on the ward were most unsettling: a harsh hawking cough, followed by a protracted bout of spitting; elsewhere, the sound of stifled sobs punctuated by pauses, as if the patient stopped breathing from time to time. And a conversation was going on that he couldn't help but overhear, between the occupant of the adjacent bed and a big, blowzy woman – the only other visitor.

'No, I didn't bring the red one. I brought the blue one. It's warmer, Gran. Stop fussing.'

He slumped down in the clammy leatherette chair. Red *what*, he'd like to know? There was little colour of any sort here. White walls, white sheets, white counterpanes. Mrs Fraser herself was dressed in a white gown, which made her face look greyer still. Did she spell her name with an s or a z, he wondered? And was her second name Margaret, like his mother's? That would be a coincidence too far. Her eyes met his. Did he detect a faint change in her expression? Perhaps he resembled her real son, and his narrow frame and greying hair were comfortingly familiar (if hardly very distinguished).

He began to feel embarrassed beneath her unflinching gaze. There was an air of desperate pleading in her eyes now, as if she were trying to communicate. His mother would never plead; her sole mode was command.

Help me, she seemed to be saying. I'm terrified.

He understood. He had lived with fear since birth. No – before birth. Even in the womb he had heard his mother's voice, chiding him to grow faster or to kick with greater exertion.

'Gran, I've told you, twice, the red one wouldn't do. It had stains on it, and a dirty great hole in the sleeve.'

Did that woman have to speak so loudly, when other patients needed rest? Most of them were just shapeless humps and extremely ill, by the looks of it.

'In any case, it's far too short. Or do you *want* to show everything you've got? Oh, look! Here's Maeve, with your dins.'

An orderly had bustled in, carrying a tray and exuding such

cheery boisterousness, it seemed an affront to the inertia of the invalids.

'So, what's Gran got today, Maeve?'

'Chicken pie.' The orderly put the tray down on the table with a clatter.

This was his chance to speak up. But wouldn't it seem odd that he hadn't told them straight away he wasn't the right Mr Fraser?

'It was chicken pie yesterday,' the grandmother complained.

'No, it wasn't, Mrs Moore. It was macaroni cheese. And that lovely choccy pud.'

He wasn't brave enough to interrupt as they continued prattling on. Besides, he might be seen as an impostor. He already felt conspicuous – the only male surrounded by eight females in their night-clothes. His own clothes were crumpled from the drive and there were wet patches under his arms.

A second orderly appeared – black this time, her ebony skin and crinkly hair a contrast to the ubiquitous white. 'Wakey-wakey!' she shouted, placing a second, identical tray on Mrs Fraser's table.

'Mrs Fraser is not asleep,' he said frostily, roused at last to speech by indignation. 'And in her condition she can't eat chicken pie.'

'Sorry, that's what she's down for.' The woman swept out, returning with another tray for the patient in the corner bed, who *was* asleep. If not dead.

New smells assaulted his nose: Bisto gravy, cabbage cooked to ruination. He pulled Mrs Fraser's tray towards him. A raft of rigid pastry afloat on chicken mush, surrounded by a battalion of solid roast potatoes. And a stubborn slab of cheesecake for dessert. A stroke victim required tube-feeding or, at the very least, light puréed foods. If she was paralysed, how could she swallow such a stodgy meal, let alone use a knife and fork? Perhaps a nurse would come to feed her or bring her something more suitable. He glanced around expectantly, but no nurse materialized. And by now the two orderlies had vanished.

'Come on, Gran, if you don't like chicken, try the carrots. They'll help you see in the dark.'

'There's little enough to see in the light.'

Mrs Fraser also had a portion of carrots, which he surveyed with distaste. They were such a lurid colour they looked as if they'd been manufactured in a laboratory rather than grown in soil. Hesitantly, he picked up the fork and mashed a few of the bright orange discs with a rivulet of chicken pulp. Then he held the fork to the woman's mouth, anticipating rejection every second: 'If I want to eat, I'll eat, John. I don't need *you* interfering.'

But Mrs Fraser made no response whatever. Perhaps the food was too bland. His mother showered everything with salt and HP sauce. The salt was in a tiny paper sachet. He tore it open and sprinkled just a little on. Too much salt was bad for the heart. 'Eat up,' he coaxed, opening his mouth in encouragement, the way he'd seen mothers do with babies.

Her eyes were fixed on his again, trying to communicate. I *can't* eat, they seemed to say. My body no longer works.

Enraged, he put the fork down. Did they intend to starve her to death? Tube-feeding probably cost too much and was saved for younger people who could contribute to the economy. The poor defenceless woman was nothing but a corpse-in-waiting.

'Leave this to me,' he told her. 'I'll have a word with the doctor the minute he shows up. We'll get you fed one way or another.'

She was relieved – he could tell. It must be quite horrific to be locked in a cage of silence, shrivelling to skin and bone.

He edged his chair a little closer. 'Don't worry, I'll sort something out. You must eat or you'll lose your strength.'

She was hanging on his words, devouring if not her food then every vowel and consonant. She *needed* him, he realized with a jolt. Extraordinary to be needed, rather than to need.

Slowly, very slowly, he leaned across and took the claw-like hand in his, again expecting a repulse. But there was no sensation save the coldness of her skin. Cold, in a heatwave? She must be as weak as a wraith. They probably skimped on bedding, too, and left their elderly patients to shiver. He used his free hand to ease the blankets up towards her neck. The stupid nurse had left her half uncovered. Old people had their dignity – he was well aware of that.

'I would have come sooner, but the traffic was appalling. And you know what my old banger's like,' he added with a smile.

Was it an answering smile or just an involuntary twitch of her mouth? No matter. The main thing was, she was listening and with total rapt attention. His mother never listened.

'Actually, the holiday was rather disappointing. I was expecting rain. Wet weather seems to suit me.'

Her fingers were getting warmer. Amazing that he could affect her circulation, make her blood less sluggish. And amazing, too, that he wasn't contradicted. His mother would have retorted that of *course* he'd enjoyed his holiday; indeed, was lucky to have a holiday at all. Had he spared a thought for *her*, cooped up all day in a poky house? He should count his blessings.

He counted them: he could speak, he could eat, he was no longer even sweating. He could say what he wanted without fear of argument.

'I know people usually like the sun. But I find it overpowering. Maybe because of the War. I used to feel safe in the blackout. No Germans looking in.'

She understood – he knew. Perhaps she felt the same: safe only in an air-raid shelter.

'Were you widowed in the war?' he asked. 'I know what it's like. My father never returned.'

A look of infinite sadness crossed her face. She was expressing sorrow for him. How wonderful. How rare.

Astounded at his temerity, he dared to stroke her hand. He had never stroked a woman's hand before. She was still a woman, however old. Maybe a beauty in her youth.

Slowly, humbly, he let his fingers feather hers, watching her face for any sign of displeasure. But no, she seemed to like it. Her other hand stopped its restless scrabbling and her eyes had lost their haunted look. 'We'll get you better, I'm sure of it. What's important is I'm here.'

More footsteps. Damn! He let go of her hand as the orderlies skittered in again to collect the untouched trays. Did no one *care* that these helpless geriatrics were in danger of wasting away? Or was it official policy to kill them off as soon as possible, in order to free their beds for drug addicts or infertile sexagenarians?

'Is there any chance of a cup of tea?' he asked Maeve, the so-called orderly. There was a button off her overall and her hair was, frankly, a mess. 'My mother's mouth is very dry and, if it isn't any trouble, I could do with one myself.'

'We don't serve drinks till nine. You'll have to get it from the machine.'

'Machine?'

'It's one floor down, the other end of the passage.'

He couldn't interrupt his bedside vigil, even for five minutes. Already Mrs Fraser seemed upset that he was no longer stroking her hand. But it was a question of priorities. Dehydration could kill.

He poured a little water from the jug into a glass and held it to her lips. But she was no more capable of drinking than of eating. Incensed on her behalf, he unfolded his pocket handkerchief and, first checking it was clean, dipped it in the water to moisten her mouth. 'That's better, isn't it? Now let me wipe your face.'

'Gran, I'm sorry but I've got to go. Ta-ra.'

He didn't catch the grandmother's reply, although it elicited a contemptuous snort from her visitor.

'All right, all right, I'll *bring* the bloody red one!'

He would never dream of swearing at his grandparents. Not that he'd ever had any. Nor brothers and sisters either. Relations were thin on the ground.

He took Mrs Fraser's hand again, emboldened by the knowledge that he wouldn't be slapped down. Had *she* a large family, he wondered. No, only the one son. John. Named for his missing father. 'John's here,' he told her. 'He'll take charge.'

She was proud of her son – always had been. He hadn't shone at school, but she was wise enough to know that other things were as important as coming top in class. Swimming, for example. He had learned to swim at five. Swam in lakes and rivers. No tame municipal pools or chlorine in his eyes. With a sport like swimming it didn't matter if you were small for your age. 'Weedy little squit!' they'd taunted, but he was braver than the bully-boys – diving into deep treacherous water, striking out for miles, alone.

'Remember those sandwiches you used to make?' Gratefully he squeezed her hand. 'And how I wolfed them down? I was ravenous after all that swimming.'

His mother's sandwiches were miserly: brown bread, a scrape of marge, a smidgin of fish paste. Mrs Fraser's would be different altogether: cloud-soft, cloud-white and moist, oozing butter and real salmon.

He jumped as a bell clanged outside. Bells meant school, and trouble.

'Lord, Gran, there's the bell and I'm still here nattering. Goodnight. See you Wednesday.'

Goodnight – so early? The sun was still shining outside. He didn't remember it shining in the war. Things had known their place then, restrained themselves for the sake of a beleaguered nation. These nurses wouldn't know. The war for them was as distant as the Flood.

A nurse came in at that moment to check that the visitors had left.

'*You* can stay, Mr Fraser. I'll draw the curtains round your mother's bed and give you some privacy. How is she?'

'Much better than she was.'

The nurse raised a sceptical eyebrow as she took Mrs Fraser's pulse. 'I can't see any change.'

Then you're blind, he thought. Any fool could see the vast improvement.

'If you do notice any sign of distress, just press this bell immediately. I won't be far, if you need me.'

I shan't, he muttered under his breath. And nor will she. It's me she needs.

And peace and quiet, although there was little chance of that. A trolley had been wheeled in and was juddering over the lino. And a shrill Irish voice was asking who wanted sleeping pills. Half the patients were asleep already.

'Just relax,' he whispered to Mrs Fraser. 'Try and let go of the tension. It may help if you shut your eyes.'

Her eyelids didn't move. Ah – he understood: she didn't want to let him out of her sight. 'Don't worry, I shan't go,' he told her. 'I intend staying with you all night.'

He frowned at another disturbance. Bedpans, by the sound of it, although no one had offered one to Mrs Fraser. Nothing in, nothing out, they obviously assumed.

He closed his ears to the obscenely intimate noises, hoping

she could do the same. At least the sun was going down, and within the sanctuary of the curtains it was tolerably cool and dim.

'We'll get you moved in the morning. I'll insist on a single room. And I'll buy some flowers to make it look more cheerful.' Red roses. 'What's your favourite colour? Oh, pink, I see. Yes, it's a hopeful colour, isn't it?' In the pink; the pink of health. Hope was essential, if sometimes near impossible. You had to fight to keep it alive, like those tiny premature babies who only survived on ventilators.

He felt so exhausted suddenly, he could do with resuscitation himself. Even breathing was an effort. He seemed to have been fighting the whole day – the whole of his life.

He let his eyelids close. He wouldn't sleep, just rest. Sit quietly beside the patient and offer his silent support.

He woke with a start. It was dark. The lights had been turned down; just one low-wattage lamp casting eerie shadows across the still-drawn curtains. Mrs Fraser's eyes were open and peering at him anxiously. 'I'm sorry,' he whispered, shame-faced. 'I must have nodded off.'

He glanced at his watch: two o'clock. Normally he loathed the early hours, when hope guttered like a candle in a draught. Now, though, he wasn't purposeless, or solitary, but enclosed in a white haven with another human being who needed and relied on him. It was clear from her expression that she was relieved he had woken up – indeed drawing strength from his presence. The other patients were all fast asleep, judging by their laboured breathing, and shut out anyway. Inside the curtains, nobody could see him as he laid his fingers against the cool grey cheek.

'It's better like this, isn't it? Nice and peaceful. Just the two of us.' He had to reassure her, make up for his negligence. It had been crass of him to doze off.

He took her hand in both of his, this time, and drew it gently towards him. She didn't recoil – far from it. Her eyes were almost seductive as they searched the depths of his. What matter if she couldn't speak when he knew the words already.

'My son, my dearest son.'

'Go on,' he urged her silently. 'There's more.'

'My darling John. My pride and joy. My comfort.'

He sat drinking in the endearments, couldn't get his fill. He had waited sixty-seven years for this. Winter years. Now spring had come.

'Brilliant son. Beloved son. The best thing in my life.'

He shook his head in wonder. He had dreamed such words throughout his childhood, manhood. Brilliant. Best. Adored.

'I was so proud of you when you won the cup for swimming. See it on the mantelpiece?'

Yes, solid silver, engraved with his name.

'And when you gave me your first pay packet I was almost moved to tears. It was so generous of you, John, dear, not keeping back a penny for yourself.'

A routine job. Dull. No power. But his mother had needed the money.

'In fact I couldn't have managed without you, not in any way. I give thanks every night for such a devoted son.'

He was vaguely aware of footsteps clack-clacking past the open door of the ward. No – there *was* no ward. They were safe at home together, on their own. It was private, solemn, hushed, and they had all the time in the world. Time to get to know each other; time to touch, caress. He was free to stroke her hair, trace the coil of her shell-ear, let his hand linger in the sweet hollow of her neck.

'Even as an infant you were special. And so precious.'

He could hardly take it in. His existence made worth while, at last; the barren decades redeemed.

'And now I'm old, you're my reason for living, the best son a mother could have.'

He repeated the phrases after her, over and over and over. The ice in his heart was cracking. With every repetition he felt another brittle shard begin to melt.

Then, all at once, she shuddered and fell sidewards on the bed.

'Mother, what *is* it? What's wrong?'

He strained his ears to listen. He alone could hear her faintest whisper, sounds no one else could detect. But there was no sound at all. No breath. Just silence. Gaping silence.

He did not press the bell. She needed no one but him.

With infinite tenderness he stretched out on the bed and pressed the frail and yielding body close to his. Her hair was soft against his neck; his lips wet with her saliva.

'I love you, Mother,' he said.

Paraquat

'Twelve large farmhouse loaves, please. Crusty ones.'

'*Twelve?*'

Mr Lely didn't answer. He had spoken quite distinctly. If that wrong-side-of-fifty bag of bones couldn't understand plain English, then . . .

'Having a party, are you?'

He removed a piece of fluff from his lapel. Party! He never saw a soul. There wasn't room. He needed all the space himself.

'Got a bag, love?

He opened his four capacious carriers and let her put the loaves in. He was nobody's love. Blubber precluded love.

'That'll be £10.80, sir.'

Oh, he was sir, now, all of a sudden. Or was she taking the mick? People always did. Fat was funny. Ha ha ha. She wasn't so hot herself, with that unsightly raised mole just below her eye and a powdering of flour on one leather-look veined cheek.

He counted out the sweaty coins. His hands were never dry. They had forecast sleet this morning and his shirt was sticking to him. He picked up the bags, two in each hand. He could smell the wooing grease-and-sugar reek of freshly cooked doughnuts. He kept his eyes down, refusing to look at the bewitching ooze of jam, the loose sugar snowing up the cake-tray. Thirty, forty, fifty doughnuts side by side by . . . He turned away. Doughnuts were Thursday. Today was only Tuesday.

'Good day, sir.' She squeezed past him to the window and started arranging fat iced buns in alternate rows. Pink, white, pink, white, pink, white, pink . . . Half a glacé cherry glossy on each one.

'Good day.' He repeated it himself. It sounded strange. Why not say good morning? He couldn't count on it being good in either case. So many things could let you down: door frames getting narrower, bread less fresh than yesterday's, strawberry jam running low on fruit. He had counted the strawberries once in all the brands. Messy, but worth it. Hartley's Pure-Fruit Super Jam came top with twenty-eight. Some of them had none, just mangled shreds and pulp.

He never started with jam. That came later. Savouries first – Marmite, peanut butter, bloater paste, Velva Cheese Spread. Velva was more expensive than the Kraft but creamier and smoother. Naturally, with a name like that. He had named his girlfriend Velva in its honour. Smooth skin, creamy pale. Velva Josephine, Velva Louise May. He hadn't met her yet. Women laughed at him or kept away. Velva wouldn't, though. She was big herself: huge breasts, flesh you could get lost in.

Having put his bags down to rest his arms, Lely mopped his forehead with a handkerchief. Walking was a strain these days, and the doctor had warned him not to carry heavy weights. The doctor was a woman – a Vera, not a Velva. Vera L. Baines, MB, BS, DRCOG. He wondered what the L was for. Lonely? He had two Ls in his own name. He wished he'd been born a Jones or Smith or even Barraclough. Lely invited sniggers – it sounded French and frail when he was neither. It could be worse. Lily, for example. They'd piss themselves at Lily.

Perhaps he should take a detour to the park, lighten his
load by eating one of the loaves. No, it was never right in the
park. You had to be so underhand; break off tiny pieces and
convey them to your mouth under cover of a newspaper; try
to chew without moving your mouth. And then the pigeons
were a nuisance. He liked birds but not in public. He fed them
at home, always saved the last loaf. They were getting fat, his
birds. Join the club. His robin was twice the size of any normal redbreast. And twice as tame. Nowadays it hopped inside
the kitchen window, right on to the draining board, even fed
from his hand.

'Morning, Mr Lely. Not so bright this morning, is it?'

The woman from the paper shop. Pigeon legs and pimple
breasts. He could see her peering at his loaves. Counting. The
shop girl should have wrapped them properly, not used those
scrimps of tissue that didn't hide a thing. *The books will be
sent by return of post under plain brown wrapper.* He had torn
the wrapper open, spent half a day staring at the girls. Velvas,
all of them, in black suspender belts or sprawled on tiger-skin
rugs. (*He* had vinyl mats – they stopped you slipping.) Half the
girls were eating: teeth marks on bananas, ice-cream cornets
thrust halfway down red throats. They never ate bread.

He turned into his cul-de-sac. No one around, thank God.
Only Mrs Stephens' tomcat, slinking between the cotoneaster
and the dead hydrangea. He loathed that cat. Thin, black,
mangy scavenger stalking and strutting on its foam-rubber
feet, weighing less than nothing, air and fur stinking out the
path; supercilious eyes narrowed and appraising, sniffing
things only to disdain them, pissing on the pale pink faces of
the periwinkle flowers; murderous claws sharpened on his
fence.

Lely slammed the front door behind him, puffed into the
kitchen, then lowered himself gingerly on to a sturdy wooden

stool. He'd had to give up chairs – the arms were too close together. He lived mostly in the kitchen now and never used the upper floor. Stairs were dangerous: strain on the heart. Dr Baines's stethoscope swooped cold against his chest again, stern hand on his pulse, her finger lassoed with a worn gold wedding-ring. Mr Baines was dead. Died of stairs, most likely. The not-so-merry widow had passed a diet sheet across the desk, discreetly folded like a love letter. His hands were trembling as he opened it.

STOP! was printed on the top in red – red for danger – and then a list of dangerous foods: cakes, sweets, pastries, biscuits, bread . . . *Bread.* He closed his eyes. 'Be careful, said the amber light winking in between.' He had learned that off by heart at school: the Highway Code In Pictures. Here it was again. The Highway Code Diet Sheet with an amber band in the middle with foods you had to eat in moderation. Peas, he read, beans. Underneath was GO! (in green) and a whole salad-drawer of foods that were mostly green themselves. Sick list. Celery and lettuce, artichokes (no dressing), endive (endive?), cabbage, raw or cooked, Chinese cabbage, watercress . . .

He turned back to the red, his favourite (robust) colour. Nuts, chocolate, raisins, figs, confectionery. Pretty word, confectionery. Old-fashioned and somehow feminine. Velva Confectionery Louise. He had filed away the diet sheet under H for Highway Code. He had never learned to drive. Cars were the wrong shape.

Struggling up, he clutched at the dresser a moment to recover his breath, then lumbered to the sink and washed his hands. You couldn't be too careful. Germs preferred well-upholstered people: more to feed on. He fetched jars and tins and paste-pots from the larder, placed them on the table with the loaves and arranged them in a still-life. Far too crowded. Mr Fern had told them to keep it simple – half a loaf or lemon, a vase with a single bloom. They had done still-lifes at his Beginners' Painting Classes at the Brookfields Centre (second term) in the days when he still went out beyond the shops. Augustus Fern was a nice name for a painter, although there wasn't much of him. Even his voice was thin, with a tendency to stutter if excited. He had taught them to look at things – really look – understand their structure, note down all the details before they touched a brush.

Lely pulled up his stool and gazed at the loaf nearest him. Work of art itself. Crust gnarled, uneven, cracking across its ridged and rutted summit, dusted with flour-snow. Corners not quite regular, sides sloping away, paler than the top. Brown shading into gold. Painters' colours – ochre, sepia, umber. One end freckled, crusty; the other dimpled, pale. Both sides bulging slightly over deep voluptuous curves. He traced one curve with a finger, gently squeezed. Springy, yielding, promise of soft flesh inside. Moistness, whiteness. He never ate brown bread. Wholemeal loaves were like plain women: coarse, with open pores and sallow skin.

He picked up the bread knife, turned the loaf towards him and cradled it a moment, delighting in its warmth and doughy fragrance. Tiny shreds of crust were adhering to the rough tweed of his jacket, flour talcuming his palms, tickling in his nostrils. He plunged the knife in, sawed along the full length of the loaf. Cut that way, a slice measured thirteen and a quarter inches, as against the normal six by five. He laid the slice on a meat plate, crumb side up, fingering its pillowy plush.

His hand was damp as he reached across for the butter. Butter was important. Soft, of course. He always kept a few pounds at room temperature besides his cold store in the fridge. It was the brand that mattered, though. Anchor for grey and insecure days. He loved the bold red anchor on the wrapper – solid, reassuring, its twist of rope promising rescue if the sea should swell too high. Choice Normandy in fancy silver giftwrap for birthdays, celebrations, days when lighter men might have booked themselves a day trip to Dieppe. Country Somerset, with its picture of a milkmaid on the paper, for parching summers when the city choked in dust.

He unwrapped the Anchor – a bold brilliant yellow like the awning of the café in the Van Gogh poster they'd tacked up in the Brookfields Centre classroom, just above the sink where you washed your brushes. He couldn't forget that poster. Even when he had given up the classes the colours sang on in his mind. The whole café was a gutsy yellow, with greenish shadows and what looked like an exotic orange carpet spread outside beneath the chairs and tables that strayed on to the cobblestones. The place had an air of suppressed excitement, as if they were cooking something rare and rationed behind that tantalizing yellow wall. He had often stood in front of it, longing to walk in and storm the kitchens, but the doors were strange gold oblongs with no proper handles and far too narrow for his bulk.

The chairs on the cobblestones hadn't any arms, so at least he could perch on one of those and watch the blue mysterious buildings pool and blur on the far side of the street. He worried sometimes that there was no food on the tables, but maybe it was on its way. There was a figure dressed in white who could well have been a waiter and definitely had something in his hands, and a Quink-blue sky with huge Chelsea-bun stars spinning in their nebulae of sugar.

Once, he had tried to make a copy of the poster, so he could take the café home with him and double the width of the doors. It hadn't really worked. He couldn't get the yellow fierce enough or reproduce the whole sparking flurry of the night, which made even the ground look hot and sort of bubbly like macaroni cheese snatched sizzling from the grill.

He had asked Augustus Fern about the place and was told it was in Arles – which could have been the moon for all that he could get there. He'd had to make do with Brookfields' own cafeteria – a dingy little snack-bar skulking in the basement rather than smiling at the stars. It only opened when they had the staff, and sold orange squash in polystyrene cartons and dwarf-sized Bounty bars. The cobblestones were scuffed brown lino, the moonlight fluorescent.

The last class of term, they had used it for a slide-show – drawn the squiggly curtains and arranged the chairs in rows. (Bounties under glass.) They'd seen Van Gogh again, and yellows – not the café but a chair with a pipe on it and a sad bloated woman with her hand up to her face. There had been other painters, too, all with foreign names. You never got an artist called John Anchor, something safe you could pronounce. He'd enjoyed the slide-show, though. They had switched the lights off and he felt safer in the dark, shed a stone or two.

Afterwards, they'd gone back to the classroom where Mr Fern had pinned up their paintings on the walls, like a proper gallery with names and dates. His robin portrait had been given pride of place. He had to admit it did look very lifelike – eye bright, head cocked, every feather distinct. Watercolours weren't that easy, yet he had got the red exactly right. Used a mixture of vermilion and alizarin crimson, then muted it with a touch of Payne's grey. Fern had been bubbling over.

'B . . . beautifully observed,' he'd stuttered, peering closely at the image. 'A most sk . . . skilled and luminous handling of a very tr . . . tricky medium.' Lely had sucked his words like sweets – the 'luminous' as translucent-cool as peppermints; the 'skilled' shiny golden butterscotch.

Even better, Fern had called him into the office and urged him, still stammering, to enrol in Intermediate. If buses were designed with wider seats, and much more space between them, and a lower step on and off the platform, he might well be in Advanced by now; his gilt-framed works lording it on the walls. It was a pity paintings couldn't sing. His robin sang all the time. He could hear it now, twittering on a branch.

'You'll have to wait,' he called. 'I haven't finished yet.'

Hardly started. He dug into the butter. The proportions had to be correct. A quarter of an inch of Anchor to every three-quarter-inch slice of bread, and spread to smooth perfection. If the bread was your canvas, then you must cover it properly. No naked corners or flecks of white accusing through.

The robin swooped down to the sill, bright black eye fixed on Lely's pale one. Brave, pert, greedy little blighter with its cheerful scarlet chest. Lely smiled. His favourite colour on his favourite bird. Nine months he'd been feeding it. It had become his baby now and trusted him completely. All the same, it would have to wait. He had only just sat down, needed a winch (or wings) to get to his feet again without distress. It could forage for itself a while.

He removed the Velva from its carton – a glistening triangle of silver foil – and pulled the tiny blue tag to cut through to the creamy wedge below. He used a different knife. Always kept things separate. A broader knife to mash. The robin was still eyeing him. You couldn't be lonely, really, not with birds. He had fixed up a nesting-box, although the robin hadn't used it. Perhaps it was a male. He couldn't tell, but he hoped not. Female robins did the courting – he had read that in his bird book – went a-hunting in midwinter for a mate. Nice to be a robin and have a female woo you. After they paired, the male brought titbits in his beak. Courtship feeding, it was called. He would be good at that. Even at Brookfields he had always shared his Bounty bars, broken them in bite-sized pieces and passed them round the class. Mostly they refused – preferred to cadge smiles and Silk Cut from Mr Tom Munro, the only other man in the class. *Only* man in the class, as far as the females were concerned. Daytime classes attracted mainly housewives (which was why he'd enrolled in one himself). Munro was a thin type – skinny as a liquorice stick, with lank black hair brushed back and grey ash always flicking on his corduroys. Everything he painted turned out thin: starved Scots pines, gaunt and hungry shadow-men with his own scraggy neck and hollow cheeks. Velva wouldn't have spared him a second glance – far too busy with the bite-sized pieces. She would have scoffed the lot in a trice and then suggested Twiglets. She'd find him; give her time. It wasn't midwinter yet. Another week or so to go.

The ninth loaf was the hardest; always was. Having worked through all the savouries – sandwich spread, liver pâté, sardines mashed with mayonnaise – he moved on to lemon curd and clover honey. The robin had been back and forth, filling up with insects while it waited for its share. Velva had stopped eating (she didn't have his stamina) and nodded off against his shoulder; a glimpse of camiknicker beneath her red chemise.

He, too, could do with a rest, a brief digestive pause. He covered the three and three-quarter remaining loaves with a clean white napkin, replaced the lids on the various jars, threw away the empties, checked the level of lemon curd and wrote it on the shopping list. He'd be a credit to a Velva. Neat, well organized.

His bed was in the dining-room: a sofa that pulled out. He was panting as he tackled it. Difficult to move now. Pain in his heart, except his heart had shifted stomachwards. He would sleep for an hour and then start work – cut out all the food pictures in the *TV Times*; compare the ratio of tomato sauce to pilchards in John West and Sainsbury's own brand.

'Hush,' he called to the robin, as he eased himself slowly back. 'I can't sleep with that din!'

Only teasing. Nice song, really. Cheerful. Little bursts of trills. With most birds it was only males that sang. But female robins did their bit as well, at least in winter. It was all part of the ritual. His bottom touched tweed base. He swung his legs up and closed his eyes. Velva warbled to him, strawberry-jam lips fat and soft like worms.

It was dark when he woke, way past tea-time. That was the trouble with sleeping – you lost all track of meals. He hadn't worn his watch since the strap shrunk. He stretched and yawned. Something hot for supper. Nice piece of fish, perhaps. There was plaice in the fridge; whole Dover sole in the freezer, on the bone. He'd ditch the loaves – tomorrow morning's breakfast for the birds. They'd have gone to roost by now, the robin on its branch or snuggled up in a hedgerow, red muffler round its neck.

He groped to his feet, bursting to relieve himself. The garden privy smelt of damp and tomcats, and things dropped on you when you were sitting with your trousers down. But better to brave the spiders than risk upstairs.

As he shuffled along the path, the unpruned rose bush caught at his clothes, surprising him with a sudden strafe of raindrops. Velva wore red roses in her hair in the evenings – except evenings never happened, not to him. Only shopping time and meal times and recovering-from-meal times, and after that it was always night, like now.

Deep night in the garden. Moon a measly cheese-rind, anorexic stars. His foot sank into something. That damn cat was always scavenging in the dustbin bags, leaving trophies on the path: mutton bones and fish-heads. He bent down – awkward – caught his breath, wobbled back to vertical. Tried again, wheezing painfully. It didn't look like a fish-head. He jabbed it with his foot. Soft. Soft as feathers, soft as bread. He grabbed at the wall, heart thudding. Shock was worse than stairs. Mustn't panic. Probably mistaken. Better get a torch.

A strain to walk at all now; torch a dead weight in his hand. Someone else's shadow creeping along the fence, sleuthing him, slowing down when he did. He turned his back on it, flashed the torch beam on the path, tottered, almost fell. Could be just a nightmare. He shut his eyes, opened them, pinched himself, peered again. Robin redbreast red with blood. *Remains* of robin redbreast. Beak, feathers, scrawny legs. A wing had been ripped off and flung across the flower-bed; the plump white stomach mauled, leaving only skin and bone. Lely collapsed on to his knees. It must have been that cat. Killer. Hoodlum. Thug. His robin dead before she had found her mate, gobbled up before she had nested, scrunched while she was singing. He hadn't even fed her – not a crumb – had stuffed his face and left her starving. A tomcat's tea when she was weak and empty herself.

Tenderly he swaddled the robin pieces in his handkerchief. The feathers were still warm, blood sticky on his fingers. The cat would be smirched with that same blood, congealing on its paws, grinning round its mouth. Nothing new in that. Tom was tooth and claw, always pouncing and destroying. It had wolfed a bluetit once, head and all, butchered a whole family of voles, slugged and thrashed its own kind. Its whiskers on the right side were shorter than on the left – shaved off in some alley fight. Even coupling it turned into combat. No soft blandishments or melodious trills and warblings for a mate. Just screech, pounce, scat. No discrimination. Any mog in season. Any skirt in class.

Even now, it would be out on the tiles, scattering sperm and rivals, drawing blood again. Thin types were always dangerous. Nothing in their bellies but the limp grey smoke from Silk Cut, the scum on small black coffees. They couldn't use their energies on peaceful things like digestion or absorption, napping after meals, so their whining hollowness had to find more violent outlets – murdering, marauding, sneering at the Bounty bars and hogging the women instead. Goebbels had been thin.

There was weedkiller in the garden shed, old but still effective. Lely had never killed before – well, only dandelions. Six million golden heads guillotined with Paraquat, and that was years and years ago when he still had knees and you could buy the stuff without a special licence. His was in a Coca-Cola bottle; an offering from a gardening friend.

Lely placed the shrouded robin on a ledge, did his business in the privy, then fumbled to the shed. Ghostly objects trembled in the torch beam, memories from his past, things that had either changed their shape or become too heavy or bad-tempered for him to handle now. The Qualcast mower lay crippled on its side, the rusting grassbox banished to the opposite corner like a head severed from a body. The gallows of a deck-chair had lost its red-striped canvas lap; the Black & Decker drill trailed its drooping black intestine flex. And splitting bags of compost had leaked their contents all over the place, mulching his abandoned paints and easel, his retired spade and fork and rake.

The Coca-Cola bottle stood cobwebbed on the topmost shelf. Lely craned his neck to look at it, trying to judge the distance. Dangerously high. He removed his jacket and clambered on to a wooden crate, feeling triumph dulled with fear. The rickety wood grumbled under his weight, threatening to cave in. The bottle looked no nearer, yet the floor had fallen away.

He heaved himself up on the work-bench, hoping to fuel his courage with revenge. There were spots before his eyes, shadows from the flickering light unweaving walls and rafters. He dared not hold the torch; he needed both hands free. He made a grab for the bottle, almost losing his balance. Sweat was pouring down his face, soaking into his shirt. His fingers closed on air. Still not high enough. Holding his breath, he slowly hoisted a foot up on a ledge. His leg brushed against the scratchy mesh of a hammock, suspended from a nail. A hundred years ago it had been strung between the plum tree and the privy walls, and he had rocked back and forth, back and forth, eyelids exploding scarlet in the sun. He could feel the scarlet again, smouldering in his chest, the queasy sensation as the hammock pitched and swung. He wound his fingers through the mesh, trying to steady his breathing.

All he had to do now was swing the other foot up. He would count to three for strength. One. Two . . . Suppose he crashed down like a flowerpot from a shelf? Coward, dumpling, lump of lard. One. Two – *two* . . . he'd show them, teach them to call him names . . .

THREE.

Empty space was soaring past his foot. In a last desperate lunge towards the rafters, he grabbed air, ledge, shelf, bottle – slipped, scrabbled, scraped his leg but still clung grimly on.

Now for the descent. He had better take it quickly, before he lost his nerve. His hands were already out of commission, cemented to the bottle. He could hear the liquid slapping against the glass, as if it, too, were dizzy as they lurched and juddered down. The floor came up to hit them, seesawed underneath them. The world was a top that God had started spinning. Lely turned to face the wall, leaning his head against rough, splintery wood. The top slowly came to rest.

For five minutes he did nothing save listen to his breathing, which sounded like a motor-bike revving at the traffic lights. When they finally changed to green, he hobbled back to the kitchen, robin in one hand, poison in the other. No cat would eat plain poison – it would have to be mixed with fish, used discreetly as a seasoning. Plaice au Paraquat.

He opened the fridge and took out the two fresh plaice. He had bought them yesterday, trudged all the way to the fish-monger's, which meant passing the Oxfam shop. Oxfam made him nervous. He sent them a cheque each Christmas, but whatever sum he wrote on it turned instantly to noughts – noughts with swollen bellies.

He wiped out his largest frying pan, chopped garlic, squeezed a lemon. Plaice deserved good cooking. He scooped a curl of Normandy butter from its swanky silver wrapper and drizzled in first-pressed olive oil. Turning up the heat, he let them froth together in the pan. He floured the fish, confettied it with herbs, added a shake of salt and a generous grind of pepper. The smell of mingled oil and butter was unaccountably soothing; numbed his pain like aspirin. He wondered how Paraquat killed. Slowly, he hoped, with convulsions.

The bottle had a stubborn cap. After a tussle he succeeded in wrenching it off and measured out a lethal spoonful which he poured into the pan. It was a deep shiny brown like Worcester sauce, except the smell was wrong – menacing and tarry. He added real-thing Lea & Perrins to disguise it and sim-mered it a while, listening to the satisfying splutter. The fish were already crisp, frilled along their edges. He flipped them out on to an enamel plate and poured the juices over. They looked appetizing, innocent. But what if cooking weakened poison, diluted its potency like alcohol? He trickled a second dose of Paraquat neat across the fish, watching it soak into the flesh.

His legs were buckling with exhaustion. The shock, the climb, the cooking – too much for one night. He panted to the window and opened it a crack, grateful for the slap of clean cold winter air. He had left the privy light on and a thin gold finger was pointing across the path, showing up the cracked paving stones, the ugly frieze of moss.

Suddenly he froze. In the picture frame of the window, the picture was changing dramatically – no longer just a static nightscape of sick lawn and sullen sky but a vivid action-painting: the garden path unrolling in a streak and spit of black – Mrs Stephens' cat back from its debauchery, eyes electric green, glowing on dark canvas. Lely jerked back from the window, seized the enamel plate and, trying to match the lecher's speed and litheness, lolloped out of the back door.

'Tom, Tom, Tom . . .' he gasped.

The cat had disappeared. If it had already skylighted in to Mrs Stephens' house, then he had lost his chance. It would be stretched supine on a sill, or draped along a sofa-back, too indolent to tackle a big meal.

Grunting with exertion, Lely bent towards the path, nearly toppling over as he lowered the plate to the paving stones, and having to clutch at a thorny berberis to steady himself. Although scratched and shaken, at least he'd positioned the fish. Now for the cat.

'Puss, puss, puss,' he called again. His tongue was dry and heavy like stale Madeira cake. He could hardly shape the words. 'Fishums, lovely fishums.'

There was a ripple in the lavender bush, which hatched a lean black head and then a body. The body shook itself, sniffed the air in the direction of the plaice.

'*Eat*,' Lely murmured under his breath. His heart was like an obstreperous child, rampaging round his ribcage He forced it to sit still as he watched the cat take two steps forward, then stop – back arched, long liquorice tail held vertical and wary, one ear bitten, ragged.

Lely plucked a berry from the berberis, pulped it in his fingers. His hands were red and sticky, his breathing made a dangerous rasping sound, as if he had tried to use his rusted drill. The cat stood motionless, only its tail twitching like a separate stealthy creature. Lely held his breath. The cat had crept up almost to the plate, a crouched black shape, belly to the ground. Half an inch of tongue protruded from the pointed trap of teeth, gleaming plate reflected in green-glass eyes, ears laid back, brief suspicious sniff.

Lely switched off his torch. The cat might eat more freely in the gloom. The light from the privy was only weak and grudging; the light from the kitchen barely reached the path. Shadows slithered down the fence, uncurled themselves from bushes. A second shadow-cat was still in contact with a second shadow-plate.

Lely shut his eyes. 'Please God,' he whispered soundlessly before opening them again. The cat and its shadow gave a sudden dismissive flick of their tails, then pranced away and scaled the Stephens' fence.

Lely kicked out at the bush, watched it bleed its berries. 'All right,' he shouted. 'Wait until the morning. You'll be hungrier then, when you've had a rest from whoring!'

It had always been the same – shaming the nights with lust, then oversleeping and slouching in late to class, too grand for watercolours, starting straight on oils; hogging the sink to wash off blood and paint, splashing dirty water on the precious Van Gogh poster, pissing on the cobblestones, ripping holes in the brilliant yellow awning, messing up the café for other decent folk, just because he had no interest in food. He even missed the coffee breaks, slinking away on his soft-soled size-nine paws to sniff around some female, rub himself against her, unsheathe his paint-stained claws . . .

Lely snatched up the plate, only to bang it down again. It could damn well stay where it was. The cat was dangerous and had to be disposed of. He'd have another shot, get up early, before the Stephens stirred and catch it off its guard: tempt it with plaice before they opened Kit-e-Kat. Even Tom might be peckish by the morning, deign to toy with a little fresh-caught fish. They had cost three pounds each, those plaice, and money wasn't easy. His father had left him a nest-egg when he died, but he was eating into it, the nest near empty now. His retirement pension barely paid the bakers' bills.

He would set his alarm to be absolutely sure. It could wake the dead, that clock – shrilled loud, louder, LOUDER, if you didn't switch it off. He hardly ever used it. He hated sudden noises and there was nothing to wake up for. The bakers didn't open till nine.

The winder was stiff, but he managed to get it going. The hands had stopped at half past eight, so he moved them forward to one o'clock – it must be about that by now – and set the alarm for six. There wasn't a sound in the street: no cars or slamming doors. He creaked back to the kitchen and sagged against the dresser. Dr Baines had told him not to stand too long. He unfolded the hankie that contained the robin remnants and, holding them very carefully, made slow laborious contact with his stool. Then he laid them on the table and tried to piece them together like a jigsaw. Half a wing was missing and there was a gap between beak and chest. The robin had never had a neck – that they'd had in common – but he had always loved her eyes. Bright and black and trusting. The tomcat had four eyes now. Its original two green ones and two black bird ones shining in its gut.

His own eyes were smarting as if someone had rubbed them against a metal cheese-grater. He must calm down, rest until the morning. Stress could kill, Dr Baines had told him. There had been a second sheet besides the diet one. Relaxation: how to lower the pulse rate by breathing from the diaphragm. (He could never locate his diaphragm – there was too much flesh in the way.)

He had filed the sheet under R. He laboured up again and plodded to his box file. He couldn't find anything about diaphragms, but he came across his portrait of the robin, the one he'd done in class. R for Robin. It still had its head.

Lely smoothed out the paper and spread it on the table – the picture on the puzzle box. He laid his own head on top of it, eye to eye with the robin, hoping his pulse rate would come down a bit. Too weary to move in any case. The sofa was twenty endless yards away and had ridged tweed seams that chafed against his bottom. Best to sleep where he was; be ready for the cat when it slunk back with the dawn.

Velva's shrilling woke him. He had never known her trill so loudly before. It was still dark outside, but she was pestering him for something. He rubbed his eyes, shivering in the cold. A blade of frosty air was scything through the window. It must be very near midwinter.

He lurched to his feet. *That* was what Velva wanted! She had come to find her mate. He understood her cry now – passionate, insistent. He stared around the kitchen. Almost four loaves left, thank God. He had to feed her, secure the bond with victuals. He tore off a chunk of bread. It was already dry and staling – hardly a lover's offering. He crammed it into his mouth, mulching it with saliva. He had read in the bird book that some male species swallowed morsels of food first and then regurgitated them to make them softer for their mates.

He pushed the bread to the back of his throat, gagged, coughed, retched it up again, then held it out to Velva. She was wearing her red chemise again; eyes elderberry black. She snapped up the titbit and opened her bill for more. Her cry was frantic still and jangling. He hacked her off a bigger piece, chewing it thoroughly first. Even while she was eating, she managed to yowl as well. He tried to speed up, squelching lump after lump of bread before disgorging them – scarcely a second's pause now between the dripping beakfuls.

He leaned across the table and dismembered another loaf. The air seemed less chilly; greyish light was filtering through the window and the sky was streaked with pink, like raspberries swirled into plain yoghurt. He must have got it wrong. It couldn't be midwinter, but already March or April, and Velva had hatched a brood. That would explain the clamour. Fledglings were always demanding. He could hear them now, squawking from the nest; Velva's scarlet-throated gape shriller than them all.

He clawed at the bread, spewing it back as soon as he had softened it. Five beaks snatched and clamped, then hinged open again at once. His head was spinning from the noise; his jaw ached from non-stop chomping. The bread was heavy, tasteless, although the fledglings didn't care; they would guzzle anything and everything. He was getting flustered trying to keep pace with them – *and* with the change of seasons. His hands were clammy, sweat snaked down his back. Judging by the heat, it was May or June by now; the Oxfam shop crammed with sloughed-off woollies. Velva must have hatched a second brood before the first had flown. Ten bills screeching and only one loaf left.

In desperation, he stuffed his mouth with crumb again and pulped it with his tongue. If he slackened, both his broods would starve. Already they were sparring, jabbing with their bills. However fast he chewed, they gobbled faster. Only crust left now. Far too hard for fledglings. Despite his attempts to soften it, he failed to produce a single drop more of saliva. Velva was complaining, a raucous jarring sound, even louder than her love-cry. He'd lose her if he didn't satisfy her. She'd be warbling to a young cock, bonded to a new provider, some crude dark upstart who disfigured Van Gogh posters, despised famous works of art.

Somehow he must find the strength to drag himself to the shops and buy in fresh supplies. Except the shops weren't open yet – only the Pakistani grocer whose cakes were all synthetic, imprisoned in curry-flavoured cardboard. He'd have to wait till nine and be first in the queue at Coombe's where everything was freshly baked. He tried to think what day it was. Fridays were custard tarts. He had better order double – triple for the fledglings – go to a different baker's; one who didn't employ crass part-time assistants full of snide remarks.

He closed his eyes and let the quivering yellow tartlets steal into his head, rows and rows and rows of them, snugged together on their heavy wooden tray. He always ate the custard first, scooping it out with a teaspoon, wobbly-moist. Next he savoured the pastry shells, smoothly rounded like his nest. He could smell the luscious pastry, see its crisp brown fragments as he munched the scalloped edges, then sucked each greasy finger so as not to miss a crumb.

Custard would be perfect for the fledglings – slip down as smooth as silk, without the need for chewing; afford him some small respite from their din. But what if it was Saturday? Saturdays were macaroons – hard again and scratchy. Fledgling beaks might break on macaroons. But he couldn't change his food plan. He had followed it for years, built his life around it.

He reached across for the last shreds and crusts of bread and, this time, swallowed them. He needed sustenance himself to withstand the deafening yammer, meet these new demands. Already, things were blurring: days, cakes, brands. He couldn't remember names – those puff-pastry slices with the icing on the top: a French name like his own but flaking into nothing along with his mind. There were new pains in his gut, squeezing like a nutcracker, and a strange steady ticking in his temples. He needed air.

Someone had tampered with the room again, putting the window further away than ever. He limped towards it, summoned his last strength to heave it fully open and gulped down draughts of chilled and flavoured morning.

Slumped against the sill, he glanced out at the garden. Tendrils of dark ivy had trespassed from the fence and wound themselves around a slim young sapling, squeezing tighter, tighter. Lely ran a nervous finger round the inside of his collar. The fence was beginning to bulge, the flower-beds were panting alarmingly.

On the path, something caught his eye. A white enamel moon had fallen there – a moon licked shining clean. He gripped the sill but lost his footing and fell against the window frame. Below him, out of focus, he could see the path bucking and up-ending; the whole taut morning poised and pulsing like a spring-board on its four black paws.

His hands flew to his face – too late. There was a leap and pounce of black; white razor teeth exploding into scarlet; green eyes blinding him with their glittering glaze of pain. He tried to shout for help, but his mouth was spewing petals. He could smell the scorch of roses – Van Gogh yellows, foreign reds, bursting into flame. He was choking on hot fur; barbed black claws skewering his gut. He closed his empty sockets, heard Velva singing somewhere far away. She had stopped her strident squawking and was warbling to him, wooing, begging him to come to her. The fledglings were silent. They must have learned to fly and gone their separate ways. He and Velva alone again together . . .

He tried to grope towards her song, swing up on the quavers, but he was falling back and back, floor and ceiling smashing around him in shards.

'Fly,' she urged him. 'Fly!'

He shook his leaking head. Couldn't fly. Grounded weakling, clawed in two. Tomcat's tea. Pathetic lump of lard. The second snap of teeth closed around his ribcage. His body was unravelling in a spurt of crimson feathers, a crunch of convulsing bones, and suddenly he was free of it, light and free and soaring, and there was a brilliant yellow awning spread across the sky and fat sugar stars spinning in the mysterious blue beneath and a great white waiter hovering high above the cobblestones showering gigantic boundless Bounty bars on all the loaded tables and the golden doors were opening wider wider and he was flying flying through them to his mate.